The Canonbury Papers

Volume 2

Freemasonry in Music and Literature

Transactions of the
Fifth International Conference
1 & 2 November 2003
edited by
Trevor Stewart

Published by
Canonbury Masonic Research Centre
London 2005

The Canonbury Papers
Volume 2 edited by Trevor Stewart
'Freemasonry in Music and Literature'
being the transactions of the Fifth International Conference
held at the CMRC in London
on 1 & 2 November 2003

Published by
Canonbury Masonic Research Centre (CMRC)
Canonbury Tower, Canonbury Place, Islington
London, N1 2NQ
United Kingdom

Telephone: 0207 7226 6256
Fax: 0207 7359 6194
E-mail: info@canonbury.ac.uk
Website: www.canonbury.ac.uk

British Library Cataloguing Data
The Canonbury Papers 2
1. History/Philosophy, Early Modern
Editor: Stewart, Trevor

ISBN: 0-9543498-1-4   978-09543498-1-3

Printed by
Antony Rowe Ltd.
Bumper's Farm Industrial Estate
Chippenham, Wiltshire, England SN14 6LH
Telephone: 01249 659705 Fax: 01249 443103
E mail: sales@antonyrowe.co.uk

Acknowledgement

The Editor of these transactions is grateful to the Trustees of the CMRC – especially to their patrons, Lord and Lady Northampton – to Professors Prescott and Stevenson for chairing the two daily sessions of the 2003 Conference, to Peter Hamilton Currie for his prompt expert technical assistance and to Mrs Carole McGilvery, the Conference organiser and CMRC administrator, whose cheerful dedication to the work of the Centre is now justifiably well-known internationally.

The opinions and facts stated in these papers are the responsibility of the authors themselves and should not be taken as indicating the views of the CMRC or any other institution.

***

Canonbury Masonic Research Centre

The CMRC was founded in 1998 as a charitable trust in order to provide what is within the UK a unique environment for the study of, and research into, all aspects of Freemasonry, together with allied traditions, and to make the results available to the general public.

Accordingly, the CMRC fosters learning about the masonic phenomenon through a continually updated programme of monthly public lectures, seminars and annual international conferences which embody the highest standards of inter-disciplinary and comparative scholarship.

The Canonbury Tower in Islington, north London, which houses the CMRC, was built in the 16th century by William Bolton, Prior of the Canons of St Bartholomew's. It stands proudly as one of London's most intriguing architectural landmarks and was once the home of Sir Francis Bacon.

*****

Foreword

CMRC is proud to deliver this second volume of *The Canonbury Papers* which form the transactions of the Fifth International Conference held at the Canonbury Tower in London in November 2003. Western music and literature have had some strong and clearly delineated influences on freemasons and likewise the ideas underpinning the Craft have found fascinating expression in various artistic forms from the earliest decades of the 18th-century, that formative period when speculative Freemasonry really began to flourish in most of the major European cultural centres. These papers reflect that amazing diversity and, like those in the previous volume, demonstrate the clear impact in both form and content which Freemasonry has in western European urban culture over the generations. It is very gratifying to note that scholars of various specialisms represented here, some of whom are not freemasons, are continuing their interest in investigating and writing about speculative Freemasonry and are thereby enabling CMRC to continue to make its useful contribution to the ever-expanding field of literature on the subject. What is especially pleasing, of course, that some of the authors here are, dare I say it, of the 'younger' generation and this certainly bodes well for the future development of this particular branch of historiography.

These papers range, in their subject topics, from England, Germany, Russia, France, Holland, Austria, Scotland and Sweden; the time-scale represented here runs from, say, perhaps the mid 15th-century to the present time; and the range of the various artistic forms examined herein is also remarkable. These three facts alone should demonstrate very clearly indeed that not only have culturally potent men of most European backgrounds found the Craft worthwhile their involvement but that this professional interest among literatii, artists and musicians has been sustained for a very long time. For these reasons alone - if for no others – the Craft merits careful, rigorous examination. That process has already been started many years ago among freemasons, of course, and slowly non-masons – who are equipped with a truly impressive range of investigatory skills and who might have been sceptical about its relevance to cultural history – have joined in the marvellous enterprise of shedding further light on to what has been wrongfully regarded hitherto as a social phenomenon of no real or lasting consequence. The late Dr. John Roberts would have been especially pleased to discover that his academic colleagues are taking seriously that famous clarion-call challenge which he issued almost forty years ago in 1969 in the *English Historical Review* and are responding herein and elsewhere accordingly.

Trevor Stewart

*****

Contents

Contributors

ANDREW PINK studied at the Royal Academy of Music and was awarded the Frederick Keene Organ Prize, the Royal College of Music's Diploma for Organ Performance - with honours (ARCM) and The Royal Academy of Music's Diploma for Organ Teaching (LRAM). His MA is from APU, Cambridge. He carried out his part-time doctoral studies in the Music Department at Goldsmiths' College, University of London.

Andrew's doctoral research is on the impact of Freemasonry on 18th-century London's musical culture. His last major project was on Benjamin Cooke (1734-1793, the organist of Westminster Abbey and director of the original Academy of Ancient Music. It consisted of a detailed biographical study, an ordered catalogue of Cooke's manuscript and early printed works, and a performing edition of Cooke's Christmas Ode (from MSS in the Royal College of Music) which was used for its first performance since the mid 18th-century in Chelmsford Cathedral, by Peter Holman and the Essex Baroque Orchestra and the Chelmsford Singers.

Andrew's recent papers include:
- *Men Behaving: 18th-century English Masonic song culture.* (May 2003);
- *The Musical Freemasons of the Philo Musicae et Architecturae lodge, London, 1724-27 - Male musical sociability in 18th-century London* (October 2002);
- *Permission and Prohibition - the performance of music by the elite male amateur in 18ᵗ -century Britain* (2002).

He is a Research Assistant for Professor Michael Worton (Vice-Provost and also Fielden Professor of French Language and Literature) at University College London.

EDWARD BATLEY is Emeritus Reader in German, University of London. From 1993-98 he was Honorary Director of the University of London Institute of Germanic Studies. Prior to that, in 1987-1993, he was Head of the Department of European Languages. From 1970 to 1987 he was Head of the Department of German, University of London at Goldsmiths' College.

Educated at University College, Durham University (1957-1964) gaining a BA hons. in German, a Post Graduate Diploma of Education and a M. Litt, thereafter Edward worked as a Lecturer in German at Goldsmiths' College, London. From 1974 until 1980 he was Vice-President of the Federation Internationale des Professeurs de Langues Vivantes and between 1980-1992 he was re-elected three times to serve of their President. He was elected unanimously to be Conseiller Honoraire de la FIPLV by the World Council in 1993. He is an active member of the Lessing Akademie (in Wolfenbüttel), the Schiller Gesellschaft (in Marbach), the Goethe Gesellschaft (in Weimar), the English Goethe Society and the Conference of University Teachers of German. In 1984 he was awarded the Jakob and Wilhelm Grimm Prize by the German Democratic Republic for his distinguished service to international understanding and the German language. In 1992 he was awarded the Comenius Medal by the Government of Czechoslovakia.

His books include: *A Preface to The Magic Flute* (1969) and *Catalyst of Enlightenment - Gotthold Ephraim Lessing* (1989). He has also published over thirty essays on German literature, including such notable figures as Lessing, Goethe, Schiller, Lenz and Hauptmann. He has also written about

- 18th-century Freemasonry in Germany, including articles for the German Quatuor Coronati Lodge;
- Singspiel and opera, including Mozart and Schikaneder;
- modern languages in education.

He has also delivered several key-note addresses at international conferences in different countries, recently in Poland and Prague. His current research is focussed on the ideas in Freemasonry and human rights and German literature in the age of Goethe. He has also been the editor of the history of FIPLV, since 1980.

DIANE CLEMENTS graduated in Modern History at Oxford and spent many years as an investment banker specialising in the international capital markets until 1995. Thereafter she applied her financial skills to the heritage field and after studying the history of Fine and Decorative Arts at Christies, she worked as project manager on a government-funded architectural project - Heritage Open Days - at the Civic Trust. She was responsible for attracting commercial sponsors and working with a national newspaper. Diane studied for a Diploma in Heritage Management at the University of Greenwich and in 1999 was appointed Director of the Library and Museum of Freemasonry at Freemasons' Hall, London. The Library and Museum has since become a Registered Museum, has maintained a regular programme of exhibitions and has been awarded a grant from the Heritage Lottery Fund for the cataloguing and conservation of archive material. In 2003 the Library and Museum launched its website which includes on-line access to the new electronic catalogue.

ANDREW PRESCOTT holds a personal Chair and is Director of the Centre for Research into Freemasonry at the University of Sheffield. For 20 years he was a curator in the Department of MSS at the British Library. He undertook his doctoral research on the Peasants' Revolt of 1381 and has published articles on that subject in *History Workshop Journal* and elsewhere. He has produced two general books on historical documents: *English Historical Documents* (1987), and - with Elizabeth Hallam Smith - *The British Inheritance* (2000). He has also produced a facsimile edition of *The Benedictional of St AEthelwold* (2003). He researched the history of the MSS Collections of the British Library which has resulted in a number of articles for *The British Library Journal* and other periodicals. Andrew is an authority on the application of digital technologies to MSS studies and was the principal British Library contact for the *Electronic Beowulf* project, which won the Library Association/Mecklermedia award for innovation. His research into Freemasonry has resulted in a number of publications. His study of 'The Unlawful Societies Act of 1799' appeared in the *Canonbury Papers* Volume 1. His major study of Charles Bradlaugh and Freemasonry was published in *AQC* Volume 116. A study of London Freemasonry appeared in the transactions of the Manchester Association for Masonic Research. Andrew was editor of the CD-ROM of *Preston's Illustrations of Masonry* which was published in 2001 by Academy Electronic Publications.

LAUREN G. LEIGHTON is Emeritus Professor of Russian at the University of Illinois, Chicago. He now lives in Madison, Wisconsin, where he continues his research in Russian literature and culture. He obtained his PhD in Slavic Languages at the University of Wisconsin and did postgraduate work at Leningrad State University. Lauren has conducted research in the Institute of Russian Literature under the auspices of the US-USSR Academic Exchange and has taught at the Moscow State Pedagogical University. His primary interest is in Russian Romantic literature, with comparative emphasis in German Romantic Idealism and English Romanticism, especially Byron. Lauren's other research interests are in translation studies, Russian culture and the esoteric tradition. He has lectured and published on this subject in Russia and the English-speaking world, and continues to keep track of new developments in that field. His recent books include *Two Worlds, One Art: Literary Translation in Russia and America* (1991) and *The Esoteric Tradition in Russian Romantic Literature: Decembrism and Freemasonry* (1994) and *A Bibliography of Alexander Pushkin in English: Studies and Translations* (1999).

MALCOLM DAVIES was awarded the Licentiate and Fellowship of Trinity College of Music, London while still at school in Caerphilly, South Wales. During that period he played viola in the National Youth Orchestra. In 1974 he graduated B.A. hons. in Music at Southampton University, and obtained a grant from the Welsh Arts Council which enabled him to pursue some post-graduate studies at the Royal Conservatory in The Hague. He graduated with an MA in choral conducting, and thereafter he conducted choirs and orchestras. He has taught early music at summer schools in France, England, Italy and Canada. Malcolm founded the Cecilia International Music School in The Hague in 1989. Its philosophy stresses the importance of matching the interests and skills of both teachers and pupils and encourages concerts, examinations, workshops and ensemble activities as well as individual musical tuition. The Cecilia School now teaches some 550 pupils from many countries. Malcolm is also Head of Music at The International School of the Hague where he teaches the IGCSE and International Baccalaureate examination groups. He has published many articles in English and Dutch on composers, recorder music, performance practice and the music of Dutch Freemasonry. His doctoral thesis - *The Masonic Muse* - was a detailed analysis of the songs, music and musicians associated with Dutch Freemasonry during the period 1730-1806. Before and after his doctoral studies at the University of Utrecht Malcolm was a guest lecturer in Lodges and at academic conferences. He is a member of a Lodge in The Hague and of several other Dutch masonic Orders.

MARIE MULVEY-ROBERTS is Reader in Literary Studies at The University of the West of England, Bristol. She had a Leverhulme Fellowship and was a Visiting Research Fellow at Australia's National University, Canberra. Her first book, *British Poets and Secret Societies,* examined the influence of Freemasonry on several poets and her second monograph was *Gothic Immortals: The Fiction of the Brotherhood of the Rosy Cross.* In addition, Marie has founded two journals and has edited over 30 books including *Secret Texts: The Literature of Secret Societies* (co-edited with Hugh Ormsby-Lennon) and *Pleasure During the Eighteenth Century* (co-edited with the late Roy Porter). Her essays on Freemasonry have included 'The Important of Being a Freemason: the Trials of Oscar Wilde'; 'Burns and the Masonic Enlightenment' and, most recently, 'Hogarth on the Square'. The latter was given at Livingstone Masonic library in New York to celebrate Hogarth's bicentenary. She has given lectures to masonic audiences in the USA and the UK, and was the first woman in England and Wales to give a lecture in a Lodge with the Brethren in their regalia. She has been working on a book on 18th-century Freemasonry.

DAVID STEVENSON is an Emeritus Professor of Scottish History at the University of St Andrews. After studying History at the University of Dublin, he moved on to do his post-graduate research on 17th-century Scottish history at the University of Glasgow, and then spent most of his career lecturing at the University of Aberdeen before transferring to St Andrews. His earliest research was on Scotland's civil wars in the mid 17th-century. In the 1980s this led him to investigate the rich records of early Scottish Freemasonry which resulted in two pioneering and complimentary books: *The Origins of Freemasonry: Scotland's Century, 1590-1710* and *The First Freemasons: The Early Scottish Lodges and their Members*, both of which were first published in 1988. David's most recent books are *The Beggar's Benison - Sex Clubs of the Scottish Enlightenment* (2001) and *The Hunt for Rob Roy - The Man and the Myths* (2004). His most recent contribution to Masonic historiography is a paper entitled 'James Anderson (1679-1739): Man and Mason', which appeared in *Freemasonry on Both Sides of the Atlantic: Essays concerning the Craft in the British Isles, Europe, the United States and Mexico,* ed. by R.W. Weisberger (2002) and in *Heredom - The Transactions of the Scottish Rite Research Society,* Volume 10 (2002).

ANDREAS ÖNNERFORS grew up in Germany and moved to Sweden in 1993. He completed his doctoral studies in the History of Sciences and Ideas Department at Lund University. He is a Fellow at a Baltic post-graduate group at the University of Greifswald, Germany. His research dealt with cultural encounters between Pomerania and Sweden during the period 1720-1815. Andreas's studies into Freemasonry started with a dissertation project aimed at investigating the Pomeranian Lodges after the 1760s that worked the Swedish Rite. He has published several papers in English, German and Swedish on this topic including a contribution to Volume 1 of these CMRC transactions. Another of his contributions was published in *Acta Masonica Scandinavica* vol. 5. Andreas became a freemason in the Swedish Order of Freemasons in 1996. He is a member of the Swedish research Lodge, Carl Friedrich Eckleff, and the German Masonic research group, Frederik.

JOHN WADE lectures at the University of Sheffield in Classical languages and literature. Recently he had a year's special leave during which he combined research on the Latin works of John Foxe, the Tudor martyrologist, with a post as Tutor in Latin and Greek to a Californian family near Santa Cruz. John's interests are wide ranging and include music. He founded and conducted charitable performances with the John Wade Singers for 18 years, has been Musical Director for the triennial Woodthorpe Festival since 1993 and until recently was a church organist and choirmaster. He is a Past Master of his mother Lodge, Fellowship No. 4069 in the West Riding of Yorkshire, and was the first Master of the Amadeus Lodge No. 9539 in Derbyshire. He is a member of many other masonic Orders, is currently President of the Sheffield Masonic Study Circle and has given lectures on masonic music on many occasions both with the Sheffield and District Masonic Choir and with smaller ensembles. John is a co-author with R. L. D. Cooper of *The Genealogy of the Sine/airs of Rosslyn* (2002), in which he translated all the original Latin charters. He has been working with other masonic scholars in the USA and England to promote some major joint masonic research events in 2005 and 2007.

*****

List of Illustrations

*****

1

'When they Sing':
the performance of songs in 18th-century English lodges

by
Andrew Pink

The role of songs in the lodges

British research libraries are brim full with 18th-century English masonic song texts, and occasionally English masonic songs with music too, and anyone wishing to make a study of such material needs to find a method of organising it. The lack of any such method has always been an impediment to the appreciation of the value of this material, not only by freemasons, but also by historians in general.

It is well known that many masonic songs had an 'informal' use during the unstructured social time that came after the close of a lodge,[1] but the 'formal' use of songs within a lodge itself is understood far less well. This is not surprising since many aspects of 18th-century English lodges remain unclear, and occasionally disputed, not least because the sources themselves never seem to provide exact corroboration with each other. In exploring the performance of songs in 18th-century English lodges, this paper proposes not only a performance framework within which to place the material, but also a contribution towards the creation of an organisational model for the material itself.

The thesis of this paper is that there were two places within a lodge in which songs had a 'formal' use; firstly at the end of a 'Lecture' (a use which can be further defined a 'formal-liturgical' use) and secondly during a lodge's meal (a use which can be further defined a 'formal-convivial' use). It is upon these 'formal-liturgical' and 'formal-convivial' uses of song that the present paper is focused, reviewing, in particular, the contemporary written evidence that describes the role and the performance practice of the two 'formal-liturgical' masonic songs that seem to have dominated the 'Work' of the 18th-century English lodge, i.e. *The Enter'd 'Prentices Song* and *The Fellow-Craft's Song*. Many 18th-century writers agree that 'When-ever a Lodge is held, the songs of the Fellow-Crafts and the Apprentices are sung'.[2] It was only after the lodge was closed that the repertoire of 'informal' masonic songs came into its own:

> [After the Lodge business] everyone is at liberty to depart or stay longer: everything of masonry is excluded: they talk of what they please, and sing various songs for their amusement.[3]

Broadly speaking, the principal activities of an 18th-century English lodge were two-fold. Firstly, lodges made freemasons and led them through the hierarchy of the three degrees of Freemasonry, which were, from the 1720s, Entered Apprentice and Fellow Craft, and (*later*) Master. The lodge members met in a private room (almost always in a tavern) and sat around a table with a space at one end of the room to perform the ceremonies necessary for the making of a freemason (fig. 1).[4] The table would have doubled, in many cases, as a meal table. The 'work' around the table comprised the 'Lectures', a process in which the formulaic questions and answers of the knowledge relevant to each of the degrees were practiced,

> by way of Catechism, or Lecture, The Master asking the Questions, and the Members, properly seated, making the Answers one after the other; this is termed Working.[5]

The following short extract from the opening of an 18th-century Fellow Craft's Lecture gives a sense of this:

> Mas. Brother are you a Fellow Craft
> Ans. I am. Try me. Prove me.
> Mas. Where was you made a Fellow Craft?
> Ans. In a just and lawful Lodge.
> Mas. How was you prepared to made a Fellow Craft?
> Ans. I was neither naked nor cloathed, barefoot, nor shod … [etc].[6]

Secondly, if not engaged in making a freemason, or rehearsing the 'Lectures', the Lodge provided the opportunity for some edifying demonstration or perhaps a lecture (not to be confused with the 'Lectures' mentioned above). Such an educational demonstration or lecture was based on a theme related to one of the Seven Liberal Arts, around which the intellectual life of English Freemasonry clung. So, for example, at the Old King's Arms Lodge, in the period 1733-1734, there were scientific papers given on themes that included 'The Structure and Force of Muscles', 'The Water Clock' and 'Optics'.[7] At the *Philo-Musicae* Society (1725-1727) the edifying emphasis was upon the study of music.[8]

The earliest English masonic songs

The earliest known English masonic song texts are *The Enter'd 'Prentices Song* (fig. 3), *The Master's Song*, *The Warden's Song* and *The Fellow-Craft's Song* (fig. 4), which all appear in James Anderson's *The Constitutions of the Free-Masons* (1723), the first official book of English Freemasonry.[9] Each of these four songs, except the last, is printed with music. Although the style of the music that is given in the *Constitutions* implies a role for instruments (fig. 5), the fact is, as far as the written evidence shows, that in almost all English lodges of the period, music was entirely vocal and unaccompanied by instruments except in rare cases, and then on rare occasions; it was not 'the norm'.[10] The four song texts in the *Constitutions* became the foundation of all English masonic song texts, appearing, as they did, time and again in English masonic books throughout the century.

According to the rubrics in Anderson *The Master's Song or A History of Masonry* is 'To be sung when the Master shall give leave'; *The Enter'd 'Prentices Song* is 'To be sung when all grave business is over, and with the Master's Leave', *The Fellow-Craft's Song* is 'To be sung and played at the Grand Feast' (i.e., at the annual meeting of the Grand Lodge) and *The Warden's Song* is 'To be sung and play'd at the Quarterly Communication' (i.e., a quarterly administrative meeting). By following Anderson's rubrics *The Master's Song* and *The Enter'd 'Prentices Song* would appear to be the only two songs of the four that are directly connected with the lodge, being both dependent upon the Master's 'leave'. But 18th-century writers repeatedly state that it was *The Enter'd 'Prentices Song* and *The Fellow-Craft's Song* that were synonymous with each other and with the (formal-liturgical) 'work' of the lodge.[11] There seems to be no written evidence to associate *The Master's Song* (fig.

5) with the degree of a Master Mason, or its ceremonies. Its length and its several toasts, make clear its suitability for use during the 'formal-convivial' meal of the Lodge. Such (formal-convivial) 'refreshment' formed a distinctive part of the Lodge, as will be shown.

The anonymous author of *Hiram* (1766) is sure that *The Enter'd 'Prentices Song* and *The Fellow-Craft's Song* provided closure to each of the Lectures of the same name. At the end of the Entered Apprentice's Lecture, *The Enter'd 'Prentices Song* was sung, after which,

> it is necessary the Brethren should have a little Respite; and, perhaps it is Nine o'Clock in the Evening, when some of the members chuse to have a bit for the Tooth. Those who have ordered any Thing for Supper retire into another Room [...] Calling the men from Work to Refreshment.[12]

Likewise, according to the same book, the Fellow Craft's Lecture 'is always closed with the Fellow Crafts Song [...] and at this Time it is perhaps between Ten and Eleven at Night'.[13] The obvious point here is that, in practice, the two Lectures followed each other, separated by time for a meal. It was at the 'formal-convivial' meal that a song like *The Master's Song* was performed, 'with the Master's leave', with the chorus and a pre-determined toast printed at the end of each of its five sections. At the end of the evening, after the closure of the lodge, the 'informal' (the more 'unbuttoned') songs were performed.

> [Then] all the officers and Brethren take the Jewels from off their necks, and each Member may go or stay as he thinks proper; nothing of Masonry must be mentioned during the remainder of the Night , and it sometimes happens, that after the Lodge is closed, some Member, being warmed with the Juice of the Grape, thinks he may dispense with the Laws of Decency, and indulge himself with an obscene Song; but though it is a Maxim pretty generally received that good Singers should be free from all restriction, yet the best sort of Free Masons have not adopted it, though they do not exclude gay and joyous songs after the Lodge is shut.[14]

Undoubtedly there were some nights when the rehearsal of either (or both) of the Lectures did not go smoothly since each Lecture is, after all, long and full of details that have to be remembered. This fact might explain why, in 1759, the author of *The Secrets of the Free Masons* wrote

> I come next to the Songs, which are in great esteem among the Masons, and sung each Night of their meeting, in every Lodge, unless their Building take up so much Time as not to admit of a Song.[15]

Songs in the exposures

The best source of information about 18th-century English lodge music and the performance of songs, comes from a series of texts that were published in London within the space of a few years of each other around the 1760s, and nowadays referred to collectively as 'masonic exposures'. The books themselves, far from being designed to undermine Freemasonry as their genre title 'exposure' might suggest, are thought to have been published as 'unofficial printed rituals',[16] a way in which Freemasonry could ensure a consistency of ritual and organisation amongst the increasingly far-flung English lodges. Interestingly, whatever philosophical and ritual differences there might have been between the two divergent groups of Freemasons that were in existence from the 1750s onwards (i.e., the so-called 'Antients' and 'Moderns'), the existing evidence from printed song material reveals a considerable degree of uniformity between them in their shared song repertoire. It seems reasonable to conclude that their musical performance practice was, before their union in 1813, similar if not identical.

The type of detailed masonic information to be found in the exposures could not have been issued officially in the name of the freemasons themselves, since the oath of a freemason obliged those who took it to conceal masonic secrets from the uninitiated. Publicly at least, these books were treated with false contempt by freemasons, but were nonetheless allowed to serve their purpose. That the contempt was false is exemplified by the production, in 1759, of *The Secrets of the Freemasons*, printed in London by J. Scott. Scott was a respected printer of mainstream 'non-secret' masonic literature. He issued several of the later editions of the hugely popular masonic *Pocket Companions*, and does not seem to have drawn down the ire of the freemasons upon himself, or his business, as a consequence of his exposure.

The specific editions of the exposures that are useful to a discussion of masonic musical performance practice are *The Secrets of the Freemasons* (1759), *A Master-key to Freemasonry* (1760), *Three Distinct Knocks* (1760), *Jachin and Boaz* (1762)[17] and *Hiram* (1766). Each of these documents gives slightly differing glimpses of the ways the lodges made use of song, but when they are read in conjunction with each other and with the song material itself, it becomes easier to gain a more coherent impression of how some things probably worked. All the musical information in these sources focuses on *The Enter'd 'Prentices Song* and *The Fellow-Craft's Song*. The reason for the sources' focus on these two songs as the distinct musical features of a lodge seems clear from their fundamental 'formal-liturgical' association with the Lectures (as shown above). These two songs' musical success, judging by their continuous appearance in collections of English masonic song texts (occasionally with their music) and in some general, non-masonic song books of the time, was due in no small measure to the simplicity and tunefulness of their melodies. Both these 'official' song texts were straightforward to sing, using commonly available musical settings that required no more musical resources than just the voices of those present. *The Fellow-Craft's Song*, the music for which is absent in Anderson's 1723 *Constitutions*, seems to have been popularly supplied by John Frederick Lampe (1703-1751).[18] Further evidence to support the fact that these two songs really were connected, as a pair, is borne out by the fact that as early as 1725, the two texts appear side by side on broad-sheets sold publicly beyond the lodge.[19]

In *Three Distinct Knocks* it appears that *The Enter'd 'Prentices Song* and *The Fellow-Craft's Song* were accompanied by their own stylised actions:

> When they sing [the Entered Apprentices Song] they all stand around a great Table and join Hands across, that is, your Right-hand takes hold of your Left-hand Man's Left-hand, and your Left-hand Man, with his Right-hand, takes hold of his left Man's Left-hand and so crossing all round. But when they say the last Verse, they jump up all together, ready to shake the Floor down. I myself have been below where there has been a Lodge, and have heard the people say 'Lord Damn their Bloods, what are they doing? They will shake the place down. I'll stay here no longer'. This they call driving of Piles.[20]

Hiram bears out this description:

> [When] the Enter'd Apprentice's Song [...] is sung, all the Brethren standing up; and at the End of each verse, they join hands crossways, so as to form a Link or Chain, and shake their Hands up and down, and stamp their Feet hard upon the Floor, keeping the Time; and this is what surprises Strangers who may be in a room underneath, or near the Lodge/ It is termed by Masons, Driving the Piles.[21]

For *The Fellow-Craft's Song*, the hands are used to clap rather than forming a chain:

> [...] holding your Left hand up keeping it square, then clap with your Right-hand, and Left together, and from thence strike your Left Breast with your Right-hand, the strike your Apron, and your Right Foot going at the same time. This is done altogether as one clap or should be, which makes a great Shaking on the Floor, and what they call driving of Piles to amuse the World. [...] I have known some Lodges that have Shores set below to support the Floor, while they have been at work as they call it.[22]

It was not only with the singing of 'formal-liturgical' songs at the end of each Lecture that actions are associated. Highly stylised actions were also part of the performance of 'formal-convivial' songs too (i.e. the songs sung during the Lodge meal), at the point when a toast is made after a song. It is the association of the text of a toast with a song that determines such songs as having a 'formal-convivial' use. In Anderson's 1723 version of *The Master's Song*, which is very long, there is a break provided, for a formal toast at the end of each of its five sections.[23] The Antient lodges' several editions of their Constitutions (*Ahiman Rezon*), from 1756 onwards used Anderson's songs as the basis of an expanded repertoire of mostly 'formal-convivial' (i.e., toasting) songs, and this expanded 'Antients' repertoire is to be found in the subsequent editions of Anderson's *Constitutions* (1756, 1784). The same toasts that appear in both books were listed in the exposure, *Tubal Kain* (1759):

Toasts Used by Masons

To the King and the Craft, as Master Masons
To all Kings, Princes and Potentates, that ever propagated the Royal Art
To his imperial Majesty (our Brother) Francis Emperor of Germany
To all the Fraternity around the Globe
To the Right Worshipful and Grand Master
To all the Noble Lords and Right Worshipful Brethren that have been Grand Masters.
To all well disposed, charitable Masons
To the Worshipful Grand Wardens
To the perpetual honour of Free-Masons
To the Masters and Wardens of all Regular Lodges
To all true and faithful Brethren &c
To all the Brethren sons of the antient and honourable Craft
To the memory of him who first planted a Vine
To Masons and to Masons bairns
And Women with both wit and Charms
That love to lie in Masons Arms
To all the female friends of Masonry[24]

All of this appears to be borne out in the text of a song published in Devon in 1763, entitled *Five Masonic Songs By a BROTHER of a Lodge at Plymouth. Published at the Request of Several of The BROTHERS*:

And after we've our Business done
Then we rejoice and sing;
To our Grand Master take a Glass,
And George the Third our King.
An to the Lodge we'll go &c

Then if the Master will permit,
Dear Brethren join with me;
To all Free Masons drink a Health,
And give them three times three.
And to the Lodge we'll go &c [25]

The anonymous author of *Jachin and Boaz* goes into some detail about how the drinking of these 'formal-convivial' toasts was stylised:

> The table being plentifully stored with Wine and Punch &c every Man has a Glass set before him, and fills it with what he chuses, and as often as he pleases. But he must drink his glass in turn or at least keep the Motion with the rest. When therefore a Public Health is given the Master fills first, and desires the Brethren to charge their Glasses, and when this is supposed to be done the Master says *Brethren are you all charged?* The Senior and Junior Warden answer *We are all charged in the South and West.* Then they all stand up, and observing the Masters Motion (like the Soldier his Right Hand Man) drink their Glasses off, and if the Master proposes the toast with *three times three Claps* they throw the Glasses with the Right Hand at Full Length, bringing them across their Throats *three* Times, and making three Motions to put them down on the table, at the third they are set down (though [they are] perhaps fifty in number) as if it was but one, then raising their hands Breast high, they clap nine Times against the Right, divided into three Divisions, which they term *Drinking with three times three*: and at the end they give Huzzah.

Although the 1738 edition of Anderson's *Constitutions* provides a toast after *The Fellow-Craft's Song,* there is no evidence that a toast was part of the performance of the song in its 'formal-liturgical' use. Thus the 1738 *Constitutions,* and subsequent volumes, suggests the possibility that 'formal-liturgical' songs could, at times, serve as 'formal-convivial songs too.

Conclusion

Here then is evidence of the establishment not only of a 'formal-liturgical' tradition, but also of a 'formal-convivial' tradition. By the 1760s, at least, drinking a health and singing were firmly associated one with the other and taking place during the 'formal-convivial' meal that came at the mid-point of the evening, under the supervision of the Master of the lodge. A certain song required a certain toast; a certain toast required a certain song. This was a practical way of establishing formality during the conviviality of the meal time and of moderating the drinking; an important consideration, given that the Fellow Craft's Lecture was very often likely to follow. It seems unlikely that every toast was used every time a lodge met; the number of songs, and thus of toasts, varying according to circumstance.

This all adds up to a lively, busy, noisy, entertaining and distinctly musical, but very controlled, evening. The singing of the songs at the end of each Lecture was accompanied by rhythmic stamping and the holding of hands in chains, while the meal time was accompanied by singing, and loud, stylised toasting, shouting, clapping and stamping. Even the distinctly proper 'work' of the lodge, as described in *The Secrets of the Freemasons* was often marked with loud cheering:

> The Applause that each Brother meets with from the whole Society, upon his duly and proportionately finishing a Piece in Architecture, is always expressed by loud Acclamations, [and] generally alarms, and surprizes [*sic*] those who are sitting by and under the Room where the Lodge is held.[26]

Although Freemasonry was practiced in secret, it seems that it was hardly discreet, and so it comes as no surprise that on 18 April 1737 a correspondent to *The Craftsman* newspaper wrote of the freemasons that

> these Men are generally look'd upon, in <u>England</u>, as a Parcel of like People, who meet together only to make merry, and play some ridiculous pranks,

and an irritable parody of *The Enter'd 'Prentices Song* appeared in the London press as early as 1725, and suggesting popular comprehension in its appeal:

> Good People give ear,
> And the truth shall appear,
> For we scorn to put any grimace on:
> We've been lamm'd long enough,
> With this damn'd silly stuff,
> Of a Free and an Accepted Mason.[27]

The Wilkins engraving (fig. 2) says it all.

Fig. 1: a mid 18th-century lodge room
'The Ceremony of Making a Free-Mason' in *Hiram* (1766).

Fig. 2: a mid 18th-century lodge room
a satirical engraving *The Free-Mason's Surprized* by T. Wilkins (London, 1754).

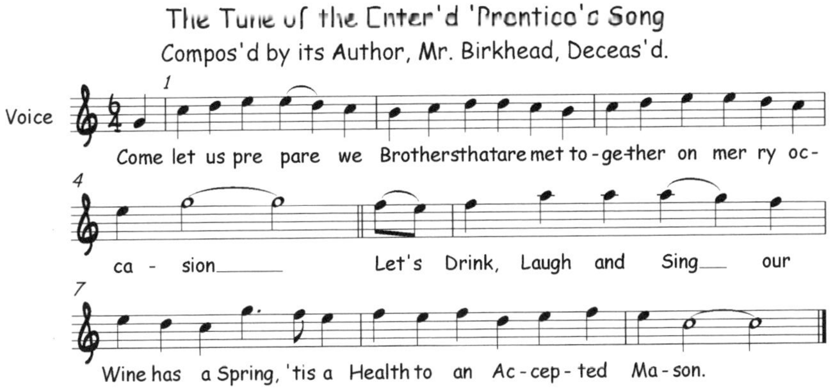

Fig. 3: 'The Enter'd 'Prentices Song' from J. Anderson's *The Constitutions of the Free-Masons*, (1723).[28]

Fig. 4: 'The Fellow-Craft's Song' by J. F. Lampe in *British Melody* (1739).[29]

The Master's Song
[Verse 5: Thus Mighty Eastern Kings]

Anderson's Constitutions, 1723

Fig. 5: 'The Master's Song' from J. Anderson's *The Constitutions of the Free-Masons* (1723).[30]

***

NOTES

1 *See*, e.g., Wallace, M.: 'Music, Song & Spirits: The Lighter Side of Scottish Freemasonry', in *History Scotland* vol. 4(1) (2004), pp. 38 - 44.

2 [Anon] *A Master-Key to Free-Masonry; by Which All the Secrets of the Society Are Laid Open;* and *Their Pretended Mysteries Exposed to the Public...* Second Edition, (London: J. Burd, 1760), p. 10.

3 From an edition of *Jachin and Boaz* by William Nichol, in A Sharpe: 'Masonic Songs and Song Books of the Eighteenth Century', *AQC* vol. 65, (1953), p. 86.

4 A.C.F. Jackson, 'Preston's England', in *AQC* vol. 89 (1977), p. 105.

5 [Anon *Hiram; or the grand master-key to the door of both Antient and Modern Free Masonry* (2nd edn., 1766), p. 23.

6 A.C.F. Jackson: *English Masonic Exposures of 1760-1769* [containing transcripts of *Three Distinct Knocks* (1760), *Jachin and Boaz* (1762) and *Shibboleth* (1765)]. London: Lewis Masonic (1986), p. 85.

7 J.F. Ashby: *Freemasonry and Entertainment* [Prestonian Lecture], London: J.F. Ashby (1999), p. 13. In J. Lane (ed.): *Masonic Records 1717-1894.* London: Freemasons' Hall (1895), p. 60 it states that the Old King's Arms Lodge was in Tower Street, Seven Dials, London.

8 M.C. Jacob: *The Radical Enlightenment - Pantheists, Freemasons and Republicans,* 2nd ed. Morristown, NJ: The Temple Books (2003), chapter 3, pp. 91-115, shows how important Newtonian science (Natural Philosophy) was, to early English freemasons, and how it had a popular audience in their lodges. Many members of the Royal Society were senior ranking English Freemasons. For the *Philo-musicae* Society *see* R.F. Gould: '*Philo-Musicae et - Architecturae Societas Apollini*' in *AQC* vol. 16 (1903), pp. 112-128.

9 J. Anderson: *The Constitutions of the Freemasons* (London: William Hunter and John Senex, 1723).

10 William Preston (1742-1818), in his *Illustrations of Masonry* (nine editions between 1772 and 1812) suggested a considerable role for both vocal and instrumental music in Lodge ritual, but there is no evidence to suggest that Preston's high view of the role music should take was adopted, attempted, or even practical, in most lodges, until the later development of permanently designated masonic rooms and halls.

11 In neither the first (1723) nor the second (1738) editions of Anderson's book do the rubrics and the songs tally satisfactorily, either with each other, or the evidence of contemporary writers. In cases of conflict I have taken the authority of the contemporary writers, who seem to agree on so much to do with practice, over Anderson.

12 *Hiram*: *op. cit.*, p. 31.

13 *Hiram*: *op. cit.*, p. 36.

14 *Ibid.*

15 *The Secrets of the Free Masons Revealed by a Disgusted Brother, Containing an Account of Their Origin Their Practices, Etc. To Which Is Added the Songs of the Masons, [...] and an Exact List of The ... Lodges. The Second Edition,* (London: Printed for the author and sold by J. Scott ... and all the booksellers in town and country, 1759).

16 R.A. Gilbert & J.M. Hamill: *Freemason - A Celebration of the Craft.* London: Mackenzie (1992), p. 28.

17 *Three Distinct Knocks* and *Jachin and Boaz* are printed in full in Jackson (1986).

18 J.F. Lampe & B. Cole: *British Melody, or, the Musical Magazine: Consisting of a Large Variety of the Most Approv'd English and Scotch Songs, Airs, &C (London: Printed for and sold by ye proprietor Benjn. Cole engraver ... & at most print sellers musick shops in town & country* (1739). Benjamin Cole was a masonic publisher and Lampe was a freemason. The date of 1739 gives no indication of the date of the music's composition.

19 For example, *see* British Library, shelfmark C.121.g.8.(9.) published by George Faulkner, Dublin, (1725).

20 Jackson (1986), *see* p. 83.

21 *Hiram*: *op. cit.*, p. 31.

22 Jackson (1986), p.92.

23 From the second (1738) edition of Anderson's *Constitutions* (and in subsequent editions), *The Master's Song* was shortened, to one section with a toast. The toasts belonging to the omitted sections of the song were attached to a series of new songs in the editions from 1738 onwards.

24 Prichard (1759), p. 24.

25 [Anon]: *Five Masonic Songs by a Brother of a Lodge at Plymouth. Published at the Request of Several of the Brothers* (Exeter: W. Andrews & R. Trewman, 1763).

26 [Anon]: *The Secrets of the Free Masons revealed by a Disgusted Brother ...* (1759), p. 20.

27 The text of the parody appeared in *The London Journal* of 10 July 1725.

28 Music and text remain as in the original; bar numbers are editorial.

29 Music and text remain as in the original, except that an *ad libitum* flute part, doubling the voice, is omitted. Where this flute part has trills not marked in the original voice part, these have been shown in square brackets. Bar numbers are editorial. This music is from a general song collection (see fn 18), and so the instrumental parts have no particular significance for the performance of lodge music.

30 Music and text remain as in the original, except for editorial accidental in bar 8 and dotted lines and bar numbers, which are also editorial.

*****

?

'The Master of Masters': The Genius of Goethe and the Manifestation of Freemasonry in his Work

by

Edward M. Batley

G oethe and Freemasonry is an old subject. Daniel Wilson's *Subterranean Passages: Goethe, Freemasonry and Politics* has helped to make it a hot topic.[1] Katharina Mommsen blames Wilson for propagating false conceptions about Goethe such as his ulterior motive for becoming a freemason. She also finds fault with the charge of inhumanity against Goethe for signing the death warrant of an unfortunate infanticide, and with the President of Germany's notion that Goethe was 'afraid of the idea of democracy', therefore, an enemy of freedom.[2] Wilson's book has, however, encouraged a reconsideration of Goethe's relationship with politics. No longer dismissed as naive, his political thinking is now under active reconsideration, his literary representation of the broadly democratic themes of the Enlightenment no longer written off as mere idealism in a cruel age of absolutism. Goethe, the Minister of State, must not be confused with Goethe, the visionary poet. Obeying the law, which a Minister was sworn to uphold, infanticide then being a capital offence, did not prevent him from persuading audiences of the inhumanity of that particular law, as of society generally, in his moving depiction of Gretchen's impending execution in the closing scene, in prison, of Part I of his epic drama, *Faust*.[3]

On 23 June 1830 the Anna Amalia Lodge in Weimar celebrated Goethe's jubilee as a freemason by making him an Honorary Member, the citation, however, failing to mention his underpinning of enlightened political thinking. Recollecting this celebration in 1880, Pietsch described him as the 'Master of Masters'.[4] Yet, according to Goethe's record after 1811, this cannot have been in acknowledgement of his regular attendance, and even the fifty years accredited to him as a freemason amounted in reality to only twenty-six. The wording of the certificate suggests that the Lodge was actually articulating the remarkable affinity between Freemasonry at its best and the multifaceted nature of Goethe's genius. It is dedicated to this 'highly honoured, fame-crowned Master of the Royal Art, the noblest example of masonic virtue', who, 'in wisdom, beauty and strength, gloriously shone the way forward for his own world and posterity, penetrating the inner secrets of nature with his brightly enquiring mind, preserving, nourishing and disseminating the sacred fire of truth, bringing together widely scattered nations by the magic of song so that the companionship of minds be shared'.[5]

Goethe's career and public activities

As early as 11 June 1775, soon after his arrival at the Weimar Court as tutor to the young Carl Augustus, Prince of the Duchy of Saxe-Weimar-Eisenach, Goethe was made Legionary Privy Counsellor and, two weeks later, was granted a seat and voting rights on the Duchy's Secret Council. Besides Carl Augustus, the Secret Council had three other members, one of whom was Freiherr von Fritsch, who had opposed Goethe's nomination. The Secret Council was the highest judiciary in the Duchy, presiding over local government and boards of trade, forestry, building and highways, the supreme councils for church and school affairs, taxes and their administration, all of which needed decisions from the Prince. In matters concerning the royal household, foreign policy, relations with the Holy Roman Emperor and the Empire, the Duchy's various estates, and the nearby University of Jena, the Prince was the highest authority. What was particularly interesting in the absolutist context of Germany as a whole, was that the members of Council were equal in principle and decisions were taken by a majority. Goethe was made Director of the Duchy's Mining Commission in 1777, Privy Counsellor and Director of the War and Highways Commission in 1779. The title 'von Goethe' was bestowed upon him in 1782. He was appointed Actual Privy Counsellor in 1804 with the title of 'Excellency'.[6]

Goethe's scientific activities included the discovery of the intermaxillary bone in man, the development of colour theory and the theory of the evolution of all plants from an original source, the study of optics, geology, mineralogy, anatomy, biology, botany and zoology. Goethe also enjoyed painting, travel, walking, and observing nature at work, both in its infinitesimal detail and its terrifying splendour, the latter exemplified in the volcanic eruptions of Vesuvius, which, given the sudden proximity of the explosions and noxious fumes, he was fortunate to survive.

His formal relationship with Freemasonry

Wilson claims that Goethe and Carl Augustus became freemasons in order to spy on their secret activities. The opening of the new Lodge in Weimar on 26 October 1764, dedicated to the Duchess Anna Amalia, had been granted on condition that it would not countenance activities against the state or against religion. The potential conflict of loyalties between church, state and Freemasonry had not proved problematic for the King of Prussia nor the Duke of Braunschweig, and Goethe had already sworn the oath of allegiance to his monarch before giving similar undertakings as a freemason, which makes it difficult to agree with Wilson's claim. In any case, why would the Prince or Goethe have felt it necessary to infiltrate the Lodge for such nefarious purposes when the Duchy's First Minister of State and President of the Secret Council, Freiherr von Fritsch, was also its permanent Master?

On 13 February 1780, prompted by Johann Joachim Bode, Goethe wrote to von Fritsch, informing him of his wish to belong to the society of freemasons.[7] The lack of this 'title', as he called it, prevented relations becoming closer with persons whom he had grown to appreciate, and he declared that it was 'this sociable and companionable feeling alone' which moved him to seek adoption. Ambition was probably not his motive, for he had already been speedily advanced to the Secret Council. On the other hand, the metaphor of the three-dimensional 'pyramid of his being', contained in his letter of 20 September[8], the apex of which he would strive to extend as high as possible, seemed to refer as much to the opportunities before him at Court as to his personal development, and he was certainly sensitive about his non-aristocratic Frankfurt origins, possibly regarding adoption as a further means of ensuring acceptance in Court society.

On 23 June 1780, the eve of the festival of St. John the Baptist, Goethe was admitted, Von Fritsch vacating the chair in favour of Bode. Lennhoff reports that Goethe refused to be blindfolded although undertaking to keep his eyes closed. The ladies' gloves he received as a mark of adoption, intended for the woman 'closest to his heart', he sent to the married Frau von Stein, Charlotte, the Lida of his poems.[9] On 23 June of the following year - actually the next meeting of the Lodge to be called - , he was promoted to Fellow Craft, the result of his earlier request to von Fritsch to be considered for further promotion as far as Master Mason. Goethe's reasons were that he wanted to spare his brothers the embarrassment of having to treat him as a stranger, adding, somewhat contradictorily, that, just as he had submitted himself to all the rules of the Order which were unknown to him, so did he wish to take further steps to move 'closer to the essence', provided this was not against the laws of the Order, signing himself 'Your Excellency's most obedient Goethe'.[10] The Prince was not made a freemason until 5 February 1782, well over a year later than Goethe, but soon afterwards, on 2 March, he was raised to Fellow Craft *and* Master Mason at the same time, Goethe also being made Master Mason on the same occasion. The various delays in Goethe's relatively tardy promotion have been attributed to Von Fritsch's opposition and the long intervals between meetings.[11]

Wilson comments on the detail of the ceremony, quoting the speech by Von Fritsch for which he identifies two of the sources, Johann August Starck's *On the Purpose of the Masonic Order* (1781) and *On the Old and New Mysteries* (1782).[12] Von Fritsch paraphrased passages which were critical of the direction taken by the Rite of Strict Observance, expressing his support for Starck's axiom that Freemasonry should be non-political. He pointed out that its laws contained nothing hostile to the state, religion or moral behaviour, and 'the better and more perfect the freemason, the better the prince, the better the citizen, the better the subject, and the servant of his lord'. Lessing had, of course, said all this, and more, five years earlier and Goethe knew his *Dialogues for Freemasons*.[13] One of the points overlooked by Wilson is the political dynamite for Germany of the first three *Dialogues*, which harked back to Anderson and focused on what Lessing regarded to be a point of principle, adoption irrespective of the candidate's religion, political opinions and social status. English Freemasonry, as Lessing understood it, was non-political in that the discussion of politics, like that of religion, was forbidden in the lodge so that freemasons could remain free of the social, religious and political divisions of the outside world. Yet English Freemasonry was progressively and dangerously political in the sense that its principles, an internally agreed constitution, secret ballots and internal promotion based on merit, however unwittingly, provided a model for society which contrasted sharply with the fundamentally absolutist states of

Germany, however enlightened they were in some things. Here servants of the three hundred or so kingdoms swore obedience to their respective sovereigns, but Strict Observance and the *Illuminati* demanded oaths of 'blind obedience' to 'Unknown Superiors'. What may perhaps best be described as the subliminal subversiveness of English Freemasonry was potentially more insidious than all the secret political planning undertaken in the higher degrees and their inner sanctums.

Wilson argues that a paragraph in a long letter of Goethe's to Lavater warning about the 'traces (...) of a huge mass of lies, stealing around in the dark, of which he (Lavater) can, as yet, have no inkling' was intended to reflect his general concern about the clandestine activities of Freemasonry. He adds that Lavater's brother Diethelm held high office in the Rite of Strict Observance in Switzerland. His subsequent analysis of the frequent occurrence of the phrase 'stealing around in the dark' in other contexts - in which the subject of concern was indeed Freemasonry – is, however, not persuasive enough to discount the fact that use of the phrase was widespread and not confined to masonic contexts, and that the broader context of Goethe's letter was not masonic at all. Even the paragraph in question refers first to 'the secret arts of Cagliostro' and Goethe's distrust of all the stories he has heard about them. It is 'our moral and political world' which he believes to be undermined by the 'mass of lies'.[14] The implication is that the stories he has heard about the secret arts of Cagliostro are part of the larger web of lies which he knows to be circulating. Goethe's comparison of subterranean activity with what goes on above ground is just as much an expression of his special understanding of the demonic presence in nature and society.[15]

Goethe and Carl Augustus were both promoted to Scottish Master, their declaration, signed on 10 December 1782 just before their Initiation, committing them to absolute silence about whatever they might learn of this fourth (Scottish) Degree, the Inner or High Order, and any other of the Order's obligations and connections, divulging nothing to persons not entitled to know, to which is added, 'nothing at all, under no pretext, and at no time'.[16] Richter refers to Goethe and Carl Augustus receiving historical instruction about the higher degrees of Scottish Master, Scottish Novice and Scottish Knight as part of Bode's plan to transfer the centre of the Rite of Strict Observance from Braunschweig to Weimar,[17] which came to nought after the Wilhelmsbad Convention agreed the formal closure of that Rite. The Weimar Lodge, although continuing half-heartedly for a while, decided to follow suit.

Given the internal discontent and Bode's growing antagonism to 'Higher' Degree systems, it was perhaps surprising that both Carl Augustus and Goethe should then be adopted as *Illuminati*. Goethe's signed undertaking on 11 February 1783, not to reveal anything, is rigorous, obliging him not only to absolute silence but also to impart nothing of the letters or documents he might receive, and to keep them under lock and key addressed to a reliable brother in case of his unexpected death.[18] Baron von Knigge, who, with Adam Weishaupt, had composed the higher degrees in the *Illuminati*, observed that '(...) the Scottish Degrees were not intended to contain anything from which the secret plan concerning the true intentions of the Order could be deduced (...)' adding in words which, unbeknown to him, were a testimony to Goethe's sense of duty as Minister of

State: 'If the man can do no better (meaning that he will not commit himself to the risks associated with secret political planning), he will remain simply Scottish Knight.'[19] These plans included rendering princes and priests redundant, introducing a religion based on reason, and, like the Rite of Strict Observance, of establishing an independent state. Schüttler states that Goethe was made 'censor' for the '*Illuminati* dirigens' within the Regent's degree[20], but, according to Knigge, the conditions of admission to that degree, one of them being that candidates be, as far as possible, 'free and completely independent of princes', would have prevented Goethe from even being considered. Since he had already been made Scottish Master in the Rite of Strict Observance, the next *Illuminati* degree would have been Scottish Knight. Knigge regarded the '*Illuminati* dirigens' as synonymous with Scottish Knight, pointing out that only in the rarely awarded degrees of Regent and Priest were the secret plans of the *Illuminati* revealed. Carl Augustus was given the alias of 'Aeschylus' and the office of 'Superior' in the Weimar Minerval Church, that is, responsible for recruitment to the Order. So, despite Wilson's contention, this kept both Goethe and Carl Augustus innocent and ignorant of the secret and political machinations of the Order of *Illuminati*.

The proximity of *Illuminati* ritual to the sacrament of communion, the revelations of defectors in Munich, their secrecy and political intrigue, whether invented or not, led to the first edict for their immediate suppression by Karl Theodor, Electoral Prince of the Pfalz and Bavaria, on 22 June 1784.[21] The work of the Weimar Lodge was duly suspended for what turned out to be a period of twenty-two years, during which the repercussions of the French Revolution reverberated throughout Europe. It was Goethe's interest in a system developed by Friedrich Ludwig Schröder which, in part, prompted him to propose reviving the Lodge. Schröder, for several years Master of the Emanuel Lodge in Hamburg, undertook a revision of the masonic system, which he considered to have been corrupted by the needless invention of innumerable higher degrees. His starting premise was that, since modern Freemasonry had originated in England and proceeded from there to the Continent, it was in Anderson's *Constitutions* and the English ritual of three degrees that the source of moral regeneration was to be found. Schröder was eventually to become Grand Master of the English Provincial Lodge of Lower Saxony. His revised system, which owed much to Johann Gottfried Herder's close scrutiny of his drafts for the rituals[22], retained the essence of the English system with only minor adaptations, added a fourth degree (possibly the model for the later *Quatuor Coronati*), and was immediately adopted in Hamburg.

On New Year's Eve 1807, Goethe wrote to fellow-freemason Voigt, opposing a move to open a new lodge in Jena and reporting a proposal he had already made to resuscitate the Anna Amalia Lodge.[23] The Masters in Weimar who had remained active were associated with the nearby Lodge in Rudolstadt, which followed - in Goethe's words – the 'very sensible system of Schröder', whom the Prince also liked. Aiming to outmanoeuvre the founding of a lodge in Jena with allegiances to Berlin, Goethe's counter-proposal, which reveals genuine concern about the general unruliness of corporations and societies in Jena, is for the Anna Amalia Lodge to follow Schröder's ritual and found a sister-Lodge in Jena, so that a 'smart triangle' could be set up linking Rudolstadt, Weimar and Jena, all – although Goethe does not say this – in the same

Duchy. This is not quite the political control that Wilson had in mind, rather a concern, whether as freemason, loyal subject or Minister, for law and order. Jena, however, jumped the gun, turned to the Lodge of the Three Globes in Berlin, from which it then received its constitution, establishing additional links with Gotha, and rendering fraternal relations with Weimar and Rudolstadt impossible. Goethe was annoyed that only *after* the event had the Jena freemasons sought Weimar's approval, which by law they needed. Needless to say, Jena's application for legal recognition was turned down. Goethe's letter to Voigt on 1 May 1808 shows him now believing it to be expeditious to resuscitate the Weimar Lodge - his words echoing his earlier approval of the Schröder revisions - 'according to the old ritual'.[24] The Lodge was re-opened on 24 October 1808 with a constitution from the Grand Lodge in Hamburg.

Manifestations of Freemasonry in a selection of his writings

Remarkably, Anderson's 'History of Masonry' (1723)[25] shares a limited kinship with an influential collection of essays published in Germany fifty years later by Herder, *The German Art and Manner* (1773).[26] The renewal of interest in Germany's national cultural heritage, reflected in three of the five essays, contrasts sharply with the cosmopolitanism of Anderson's approach, and yet both works share certain general characteristics: a rediscovery of the past, an interest in architecture as an expression of the past, the validation of the present by an imaginative re-thinking of the past, and an enthusiasm which, while inspiring, is prone to error. Goethe's contribution, 'On German Architecture', amounted to a positive re-evaluation of the Strasbourg cathedral and the hitherto much maligned Gothic style. He commented on the rules and traditions of architecture, the use of pillars, the mean-minded Italian, French and German experts in the field, but the most moving passage is his description of the impact which the cathedral made upon him. He could only marvel at the genius of the architect, Erwin von Steinbach, who moulded seamlessly together infinitesimal detail and grandeur. 'It is very hard for the human mind', Goethe wrote, 'when the work of a brother proves to be so wondrously sublime, that the mind must perforce kneel before it and worship.'[27] Such reverence is close to what he felt when first reading Shakespeare, 'as if the gift of sight were miraculously restored to one born blind', he wrote in 1771.[28] Reverence before something higher and better than yourself is what Katharina Mommsen, rightly or wrongly, finds lacking in today's world. Anderson articulated a similar concern in the Charges of 1723 when he wrote that neither 'a stupid atheist' nor an 'irreligious libertine' could gain any true understanding of the 'Art'.

Herder was made a freemason in Riga in 1766, becoming Secretary and then Orator in the Lodge of the Sword. Goethe first met him in a tavern in Strasbourg in 1770 where they discussed Shakespeare. His masonic activities continued in Weimar, although he was perhaps sensitive to the high office of superintendent which he now held in the church. He had a profound influence on the younger Goethe, but nothing is known of a specifically masonic influence other than a general affinity between the two men. This is reflected, in part, in *The German Art and Manner* and a possible link via Herder's printer, Bode, who was a friend and recent collaborator of Lessing's, had witnessed Lessing's adoption in Hamburg, and became one of the most influential and knowledgeable German freemasons of the century.

Affinities between English Freemasonry and this pre-Romantic period of German literature are to be found in Goethe's early poetry, his play, *Götz of Berlichingen, Knight of the Iron Hand* (1771), and his novel, *The Sufferings of Young Werther* (1774).[29] The revival of a mythical past, the cultural restoration of the imagined past, the re-awakening of interest in antiquity, in the chivalry, the castles and other crumbling edifices of the Middle Ages, the weighing of conventional morality and conduct against individual conscience, a universalism which ran close to the cosmopolitanism of the brotherhood of man, and the recurrent theme of the wanderer through life are themes which are common to both. In Goethe's drama of *Egmont*, begun in 1775 and not completed until 1787, the affinities become more specific. The action is set in The Netherlands between 1566 and 1568 when, on 5 June, the historical Count of Egmont was executed. It depicts, with a degree of accuracy, the events immediately preceding Holland's establishment of independence from Spain. One of the most secret and treasonable plans of Strict Observance and the *Illuminati* had been to establish an independent state in which different religions would be tolerated. Goethe had not been promoted high enough to learn of these plans, although Bode might have passed information on to him, but the idea of establishing an independent republic is central to his drama. In other respects, the drama reflects masonic principles which are closer to English Freemasonry than to Strict Observance or the *Illuminati*.

Setting the action in the 16th century of Philip II, King of Spain, the despot of all despots, when the 'single true' religion of Catholicism was enforced throughout the Empire by the Inquisition, allows the depiction of the extremes to which the absolutism prevalent in 18th-century Germany could potentially still revert. Egmont serves Philip loyally, but interprets his policies liberally. Less disturbed at the occasional public unrest in the Netherlands than his Spanish overlords, Egmont governs with common sense and humanity. Never encouraging the Dutch to worship other religions, he nevertheless tolerates it. Even into the fourth act, Egmont remains aloof from any political involvement, and when public disturbances take place, points out to the crowd that, as citizens, they enjoy already as much freedom as they need. A statesman with a clear conscience, Egmont resolutely rejects the Prince of Orange's warning to flee the Province before Philip's net closes around him. Why should he take to flight and be made to seem guilty of treason as a result?

In an absolutist and monarchic age of divine right, Egmont deports himself as a free man, which only draws attention to him. Queen Margareta of Parma's Secretary observes that, in contrast to the cautious Prince of Orange, Egmont 'walks around freely, as if the world belonged to him', and the Queen that 'he holds his head so high, as if the hand of majesty did not hover over him'.[30] The Secretary attributes such behaviour to nothing more than a clear conscience, but the Queen senses the fatal charms of the charismatic Egmont and the political dangers for Spain, should he ever become politically involved. In scenes such as these, Egmont is the enlightened embodiment of modern republicanism which the closed mind of the 16th-century potentate can only seek to eradicate, his liberal character paradigmatic of the mini-republic which the late Roy Porter saw in English Freemasonry. The drama centres politically on the freedom of conscience, social equality, liberty and brotherhood, and, after General Alba imposes martial law in Act IV, evokes the freedoms of movement and the right of public assembly by showing the dismal effects of their prohibition.

After Egmont has been arrested by Alba, ostensibly for treason, he overcomes his fear of death to become politically committed to the Dutch cause. Goethe motivates his change of heart carefully. Egmont sits in the darkest dungeon, now solitary, desolate and frightened, reflecting upon his imminent execution, not the kind of death he was accustomed to facing in the heat of battle. Ironically, it is a visit from the young Spaniard, Alba's son Ferdinand, who has never ceased to admire him for his love of horses and freedom, which helps Egmont to overcome his fear of death and recognize at last the political potential of his powerful public image, which will make him into a military leader even in death, a martyr dying for the cause of Dutch independence. He marches bravely to the scaffold rallying the Dutch to take up arms, accompanied by the victory symphony marked in the text of the play which was to inspire Beethoven's *Egmont Overture*.[31]

This is close to the moral sublimity of the Master's ritual, as it is to Schiller's moral philosophy. Karl Philipp Moritz, in his work, *The Grand Lodge* (1793), explains the masonic purpose of being confronted with the human skeleton. He writes of mastery over the thought of death as the catalyst of wisdom, arguing that the symbols of Freemasonry teach the wisdom of how closely intertwined are life and death. There must be more to the purpose of life than the skeleton, which cannot, in the end, signify the end. Man's contribution to mankind is his mind, argues Moritz, which is what generates the ideas that outlive him. The face-to-skull contemplation of the skeleton teaches that the purpose of life is to build out of destruction: 'the direct contemplation of death before us allows a glimpse behind the mysterious curtain which keeps from our eyes what is beyond the grave'.[32] Adam Weishaupt too, in a work first published before Goethe's *Egmont* and independently of the *Illuminati*, exhorts people to learn to live positively with the fact of their mortality:

> Our preparation for death is our preparation for freedom: whoever has learned to die knows how to deliver himself from bondage. (...) Dying is merely the fulfilment of the reason why we are born. Dying is merely being led down the grand highway on which, since beings have existed, we will meet a huge crowd, each bustling to arrive at their appointed hour, without distinction of quality or rank, showing neither vanity nor distrust, the great alongside the small, the rich alongside the poor, and the oppressor alongside the oppressed. (...) Live in the consciousness of God as you make your pilgrimage through life.[33]

The important issue here is not the question of influence but rather the glimpse afforded of the common inheritance shared by this variety of discourses on the subject of death.

Goethe's comedy, *The Grand Cophta*, was completed in 1791, three months after the first performance of Mozart's *Magic Flute* in Vienna.[34] It is based on the so-called 'Diamond Necklace Affair' which shook Paris between 1784 and 1785, just a few years before the Revolution, and involved Louis XVth and his mistress, Madame du Barry, later, by implication, Louis XVIth and Marie Antoinette, the Court jewellers, Cardinal Louis de Rohan, Count Cagliostro, and the real villain, Madame de la Motte-Valois, and her husband. Louis XVth died before the matter came to court, Madame de la Motte-Valois was found guilty of theft, the Cardinal was revealed as the gullible victim of the intended heist, and Cagliostro was acquitted.[35] Goethe makes Cagliostro the focal point of his comedy, associating deception with criminal intent with the illusory deceptions practised by Cagliostro in his Lodges of Egyptian Freemasonry.

The text merits a full critical analysis, which cannot be given here. The most striking features are what Goethe adds to history and how it reflects his disillusionment with all those 'Higher' Degree systems which had 'Unknown Superiors' demanding absolute obedience. Goethe reveals no masonic secrets, but he does parody ritual, using the non-masonic terms of 'pupil' and 'companion' to differentiate between the two degrees, and the term 'Master' with a degree of profligacy. Like Egyptian Freemasonry, the Lodge which he depicts admits men and women, but there is no equality of the sexes, as there was in Egyptian Freemasonry, the symbol of women being the Moon 'because they emit no light of their own, receiving their reflected light from men'. If women obey Count Rostro's commands, 'heaven will guard them from the waning light, the wretched condition of widowhood'. The motto of the First Degree – 'Do unto others as you would be done by!' - is contradicted by that for the Second - 'Do NOT do unto others, as you would be done by!'

Count:	Where is the centre of the world to which everything must relate?
Cardinal:	In our heart.
Count:	What is our supreme law?
Cardinal:	Our own profit. (...)
Count:	Who is the wisest?
Cardinal:	Whoever doesn't know anything, and doesn't want to either.
Count:	Who is the cleverest?
Cardinal:	Whoever makes profit from whatever he encounters.[36]

The Knight is outraged, but Count Rostro wins him over by explaining that such outrage qualifies him immediately as Master Mason.

Goethe presents on stage the ceremony at which the Grand Cophta appears in person. There is chanting and burning incense. The songs refer to temples, halls, preparation room, graves, pillars, wise men and hallowed places. A person clad in gold reclines in an arm chair, his head covered with a white veil, the leading characters of the play kneel before him. Whose face is revealed when the veil falls? Count Rostro's! The Cardinal is astounded, the Knight speechless, the wicked Marquise struck by the Count's shamelessness, and the Marquis wonders, what next? This would have struck a chord in any member of the audience who knew of Knigge's disillusionment at his own discovery that the much-vaunted 'Unknown Superior' of the *Illuminati* was none other than a

Professor of Canonical Law, Adam Weishaupt, knowledge of which was by now in the public arena. In the end, it is the dour, practical, down to earth, unpretentious nature of the Swiss Guard sent to apprehend the miscreants, which physically overwhelms the Count's compulsive protestations of innocence:

> Count: Do you know who I am? I'm the greatest of all mortals. Know that I am the *Conti di Rostro, di Rostro impudente*, an honest, widely admired stranger, a master of all secret knowledge, lord of the spirits (...)
> Swiss Guard: Tell that to *our* Superior, the General. He understands Italian, look you, and if you don't walk straight ahead, we'll poke you left and right in the ribs to show you the way, as commanded! (...)[37]

'The Mason's Journey / Is like Life, / And his Striving / Is like Trading / With Men on Earth' wrote Goethe in his poem 'The Symbol' (1815).[38] His novel *William Master* made the journey, as a metaphor for the learning experience of life, into its binding theme. Started in March 1782, the novel, in two volumes, *The Years of the Apprentice* and *The Years of the Journeyman*, was not completed until three years before his death. When the Weimar Lodge re-opened in 1808, it adopted Schröder's rituals, and it is hardly surprising that the novel should reflect Goethe's by now closer affinity with Schröder's revisions of English Freemasonry, which it does particularly in three extensive sections: the Society of the Tower, the Education Province, and the two communities led respectively by Lenardo and Odoardo.[39]

William's moral education progresses in clearly marked stages. The interactive relationship between inner being and outside world is reflected morally in the translation of self-knowledge into positive action for the good of the community and its members. As an inducement to that, the distinctive differences between monotheistic religions are tolerated as a matter of principle. Other features of the English tradition are the tripartite system of degrees, the metaphor of the edifying edifice, the arts and sciences of Freemasonry, friendship and universal brotherhood, the confrontations with death, and the wisdom of discretion, the materials of masonry (stone, granite, cedar, corner-stones, etc.), the associated crafts of carpentry and stonework, the arts of music and painting, and the sciences of architecture, mathematics, geometry and astronomy.

In the 'Education Province', the 'Superior', one manifested in three, does *not* demand blind or unthinking obedience, nurturing instead individual growth and independence within an orderly framework. Although the Province has an educational aim, pupils are not allocated to the three degrees by age, but by their different levels of achievement. Since pupils may not talk about these among themselves or with strangers, each level is new to them at the point of entry. The Warden observes that certain mysteries must be maintained by a cloak of silence, for this has a salutary effect on morality and the sense of shame. William cannot at first make sense of the three-fold symbolism of gestures and greetings, but these told the Warden immediately each pupil's educational level. In 1965 Wagenknecht explained the symbolic meaning of the three groups of pupils who look respectively to heaven, earth and their comrades: the masonic godhead was 'the light above us', conscience 'the light within us' and humanity 'the light around us'.[40]

The 17th century beginnings of modern English Freemasonry were predominantly Christian, with some circumstantial evidence that men of other religions might have been admitted as early as 1660.[41] Goethe's 'Education Province' has no regard for any religion which divides the self by being based on fear. His categories of ethnic, philosophical and Christian religion each encourage reverence. Reverence of all three produces true religion, from which emerges the highest form of reverence, that of the self. This allows man to achieve his highest potential, to see himself as the highest product of God and Nature. Lenardo's community of emigrants, despite the caution shown towards the race of people blessed by eternal wandering, is bound by three obligations: to honour all forms of religious service, to allow all forms of government to have equal validity, and to practise and promote morality without pedantry or unbending harshness, all of this stemming from the three reverences which the community professes. While matters of faith will separate the Jew from the Christian, their moral code does not, for this is expressed purely in what they do and based on the commandments of moderation in all things concerning the will, industriousness in all things that are necessary. Like Freemasonry, *William Master* offers no promise of eternal salvation, one way or the other.

The 19th-century freemason and masonic historian J.G. Findel believed the interaction of inner and outer worlds to be fundamental to the Royal Art.[42] Indeed it is his understanding of the '*inner* secret' of Freemasonry, which qualifies the ritual pathways of Goethe's novel. One of the most important subjects of Goethe's later writing, as it is of *William Master*, is his exploration of the reciprocating relationship of man's inner world to the world outside him. A philosophical poem, printed in 1820 in his journal, *Morphology*, suggests that even the concepts of 'inside' and 'outside' distract from the truth of things: 'Nothing is inside, nothing is outside; / Whatever is inside, is also outside. / So grasp without delay / Mystery, sacred and public.'[43]

A few of Goethe's poems are more obviously masonic: 'The Mysteries' (1784), 'The Symbol' (1815), 'On the Lodge Celebration of 3 September 1825' and 'To the Worthy Feast of Brothers' (1830).[44] Others reflect Freemasonry in their imagery, their morality, and their attitudes to religion, but not always consistently. In religious terms Goethe is perhaps best summed up as a non-denominational believer in a supreme divine being and with a marked leaning towards Christianity, particularly to the teaching of Christ, but this did not prevent him from singing the praises of Mohammed and Mohammed's civilizing influence, from expressing defiance at the arrogance of the Greek gods, from exuding Pantheism, examining Spinozism, nor from exploring unconventional sexual relationships. Open-minded and unprejudiced receptivity to other values and other religions is the hallmark of Goethe's genius, his spirit consistently reverential towards what he once called the Architect of the World, the Creator of all things.

***

NOTES

[1] W. Daniel Wilson, *Unterirdische Gänge: Goethe, Freimaurerei und Politik* (Göttingen: Wallstein, 1999). The English translations of German titles and French and German quotations in this article are my own.

[2] Katharina Mommsen, *Goethe und unsere Zeit – Festrede im Goethejahr 1999 zur Eröffnung der Hauptversammlung der Goethe-Gesellschaft im Nationaltheater zu Weimar am 27. Mai 1999* (Frankfurt am Main: Suhrkamp, 1999).

[3] *Johann Wolfgang von Goethe - Werke*, ed. by E. Trunz (Munich: Beck, 1981), vol. III, pp.10-364 (139-145).

[4] J. Pietsch: *Johann Wolfgang von Goethe als Freimaurer* (Leipzig: 1880), pp. 27f.

[5] *Ibid.*, p. 29.

[6] *Goethes Amtliche Schriften*, ed. by Reinhard Kluge (Frankfurt am Main: Deutscher Klassiker Verlag, 1998-99), vol. I, pp. 820-21.

[7] *Goethe: Das erste Weimarer Jahrzehnt. Briefe, Tagebücher und Gespräche vom 7. November 1775 bis 2. September 1786*, ed. by Hartmut Reinhardt (Frankfurt am Main: Deutscher Klassiker Verlag, 1997), p. 242.

[8] *Ibid.*, p. 299.

[9] *Internationales Freimaurer-Lexikon*, ed. by Eugen Lennhoff, Oskar Posner, Dieter A. Binder (München: Herbig,[2] 2000), p. 353.

[10] *Goethe - Das erste Weimarer Jahrzehnt: op. cit.*, pp. 342f.

[11] T. Richter: 'Der Geheime Rat Goethe als Freimaurer und Illuminat', in *Jahrbuch: Quatuor Coronati*, vol. 36 (1999), pp. 45-89. Richter's precise, detailed, and comprehensive article appeared immediately after Wilson's *Unterirdische Gänge Goethe, Freimaurerei und Politik*. As far as Goethe's formal relationship with Freemasonry is concerned and judged from the internal perspective of Freemasonry, Richter set the record straight.

[12] J.A. Starck: *Über den Zweck des Freymaurerordens* (Germanien [Berlin]: Himburg, 1781); *Über die alten und neuen Mysterien* (Berlin: 1782). *See* Wilson: *op. cit.*, pp.73-76.

[13] *Ibid.*, pp. 80-87. G. E. Lessing: *Ernst und Falk - Gespräche für Freimaurer*. In *Gotthold Ephraim Lessing. Werke*, ed. by H.G. Göpfert (München: Hanser, 1979), Lizenzausgabe für die wissenschaftliche Buchgesellschaft (Regensburg: Pustet, 1996), vol. VIII, pp. 451-488. Adolph Freiherr von Knigge: *Über Jesuiten, Freymaurer und deutsche Rosencreutzer* (Leipzig: 1781).

[14] Wilson: *op. cit.*, pp. 20-24.

[15] *Goethe - Das erste Weimarer Jahrzehnt: op. cit.*, p. 360.

[16] *Ibid.*, pp. 461f.

[17] Richter: *op. cit.*, p. 51.

[18] *Goethe - Das erste Weimarer Jahrzehnt: op. cit.*, pp. 468f.

[19] *Die neuesten Arbeiten des Spartacus und Philo in dem Illuminaten-Orden jetzt zum erstenmal gedruckt, und zur Beherzigung bey gegenwärtigen Zeitläuften herausgegeben* (1794), p. 14.

20. *Johann Joachim Christoph Bode - Journal von einer Reise von Weimar nach Frankreich im Jahr 1787*, ed. by H. Schüttler (Munich: ars una, 1994), p. 22.

21. C. Bröcker: *Die Freimaurer-Logen Deutschlands* (Berlin: Königliche Buchhandlung, 1894), p. 146.

22. *Johann Gottfried Herder. Briefe. Gesamtausgabe* (Hermann Böhlaus: Weimar, 1988), vol. IX, pp. 625-661.

23. *Goethe: Napoleonische Zeit II (1805-1811), Goethes Briefe, Tagebücher und Gespräche vom 10. Mai 1805 bis zum 5. Juni 1816*, ed. R. Unterberger (Frankfurt am Main: Deutscher Klassiker Verlag, 1993), pp. 41-44.

24. *Ibid.*: pp. 44ff.

25. J. Anderson: *The Constitutions of the Free-Masons, containing the History, Charges, Regulations, etc. of that most Ancient and Right Worshipful Fraternity* (London: Hunter, 1723).

26. *Von deutscher Art und Kunst*, ed. by E. Purdie (Oxford: Clarendon, 1924).

27. *Johann Wolfgang Goethe, Von deutscher Baukunst, D.M. Ervini A. Steinbach 1773*, ed. by L. Unbehaun (Rudolstadt & Jena: Hain, 1997), p. 12. *Johann Wolfgang von Goethe - Werke*, ed. E. Trunz (Munich: Beck, 1981), vol. XII, pp. 11f.

28. *Ibid.*, vol.. XII, p. 225. 'Zum Shakespeare-Tag'

29. *Ibid.*, vol. IV, pp. 73-175: *Götz von Berlichingen mit der eisernen Hand. Ein Schauspiel*; vol. VI, pp. 7-124: *Die Leiden des jungen Werther*.

30. *Ibid.*, vol. IV, pp. 381f.

31. The Viennese Court Theatre commissioned Beethoven to write incidental music for Goethe's play in the autumn of 1809. It was finished in June 1810, the overture being finished last.

32. K.P. Moritz: *Launen und Phantasien*, p. 292. *Die Große Loge* was printed in Berlin in 1793. *Karl Philipp Moritz – Werke*, ed. by H. Günther, 3 vols. (Frankfurt am Main: Insel, 1981) includes only eight of the original entries. I am grateful to the librarian of the Herzogin Anna Amalia Bibliothek in Weimar for a microfilm copy of all of the original seventeen in the *Launen und Phantasien*.

33. *Discours Philosophique sur les Frayeurs de la Mort, Traduit de l'Allemand, de Adam Weishaupt* (Hambourg: Fauché, 1788), pp. 37f. & 43f.

34. *Der Cophta als Oper angelegt (Die Mystifizierten), Der Gross-Cophta*. In *Goethes Sämtliche Werke*, ed. by D. Borchmeyer & P. Huber (Frankfurt am Main: Deutscher Klassiker Verlag, 1993), vol. VI/i, pp. 9-109. Goethe's *Der Zauberflöte zweiter Teil* remained a fragment, see vol. VI/i, pp. 221-249.

35. H.R. Evans: *Cagliostro and his Egyptian Rite of Freemasonry* (New York: 1930), pp. 14-21.

36. *Der Gross-Cophta*, ed. cit., p. 63.

37. *Ibid.*, p. 101.

38. *Johann Wolfgang von Goethe - Werke*, ed. by E. Trunz (Munich: Beck, 1981), vol. I, p. 340.

39. For a fuller account of the reflection of English Freemasonry in Goethe's novel, see my essay, 'Die Reform der Freimaurerei in London und ihr literarischer Niederschlag bei Goethe', in *Quatuor Coronati Jahrbuch*, vol. 36 (1999), pp. 91-103.

40. C.J. Wagenknecht: 'Goethes "Ehrfurchten" und die Symbolik der Loge', in *Zeitschrift für deutsche Philologie* vol. 84 (1965), pp. 490-497.

41. *See* my essay, 'Human Rights and the Masonic Legacy, 1646-1792', in *The Social Impact of Freemasonry on the Modern Western World* [The Canonbury Papers vol. I], ed. by M.D.J. Scanlan (London: Canonbury Masonic Research Centre, 2002), pp. 22-24. In the second 1738 edition of *The Constitutions*, Anderson refers specifically, when discussing the achievements of the Mohemmedans, [*sic*] to 'leav(ing) every Brother to Liberty of Conscience'. *The New Book of Constitutions of the Antient and Honourable Fraternity of Free and Accepted Masons* (London: printed for Caesar Ward and Richard Chandler, 1738), p. 23.

42. J.G. Findel: *Schriften über Freimaurerei* (Leipzig: ²1882), vol. I, p. 225.

43. *Johann Wolfgang von Goethe - Werke*, ed. by E. Trunz (Munich: Beck, 1981), vol. I, p. 358.

44. 'Symbolum', 'Zur Logenfeier des dritten Septembers 1825' and 'Dem würdigen Bruderfeste, Johanni 1830' are all available in: *Johann Wolfgang von Goethe - Werke*, ed. by E. Trunz (Munich: Beck, 1981), vol. I, pp. 340-343; the unfinished epic poem, 'Die Geheimnisse' in the same edition, vol. II, pp. 271-81, followed by Goethe's essay on this fragment which was published in the *Morgenblatt* of 1816.

*****

3

Sir Michael Costa 33°
'the most popular *chef d'orchestre* in England'

by

Diane Clements

Introduction

The bi-centenary of the birth of the French Romantic period composer Hector Berlioz was 2003. He visited London several times during his career, he married an Irish actress and his music was more popular in London than in Paris. However, the first performance of his opera *Benvenuto Cellini* at Covent Garden in 1853 became notorious not for the quality of his music but for the demonstration against French music which occurred. Despite the presence of Queen Victoria throughout, members of the audience played penny whistles, rattled door keys, whistled and hissed to drown out the music. The singers were heckled and the orchestra was booed. The performance was a rout. The co-ordinator of this demonstration was popularly assumed (although without foundation) to be the Director of Music at Covent Garden, an Italian called Michael Costa[1] (*see* fig. 6).

At the time Costa was a far more important figure in musical life than Berlioz but in the 150 years since this famous performance Berlioz's fame has grown whilst Costa features only as a bit player in the biographies of other 19th-century figures including David Cairns' biography of Berlioz[2] and a recent biography of Sir Henry Cole, the first Director of the Victoria and Albert Museum, where Costa is described as Cole's 'tame conductor'.[3]

In this paper, I would like to try to re-establish Costa's reputation and suggest how a study of his career in music and Freemasonry might act as an indicator of changing perceptions towards Freemasonry in the second half of the 19th century.

Costa's early career

In the autumn of 1829, a twenty-one year-old composer, Michael Costa, arrived in Birmingham. He had been sent from Naples by his music teacher, Zingarelli, to conduct Zingarelli's sacred cantata at the City's prestigious music festival. The directors of the festival, 'doubting his ability on account of his youth', refused not only to allow him to conduct the work but also refused to pay him any fee whatsoever unless he undertook to sing at the festival. He was first heard on 6 October 1829 when he sang a duet; he then sang two other solos and in some of the choral numbers. The critics were not impressed: as a singer he was described as far below mediocrity. Fortunately the composer, pianist and music publisher, Muzio Clementi, noticed Costa arranging some music of Bellini and declared him to be a composer rather than a singer[4]. Clementi was an influential teacher and composer, one of the original directors of the Philharmonic Society, and it would not have been uncommon at the time if he was influential in getting Costa an appointment at the King's Theatre in London. Costa's talent was recognised and in 1832 he was promoted to the position of Director of Music at the King's Theatre.

Costa and music

Since 1737 the King's Theatre had had the monopoly on the performance of Italian opera in London in the same way that the performance of English spoken drama was restricted to the two 'patent theatres' – Drury Lane and Covent Garden. Italian opera was the fashionable art form throughout Europe, patronised by the aristocracy. Costa made an immediate impact as Director of Music. He became known for his authoritative method of conducting and particularly the use of a baton. This was a new idea (Berlioz was one of the earliest advocates of this). Previously the principal violinist or the pianist had directed orchestras.

The leading contemporary music journal, the *Musical Times*, summarised Costa's ability in its obituary of him thus: 'He had, what all conductors should possess, the secret of command.'[5] Costa's approach as a strong disciplinarian was confirmed by James Henry Mapleson[6] with whom he worked closely in the 1870s who remarked that 'Costa was born with the spirit of discipline strong within him. As a conductor his love of order, punctuality, regularity in everything, stood him in excellent part'[7]. Apparently he never began a performance a minute late whether or not all the orchestra were in their seats. Another contemporary, the Leeds musician William Spark, devoted the first chapter of his book *Musical Memories* to Costa. Again he emphasises the extent of Costa's control: 'One source of his success as a conductor was his personal attention to detail, nothing seemed too small for his observation, inspection and strict surveillance'[8].

Costa's method enabled him to achieve a noticeable improvement in orchestral performance. Although it often caused strained relations with the theatre managers he worked with, Spark asserts that 'undoubtedly he was the most popular *chef d'orchestre* that ever resided in England'. He was successful; his reputation meant good audiences which meant steady employment for the musicians. While he insisted on punctuality and high standards he was known to be generous to orchestra members often paying for convalescent trips to the seaside[9].

A further element of Costa's success is indicated by James Davison, music writer of *The Times* and rather a critic of Costa on a professional basis for his lack of support for new composers. He relates a story of a concert at one of the Birmingham Festivals where female members of the Birmingham Festival Choir asked for Costa's gloves so that they could be torn into strips and cherished as souvenirs, the sort of celebrity with which many modern performers would be familiar![10]

Public performances of music in 19th-century London

In 1843 the Theatre Regulation Act abolished the patent theatres' monopoly over dramatic and musical performances and opened up competition in all types of performance. This 'deregulation' exacerbated the trend towards increasing commercialisation of musical performance.

London theatrical and musical performances did not have the benefit of either state or princely patronage such as existed in Paris or the German states at that time. The need for individual theatres to be profitable had its effect on musical performance and on the type of material that was performed. To limit the costs of musicians, rehearsal times were kept to a minimum. This encouraged the tendency to perform works with which the orchestra and the singers were familiar. It was often difficult to get new material performed and, if it was, to ensure that the standard of performance was satisfactory.

Management of a theatre or concert series was a high risk business, particularly after deregulation. Costa's reputation for orchestral discipline which helped keep costs down and audience numbers up meant that he became a key player in the changes in management seen in this period and their subsequent success or failure. In 1846 Costa was asked to become the first permanent conductor of the Philharmonic Society, the leading orchestra at the time. The Manager of Her Majesty's Theatre, as the King's Theatre had been renamed in 1837 on the accession of Victoria, Benjamin Lumley, was reluctant to allow him to take up this appointment. Costa took fifty-three of the eighty member orchestra and a number of singers and moved to the Covent Garden Theatre in protest where he founded the Royal Italian Opera with himself as Music Director[11]. From 1849 the Covent Garden Theatre was managed by Frederick Gye, one of the most successful of the managers of this period.

Music in the provinces then

Outside London musical life was less obviously commercial. A number of provincial cities had a tradition of music festivals that were flourishing during the middle years of the 19th century. Their profits were often used to provide finance for hospitals and other community facilities but provincial status was also important. Many were of international repute, including Birmingham, one of the oldest, with its origins in the 18th century and which had first brought Costa to England. Costa became conductor of the Birmingham Festival in 1849 and held that position until 1882. This also led to his involvement with the short-lived Bradford Festival from 1853-1857 and the Leeds Festival of Music from 1874 to 1880[12].

The programmes of these provincial festivals were underpinned by oratorio, sung with no scenery rather than staged, based on biblical themes and involving large numbers of singers and musicians, for which Costa's talent for musical discipline was particularly well suited.

In London the standard of choral singing was raised by the formation of the Sacred Harmonic Society in 1832 from a coalition of non-Conformist choirs and it performed at Exeter Hall, the focus of London non-conformity. Costa further expanded his musical appointments in 1848 when he became Director of the Society. In this position he also directed the triennial Handel Festivals, which were held at the re-sited Crystal Palace at Sydenham in southeast London. These were the London equivalents of a provincial festival. Each of these festivals was a large-scale event with a choir of 4,000 and an orchestra of 450 that attracted total audiences of over 80,000 people over the four days of the event.

Thus, by the late 1840s, Costa had become an important figure in the musical life of London and the provinces. He was Director of the fashionable Royal Italian Opera and conductor or Director of Music of the major symphony orchestra and the most important musical festivals of the time.

Costa as a composer

Costa had begun composing at the age of fifteen when he had written a cantata for the musical college in Naples where he was studying. In his early years at the King's Theatre he wrote a number of ballets and operas but his most enduring compositions were both oratorios first performed at the Birmingham Festival. *Eli* dates from 1855 and *Naaman* from 1864. These seem to have remained in the oratorio repertoire in Costa's lifetime but are now rarely performed. The verdict of contemporaries was mixed. Rossini, whose works were performed regularly by Costa, commented on an unidentified work by Costa: 'Kind Costa sent me the score of an oratorio and a Stilton cheese, the cheese was excellent'[13].

In the 19th century it was quite common for composers/conductors to rearrange or in their eyes 'improve' the scores of earlier composers. For example, Costa added trombone parts and drum passages to Handel's *Israel in Egypt*. Berlioz, whose work was not supported by Costa, criticised this tendency and when Costa rearranged a piece by Mozart he likened it to 'slapping a trowelful of mortar on a Raphael painting'[14].

In some cases this type of rearrangement was successful. In particular Costa's orchestration of the 'National Anthem' has been described by a leading historian of empire as 'holding sway throughout the latter part of Victoria's reign'[15][16]. As late as 1916 this version of the National Anthem was specifically requested by George V for a Red Cross concert.[17]

Costa's later musical career

Costa's collaboration with Gye at the Covent Garden Theatre was initially successful both artistically and financially but on 5 March 1856 the theatre burned down (in half an hour) and opera during the seasons of 1856 and 1857 under the management of Gye and directed by Costa was performed at the Lyceum Theatre. Gye was closely involved in the redevelopment of Covent Garden that reopened in April 1858.

Gye was primarily a businessman and was involved in a series of negotiations in the 1860s to amalgamate Covent Garden and its old rival, Her Majesty's Theatre, then managed by Henry Mapleson, as a way of reducing capacity and improving profits. This was achieved in 1868. Gye and Mapleson decided that they, as managers, wanted the right to engage the members of the orchestra, a role usually undertaken by the Director of Music. Costa was dissatisfied with the loss of artistic control and resigned. Mapleson described him as 'a despot'[18].

Despite two successful and profitable seasons in 1869 and 1870 Gye and Mapleson fell out and Mapleson took over management at the Drury Lane Theatre where he proceeded to re-hire the 'despotic' Costa. He then returned to Her Majesty's in 1877 still working with Costa. The relationship between the two men finally broke down in 1880 when Costa sued Mapleson for non-payment which caused Mapleson to be held briefly and technically bankrupt.[19]

Costa's masonic career

1848, the year Costa became Director of the Sacred Harmonic Society, was the year of revolutions in Europe with the overthrow of the constitutional monarchy in France and upheaval throughout Europe. Political upheaval created an uncertain employment situation for many musicians. Many court musicians found themselves unemployed. Performances were cancelled as audiences stayed at home. Although Chartist protests in England led to an atmosphere of unease and plans were put in place to evacuate the children of the Royal Family to the Isle of Wight, London proved to be a safe haven for many European musicians. Berlioz was already in London and had to delay his return. Other émigrés to England included Charles Halle and the Ganz family who were all to make a substantial contribution to the musical life of England.

1848 was significant for Costa in a different way as it was on the 3 May 1848 that he was initiated as a freemason in the Bank of England Lodge (*now* No. 263). As the Lodge Minutes for this period have been lost it is not possible to establish who proposed Costa. His brother Raphael had been initiated in the preceding year but there were also a number of other lodge members with musical connections. William Hammond, described as a music dealer, had been in the Lodge since 1836[20]. Benedict Negri, a composer, had joined in 1839 (the register says 'from Milan'), Scipio Brizzi (initiated 1842) and Maurizio Sardelli (initiated 1846) were both described as 'Professors of Music'. The *Grove Dictionary of Music* has no listings for any of these names.

The Bank of England Lodge had been founded in 1788. It took its illustrious name from the financial institution where two of its founders worked but there was no other direct association with it. By the middle of the 19th century the Lodge had a fairly eclectic membership with the professions and trade represented. A number of notable figures in Freemasonry were also members of the Lodge including Dr. Robert Crucefix, founder of the Home for Aged and Decayed Freemasons who had battled with the Duke of Sussex over the issue of provision for elderly members. Crucefix was also publisher of the first masonic periodical, *The Freemason's Quarterly Review*, which, in common with other periodicals of the day and with which it strove to be compared, included comments on matters of general artistic, musical and literary interest as well as specifically masonic content. Another member of the lodge was

Richard Spencer, publisher of the *Masonic Mirror*. Michael Costa served as Master of this Lodge in 1852 and 1853[21].

In July 1849, shortly after his brother, Michael Costa was exalted into the Royal Arch Chapter of Fidelity No 3. The Bank of England Lodge had no Royal Arch Chapter attached to it and many other members of the Lodge had also joined this Chapter including Richard Spencer, Richard Graves and Scipio Brizzi.[22]

The 1840s was also a period of unrest and change in English Craft Freemasonry. The death of the Grand Master since the Union, the Duke of Sussex, in 1843, resulted in a reaction against his authoritarian control. This reaction was particularly manifest in the increased activity in the 'extra-Craft Degrees', in Daniel's terminology, which had been largely kept dormant by the Duke of Sussex[23]. Costa and his brother also joined many of these other degrees. On 21 September 1849 Michael and Raphael Costa both became members of a Knights Templar Encampment, Cross of Christ (*now* the Preceptory of St George)[24].

Costa was appointed Grand Organist of the United Grand Lodge in 1851 and held the post for two years. He held the equivalent position in Supreme Grand Chapter and in the Grand Conclave of the Masonic Knights Templar.

Many of the men Costa knew from his Lodge and the Chapter of Fidelity were also involved with the establishment of another masonic organisation in England - Mark Masonry. Richard Spencer and Richard Graves were signatories to the Petition submitted to the Bon Accord Royal Arch Chapter of Aberdeen to found the Bon Accord Mark Lodge in London, which held its inaugural meeting at the Radley Hotel, Bridge Street, Blackfriars on 19 September 1851. Michael and Raphael Costa were both advanced to the 'honourable degree of Mark Master' at this meeting and they joined the six founders of the Lodge in presenting the Lodge furniture. Both were invested with offices: Michael Costa as Registrar of Marks and Raphael as Director of Music and Ceremonies. Although members of this Lodge were later instrumental in forming the Grand Lodge of Mark Master Masons in 1856 and were appointed the first Grand Officers, neither of the Costa brothers appears to have played any part in that event or more generally in the development of Mark Masonry in England, although Michael Costa was later one of the founders of the Studholme Mark Lodge No. 197 in the 1870s.[25]

In July 1846, Robert Crucefix obtained from the Supreme Council of the Northern Jurisdiction of the USA a Patent authorising him to establish the Ancient and Accepted Rite for England with a Supreme Council of the 33°. Costa also joined this Rite and by October 1853 is recorded as playing the organ at the consecration of the St Peter and Paul Chapter at Bath.[26] He attended a meeting of the Rite called by its Supreme Council in February 1854 by which time he had the rank of Grand Inspector Inquisitor Commander (31°) whilst his brother was Grand Elected Knight Kadosh (30°).[27] He was appointed to the Supreme Council itself in 1869, the Council Minutes state that he was already an Honorary Member of the 33°.[28] Costa's documented involvement in the affairs of the Supreme Council is small. He advised on the specification for the organ to be installed in the new Masonic Hall built when the premises at Golden Square were extended in 1872.[29] In that same year he was also a member of a small committee with Henry Clerk and Dr Robert Hamilton which considered favourably the recognition of a Supreme Council at Turin in 1872 as the governing body for the Ancient and Accepted Rite in Italy, a rather delicate question which involved rejecting the claims of the more politically inclined Supreme Council at Palermo associated with Garibaldi.[30] Costa's professional knowledge and language skills were probably the reason for his involvement in these two issues. (His brother is also described in the history of the Bank of England Lodge as 'Italian Consul'). Nevertheless the Supreme Council of the Ancient and Accepted Rite had fewer than a dozen members and Costa had a significant, if honorary, position as Captain of the Guards within it.

In 1851 Costa had also joined Royal Alpha Lodge No. 16. Since 1814 this Lodge had held a unique position, with 'its membership ... a highly prized masonic honour' in the view of the Lodge historian. Membership was limited in number and generally granted only to those who had high office in Grand Lodge, with all candidates for admission either proposed or approved by the Grand Master (an understanding which had become a rule after 1843). Costa continued as a member of this Lodge until his death in 1884.[31]

Costa also signed the Petition for the Friends in Council Lodge No. 1383 which was consecrated in 1872, having been established by Lord Carnarvon (Deputy Grand Master) as an additional means of communication between the Craft and the other masonic Orders. The Lodge was to provide the Supreme Council and its friends with

> an opportunity of meeting not to discuss not the affairs of the Order but those of the Craft, with the purpose of acting together by a previous exchange of views on such subjects...with which it is the function of Grand Lodge to deal.[32]

Costa attended the Consecration and was appointed as the first Treasurer but his membership ceased in 1878.

Costa's membership of both these Lodges is significant in terms of their prestige and potential influence (although that of the Friends in Council Lodge was probably rather less than its petitioners had anticipated.).

Costa and masonic music

In 1849 Costa composed a simple 'Grace' for the Bank of England Lodge.[33] At the Installation of the Prince of Wales as Grand Master, which was held at the Royal Albert Hall on 28 April 1875, Costa played an especially composed processional 'March' as the Prince and his sponsors entered the Hall. In recognition of this he was invested with the senior honorific rank of Past Junior Grand Warden.[34] This 'March' was played again by the Band of the Coldstream Guards in June 1876 at a masonic fete held in the grounds of Wadham College, Oxford attended by Prince Leopold, as Provincial Grand Master and other eminent men, both freemasons and non-masons.[35]

Costa and the Royal Family

Victoria and Albert shared their approach to music with much of the aristocracy. They occasionally attended opera at Covent Garden, they expected to have music performed at major public events and they developed an active musical life within their family. Although he never held any musical position within the Royal Household, Costa came into contact with members of the Royal Family from an early stage in his career. He accompanied the singer Madame Malibran at Queen Victoria's 16th birthday party in 1834. In June 1853 he attended the baptism of their youngest son Prince Leopold (*later* Duke of Albany) at Buckingham Palace where the boy chorister Arthur Sullivan sang an anthem, *Suffer the Little Children,* composed by Costa. Costa also gave piano lessons to Princess Victoria, the Princess Royal, and kept in contact with her when she moved to Germany as the wife of Frederick William of Prussia.[36]

Costa's masonic career also brought him into contact with the Royal Family. Prince Albert was not a freemason but the Prince of Wales was initiated into Freemasonry in Sweden in December 1868 and was subsequently invested as Past Grand Master of the United Grand Lodge of England in 1869. He joined Royal Alpha Lodge in 1870 by which time Costa had been a member for nearly twenty years. The Lodge subsequently saw an increase in the number of peers as joining members, many members of the Court or from the Prince's circle of friends.

Costa and public life

The second half of the 19th century was the great age of International Exhibitions starting with the Great Exhibition of 1851. A central feature in the original concept (which led initially to the establishment of the South Kensington Museums) was a Great Hall. After Prince Albert's death plans for the Hall fell into abeyance but were revived in 1865. Repeating his role in the organisation of the Great Exhibition, Sir Henry Cole was a key figure in arranging the design and construction of the Hall. At the foundation stone laying in May 1867 the ceremony included a performance of a composition by the Prince Consort called *Invocazione all'Armonia* with the Royal Italian Opera orchestra conducted by Costa. Cole also consulted Costa about the Hall's acoustics (which have never been entirely satisfactory)[37]. At the official opening in March 1871 Costa conducted his own specially-composed cantata involving more than 1200 performers. The *Musical Times* commented that it is but fair to say that the composer has successfully struggled against the difficulties presented to him in the libretto – which seemed thrown together by accident'.[38] Undaunted by this the Prince of Wales, in gratitude, presented Costa with a gold ring bearing an engraved seal of the Royal Albert Hall on behalf of the Commissioners.[39]

Sir Henry Cole's interest in arts education extended to music. At his powerbase, the Society for the Encouragement of Arts, Manufactures and Commerce, he organised a Committee in the 1860s to consider the paucity of British composers and musicians. Costa gave evidence stating that England had abundant talent but gave it no encouragement. The Committee's report helped establish a National Training School for musicians and then the Royal College of Music. The College was also patronised by the Prince of Wales and thus was also initially supported financially by a number of masonic donations.[40] Costa seems to have supported the institution by donating a number of scores now in the Library there.

Costa also came to be held in regard by other more academically inclined musicians. Also in the Royal College of Music Library is the score of a cantata by George MacFarren, dedicated to Costa in 1883, called *May-day*. MacFarren became Professor of Music at Cambridge in 1875 and Principal of the Royal Academy of Music in 1878.

Costa was knighted in 1869, only the second musician to be so honoured. His standing and fame continued for some years after his death. The centrepiece of an exhibition in 1897 for Victoria's Diamond Jubilee held at the Crystal Palace - the scene of some of his greatest musical triumphs - was his music collection.[41]

Costa and Freemasonry

I have yet to find any diaries or letters left by Costa which shed light on his decision to become a freemason. At the time of his Initiation he was already one of the most important figures in London musical life, a central figure in the most prestigious and fashionable art form - Italian opera - and of major importance in the more popular oratorio and concert life. He was already a man of some wealth, living in Eccleston Square, making significant donations of furniture to both his Craft Lodge and his Mark Lodge and as a patron of the other masonic charities. It seems unlikely in this position that Freemasonry could offer him opportunities to benefit his career in the world of commercial music and opera.

Costa had spent his formative years in Italy where he had seen his teacher, Zingarelli, knighted by King Ferdinand I of Naples for his contribution to music. He would have been aware that in much of continental Europe creative musical achievement in itself conferred eminence and status. In Victorian England, making music did not, of itself, lead to social acceptance. Did Costa see Freemasonry as offering a route to social acceptance?

The *Musical Times* highlighted in 1868 the perceived low social standing of musicians when it reported that Costa's membership of the Athenaeum Club had been blackballed by 20 members (over 170 voting in favour), 'it was a question whether so dignified an assembly could admit a man who... [is] styled a "professor of music'. The *Musical Times* chose to regard this as a slight on all musicians,

> Mr Costa is a representative man; he has done much for art and artists in England: and in passing a slight upon him, every musician who has obtained a public representation in this country feels himself to a certain extent aggrieved. [42]

An unnamed contributor to Crucefix's publication *The Freemason's Quarterly Review* wrote the following in 1849,

> The growing reputation of this lodge [i.e. the Bank of England Lodge] which ranks second to none in the Craft, is attributable no less to the refined intellectuality of its social engagements, than to the perfect and effective manner in which its ceremonies are conducted, and we

> consider it an enviable distinction to rank as one of its members. To every brother…who has a yearning to participate in all the pleasures which crown the social board of gentlemen and men of education we should say – pay a visit to the Bank of England Lodge.[43]

In his response to Daniel's 1993 paper on 'Pure - and Accepted – Masonry…' Gilbert points out that the great number of unofficial printed rituals that began to be issued in the 1830s and 1840s evidence growing interest in Freemasonry and demand for information.[44] In its second edition published on 1 July 1834, *The Freemason's Quarterly Review* published a selection of reviews of its first edition. This quotation from *The Age* is a typical response in its surprise that the magazine could interest the general reader as well as the members:

> At first sight we expected to find some mystical writing, interesting to the order alone. We have been agreeably disappointed. The articles on freemasonry are so agreeable as to prove equally interesting to the general reader.[45]

Perhaps Costa was one of those who read about Freemasonry and but possibly surmised that involvement with a well-regarded Lodge such as No. 263 could advance his status. Subsequently his membership of Royal Alpha Lodge and his 'extra-Craft' activities brought him into contact with many senior figures in society that may have compensated for the general lack of status suffered by musicians in England at the time.

It is noticeable that a number of important musicians and singers whom Costa would have known joined the Bank of England Lodge in the late 1840s and 1850s when Costa's interest in the Lodge was at its highest and although we do not know whether it was entirely due to his influence, their involvement may have mirrored Costa's own reasons for joining. These included Enrico Tamberlik, an Italian tenor who became immensely popular in London and sang at Covent Garden for fourteen years, made his London debut there on 4 May 1850, the same month in which he was initiated.[46]

Few new London lodges were formed in the first half of the 19th century but this changed at about the time that the Prince of Wales became Grand Master. There were 109 London lodges in 1844, 204 in 1874 and by 1900 the number of lodges in the capitol had more than doubled to 468. This partly reflected the huge growth in the population of London at this time but a full analysis of the reasons for this expansion, how it was effected and the implications it had for the social status of the membership remains to be undertaken.

Amongst the new lodges formed in this later period was the first lodge drawn largely from the musical and theatrical professions - the Lodge of Asaph No. 1319 - established in 1870. Although musicians and actors had joined lodges from the earliest days of organised Freemasonry in the 18th-century, the petition to form this new lodge argued that the members of such professions

> are unable to attend a lodge in consequence of professional duties requiring their services at the time Masonic meetings are usually held and are thereby precluded from accepting office, and advancing the interests of Freemasonry without great pecuniary sacrifice and detriment to themselves and families.

The lodge was to meet 'at an early hour' so that the members could then go on to their professional occupations[47] The lodge was sponsored by Montefiore Lodge No. 1017 and the petitioners included Charles Coote, described in the petition as 'a Professor of Music' but in the lodge's history correctly as 'a music publisher'; Edward Stanton Jones; John Martin Chamberlin and James Weaver (all described as 'Professors of Music'); George Buckland 'musical lecturer' at the Polytechnic Institute and George Martin, conductor of the National Choral Society at Exeter Hall.[48] The lodge grew rapidly in numbers. From the Grand Lodge Register information its members were mainly English orchestral players with few foreign names listed and a combination of new initiates and members joining from other lodges.[49] Perhaps Costa's eminence in the masonic world helped create the atmosphere in which the formation of such a lodge could be supported.

Conclusion

Costa died at Hove on 29 April 1884 having suffered a stroke in the previous year. He had remained active and influential until shortly before his death and the press tributes both nationally and masonically marked his passing.

Whatever role Costa had played in national events, he was essentially a professional musician in a commercial world. After his death he was criticised for not supporting 'new' music. George Bernard Shaw, the leading music critic of the time accused him of allowing 'opera to die in his grasp whilst it was renewing its youth and strength all over Germany'. But 'new' music, in the 19th century as much as now, did not attract public support and unless paying audiences went to the concert halls the economics did not work and the musicians did not get paid. Costa made commercial music socially acceptable and received a knighthood until then rarely granted to musicians not employed in the Royal Household.

Costa embraced Freemasonry and the 'extra-Craft' degrees with noticeable enthusiasm and remained actively involved with them. He did not need Freemasonry to advance his career or to meet patrons, he was already well established when he joined. In Italy his eminence in the musical world would probably have been sufficient to have brought him honours but this was not the case in mid 19th century England. His choice of lodge and his subsequent involvement suggests that he might have seen Freemasonry as a route to social acceptability.

Costa's masonic career illustrates both the changing perception of what joining Freemasonry might mean and also the greater inclusiveness of Freemasonry in the second half of the 19th century. Whether it is typical or whether it relates specifically to the changing status of musicians must await further biographical studies in this period.

***

Fig. 6: Michael Costa (1808-1884)
(with kind permission of the Library & Museum of Freemasonry, London)

***

NOTES

[1] D. Cairns: *Berlioz: Servitude and Greatness 1832-1869* (London, 1999), pp. 510 – 512.

[2] Cairns: *op. cit.*

[3] E. Bonython & A. Burton: *The Great Exhibitor, the Life and Works of Henry Cole* (London, 2003), p. 249.

[4] Entry for Costa in *the Dictionary of National Biography*

[5] P. Scholes: *The Mirror of Music, 1844-1944* (London, 1947), p. 377.

[6] Mapleson joined the Grand Master's Lodge No. 1 in May 1874 from a Scottish Lodge No. 291 (UGLE Membership records held at the Library and Museum of Freemasonry)

[7] J.H. Mapleson: (ed. by H. Rosenthal) *The Mapleson Memoirs* (London, 1966), p.130.

[8] W. Spark: *Musical Memories* (London, 1888), p. 6.

[9] Spark: *op. cit.*, p. 9.

[10] M. Hughes: *The English Musical Renaissance and the Press, 1850-1914* (Aldershot, 2002), p. 19.

[11] D. Nalbach: *The King's Theatre, 1704-1867* (London, 1972), pp. 105f.

[12] Scholes: *op. cit.,* pp.160 &162.

[13] Cairns: *op. cit.,* p. 406.

[14] *Ibid.*

[15] J. Richards: *Imperialism and Music* (London, 2001), p. 96.

[16] P. Scholes: *God Save the Queen!* (Oxford, 1944), p. 274 dates Costa's arrangement to 1883 and describes it thus: 'It begins with a drum roll, and the first half of the tune by full orchestra, followed by the first stanza in the key of B flat, as a soprano solo, accompanied merely by organ; it then modulates to the key F, so that the contralto may sing the second stanza (accompanied by the orchestral wind instruments), and returns to B flat so that the full choir may give out the final stanza (naturally with full orchestra plus organ). The orchestral accompaniment is comparatively simple.' Scholes states that there were two versions of this arrangement, one published by Novello and the other (as sung at Crystal Palace) by Joseph Williams. The Williams version also uses a running bass.

[17] Richards: *op. cit.,* p. 490.

[18] Mapleson: *op. cit.*, p. 81.

[19] *Ibid*, p. 137.

[20] This is probably William Hammond, comedian, burlesque actor and the brother in law of the dramatist Douglas Jerrold who was also a member of the Lodge. M. Slater: *Douglas Jerrold, 1803-1857* (London, 2002), p. 109.

[21] S.A. Pope: *The Bank of England Lodge No. 263, 1788-1931* (London, 1932), p. 117.

[22] Royal Arch membership records held at the Library and Museum of Freemasonry

[23] J.W. Daniel: 'Pure- and Accepted- Masonry: The Craft and the Extra-Craft Degrees, 1843-1901', in *AQC* vol. 106 (1994), p. 85.

[24] Pope: *op. cit.*, p. 118.

[25] J.A. Grantham: *History of the Grand Lodge of Mark Master Masons* (London, 1960), p. 27; Pope: *op. cit.,* p. 118.

[26] C.J. Mandleberg: *Ancient and Accepted* (London, 1995), p. 26.

[27] Mandleberg: *op. cit.,* p. 26.

[28] *Ibid,* p. 73.

[29] *Ibid,* p. 90.

[30] *Ibid,* p. 245.

[31] *History of Royal Alpha Lodge No 16* (London, 1962), p. 4.

[32] Daniel: *op. cit.,* p. 82.

[33] Pope: *op. cit.*, p. 116. The 'Grace' is still sung by the Lodge

[34] *Ibid,* p. 118.

[35] R. Hollinrake: 'The Masonic Life and Times of W. Bro. Sir Walter Parratt, *KCVO*', in *AQC* vol. 112 (London 2000), p. 191.

[36] Spark: *op. cit.* p. 11. '*The dream, a serenata'* was composed by Costa for her marriage and a score for this is in the Library of the Royal College of Music (D1005)

[37] Bonython & Burton: *op. cit.,* p. 249.

[38] Scholes: *Mirror op. cit.,* p. 209.

[39] Pope: *op. cit.,* p. 116.

[40] Hollinrake: *op. cit.* , p. 202.

[41] Richards: *op. cit.*, p. 138.

[42] Scholes: *Mirror, op. cit.,* p. 735.

[43] *The Freemason's Quarterly Review* (Second Series) (1849), p. 404.

[44] Daniel: *op. cit.,* p. 87.

[45] *The Freemason's Quarterly Review* (1834), p. 113.

[46] Pope: *op. cit.,* p. 125.

[47] Petition and associated correspondence held at the Library and Museum of Freemasonry

[48] Petition and associated correspondence held at the Library and Museum of Freemasonry

[49] UGLE membership records held at the Library and Museum of Freemasonry

*****

4

Some literary contexts of the Regius and Cooke manuscripts

by

Andrew Prescott

Þe smyth in forging, þarmorier in aremure,

In steele tryinge he cane al þe doctryne,

By crafft of Ewclyde mason doþe his cure,

To suwe heos mooldes ruyle, and his plumblyne,

Þe craffty ffynour cane þe golde wele fyne,

Þe iowayllier, for þat it is vaillable,

Maþe saphyres, rubyes, on a foyle to shyne,

Þus every þing draweþe to his semblable.

John Lydgate (*c.*1370-1449/50?),

Everything to His Semblable

The provenance of the Cooke and Regius manuscripts

On 24 June 1721, John, 2nd Duke of Montagu, was elected Grand Master of the Grand Lodge of Freemasons in London. This was a momentous event for the fledgling Grand Lodge, since it was the first time since its creation four years previously that a nobleman had accepted the office of Grand Master. Among those present was the antiquary William Stukeley, who afterwards benefited greatly from Montagu's patronage.[1] In his diary, Stukeley described how, during the meeting of Grand Lodge, Montagu's predecessor as Grand Master, George Payne, 'produced an old MS of the Constitutions which he got in the west of England 500 years old'.[2] Stukeley made drawings of the manuscript shown to the Grand Lodge by Payne which establish that it was the volume which is today Additional MS 23198 in the British Library, known, after its first editor, as the Cooke MS (hereinafter referred to as Cooke).[3]

Cooke is in Middle English prose, and the appearance of its handwriting suggests that it was not as old as Stukeley thought, but was compiled in the 15th century.[4] It contains a legendary history of the craft of stonemasonry and regulations for stonemasons. Its exhibition by Payne at Grand Lodge probably contributed to Grand Lodge's decision at its next meeting to ask James Anderson to produce a digest of the 'Constitutions of Freemasonry'.[5] In preparing this first *Constitutions of the Free-Masons*, Anderson sought to rescue these texts from the corruption introduced into them by 'Gothick ignorance' in the 'dark illiterate ages'.[6] Anderson used his own skills as a historian to try and reconstruct what he felt was the original legend, but his methods of historical criticism bore little relationship to modern procedures. Although a few passages in the 1723 *Constitutions* including the final line, 'Amen So Mote It Be', were based on Cooke and the influence of another five similar manuscripts can be detected, Anderson's work bears little relationship to Cooke or any other surviving pre-1717 'Charges'.[7]

Cooke apparently remained in the possession of Grand Lodge and the third Grand Secretary William Reid made two transcripts of it in about 1728.[8] Afterwards, however, it left masonic custody. In 1781, it was in the possession of one Robert Crowe, perhaps to be identified with the solicitor of that name who lived in Swaffham in Norfolk and died in 1786.[9] It was probably Crowe who wrote in a mock gothic hand the notes of the dates of the introduction of printing in Germany and England on folio 2 of the manuscript.[10] In 1786, the volume passed into the possession of the Norfolk antiquary Sir John Fenn, best known for his publication of the celebrated collection of 15th-century domestic correspondence, the Paston letters.[11]

After Fenn's death in 1794, the manuscript disappeared from sight, but it resurfaced in a rather Dickensian episode on a rainy day in London sixty years later. On 12 October 1859 the formidable Keeper of Manuscripts at the British Museum, Sir Frederic Madden, noted in his diary that he had been visited by an obscure woman who offered a manuscript for sale: 'A person named Caroline Baker also called with a small vellum MS. for which she asked £10, but I offered £4, which she took the day afterward'.[12] The tone of Madden's reference to Mrs Baker (we learn that she was married from a note afterwards made by Madden on the flyleaf of the MS) suggests that she was a humble person, and her willingness to accept a much lower price for the manuscript hints that she was pressed for cash. The item which Madden had purchased for the Museum was the long-lost Cooke MS.

Madden was very pleased with this new acquisition. He wrote in his diary that:

This MS. is of some little interest, since it contains a treatise in prose on the "Science of Gemetry" or Masonry, of the 15th century, and corresponds partly with the Poem on the same subject in MS. Reg. 17.A I printed by Halliwell in 1841[13] (2nd ed. 1843)[14], particularly in regard to the 'Articles'. It would be curious to ascertain which was the <u>earliest</u> form of the tract, <u>prose</u> or <u>verse</u>. The former is the fuller of the two, and at the beginning seems to agree with what Halliwell calls the 'Ancient Constitutions', and the Legend quoted from MS. Harl. 1912 and Lansd. 98 the earliest copy of which is stated to be about 1600. [15]

It seems that Madden did not undertake any further investigation of the contents of the manuscript, but, after it was incorporated in the Museum's collections as part of the sequence of Additional MSS, it came to the attention of the Canonbury freemason and self-styled 'Organist, Clerical Amanuensis, Public Lecturer and Sub-Editor',[16] Matthew Cooke. Cooke was a regular user of the British Museum, falling foul of the authorities there because of his refusal to fill in book request tickets in the correct fashion.[17] In 1861, Cooke published an elaborate transcript and pseudo-facsimile of the manuscript, made using specially cut types, the difficulty of producing which led to a legal dispute with the printer, William Smith, the printer of *The Freemasons' Magazine*.[18]

As Madden had immediately noticed, there were similarities between Cooke and another medieval manuscript in the British Museum, Royal MS 17 A. I. While Cooke is in Middle English prose, Royal MS 17 A. I is in verse and incorporates extracts from other Middle English poems. Nevertheless as Madden noted, like Cooke, Royal MS 17 A. I also contains a legendary history of the origins of the craft of stonemasonry and gives ordinances for stonemasons. Madden knew about this poem because it had been printed earlier in the 19th-century by James Orchard Halliwell (*afterwards* Halliwell-Phillipps).[19] Halliwell and Madden were bitter enemies. Madden had discovered that manuscripts sold to the British Museum by Halliwell in 1840 had been taken from the library of Trinity College Cambridge and sought to prevent him using the British Museum Library. Halliwell protested and threatened legal action against the Museum, so that his reader's ticket was restored, to Madden's great chagrin. Madden confided to his diary that Halliwell was a villainous scoundrel who deserved transportation.[20]

Halliwell was one of the most precocious literary scholars of his generation. He had begun to collect books and MSS on scientific subjects while he was still a schoolboy. At the age of 17, he published a series of biographical articles on British scientists in a leading literary journal. He was elected to the Royal Society and the Society of Antiquaries in 1839, when he was just 19. In the same year, while undertaking a systematic survey of scientific manuscripts in the British Museum,[21] Halliwell found among the manuscripts from the Old Royal Library in the British Museum a Middle English poem described in the 18th-century catalogue as 'A Poem, of Moral Duties: here entitled, *'Constitutiones Artis Geometrie Secundum Euclidem'*.[22] Halliwell, who was not a freemason but whose associates included a number of leading freemasons,[23] immediately recognised the masonic interest of this text, and described his discovery in a paper to the Society of Antiquaries in April 1839,[24] publishing an edition of the poem the following year.[25]

The MS published by Halliwell had formed part of the library of John Theyer a Gloucestershire antiquary who died in 1673, after which his books and manuscripts were acquired by King Charles II, then passed - with the rest of the Royal Collection - to the British Museum on its establishment, where it received its present official designation, Royal MS 17 A. I, representing its position on the shelf when it was moved into the British Museum.[26]   Royal MS 17 A. I was generally known by masonic scholars as the Halliwell MS until 1889 when Robert Freke Gould, conscious perhaps of Halliwell's scandalous reputation and maybe also piqued that this manuscript should have been first identified by a scholar who was not a freemason, proposed that it should be renamed the Regius MS, 'as being indicative alike of the collection – 'King's' or 'Royal Library', British Museum – upon whose shelves it reposes, and its own obvious supremacy as a document of the craft'.[27]   Gould's designation of this manuscript has been used ever since (referred to hereinafter as Regius).

The legendary history of the stonemasons' craft and the ordinances for stonemasons first recorded in Cooke and Regius were from the end of the 16th century amplified and extended in MSS which, to distinguish them from the modernised versions promulgated after the creation of the London Grand Lodge, are known as the 'Old Charges'.   While many of these post-1580 manuscripts containing early regulations for stonemasons have been traced – at the last count there were over 120[28] – Cooke and Regius are still the only medieval texts of this kind to have been identified.

Contextualising our interpretations

In considering Freemasonry and literature, it is tempting to concentrate on famous literary figures who were freemasons and to emphasise the influence of Freemasonry on their life and work.   However, Regius and Cooke remind us that literary texts, whether in the form of charges, ritual or writing about Freemasonry, are at the heart of Freemasonry itself.   But they are not of interest only to freemasons. The distinguished medievalist Helen Cam made a spirited defence of medieval local studies many years ago in which she stressed the enormous impact of the Middle Ages on modern life.[29]   Regius and Cooke are dramatic illustrations of this, since these short medieval texts have helped shape one of the modern world's largest and most influential social organisations.   They have had perhaps the most remarkable career of any medieval texts.

The critical literature on the Old Charges is immense, dwarfing the bibliographies of many more famous medieval texts.[30]   However, these studies concentrate on the classification of the surviving versions of the Old Charges and devote less attention to their historical context. This concern with classification is so intense that it sometimes almost obliterates the text itself. For example, when the discovery of a new 18th-century transcript of the Old Charges by the Newcastle lawyer George Grey was reported in 1999, the manuscript was described purely in terms of its textual relationships, making it impossible to tell what the actual manuscript says.[31] The Old Charges have become progressively divorced from their historical context, squeezing life from them.

The Chaucerian scholar David Wallace has recently lamented that the *Canterbury Tales* have suffered a similar fate and that the 'mechanical subjection of Chaucer's text to a pre-fashioned theoretical gridwork' has squeezed the life from the poetry.[32] He argued that it is necessary to restore Chaucer's text to the movement of history, 'to recognise its own sense of precariousness in occupying a time and place that shifts even at the instant of its own articulation'. Wallace's remarks refer to the effect on the reading of Chaucer of some types of modern critical theory. In the case of the Old Charges, their historicity has been undermined by a much older form of theoretical dogma, namely the view which characterised 19th-century classical studies that texts are best understood if they are grouped in textual classifications so that the purest and most original form of the text can be reconstructed. This methodology has dominated studies of Cooke and Regius since the German scholar Wilhelm Begemann first sought to classify the texts of the Old Charges in the 1890s. As a result, the texts of Cooke, Regius and the later manuscripts of the Old Charges have become de-historicised. While the critical situation in relation to the Old Charges is different to that described by Wallace in relation to Chaucer, the prescription is the same. The texts of Regius and Cooke need to be rescued from theoretical preconceptions and restored to the medieval world.

An important contribution to this endeavour has recently been made by the young American scholar Lisa Cooper in an article published in the *Journal of the Early Book Society*.[33] She seeks to establish what Regius and Cooke tell us about the mentality of medieval artisans. She shows how the texts sought to inculcate a sense of community among the stonemasons and how they reflected a pride in their work. Hitherto it has been assumed that medieval artisans expressed their self-esteem through the exuberance of their craftsmanship. Cooper points out that Regius and Cooke show that artisans could also articulate their loyalty to the craft through intellectual and symbolic constructs. She argues that in this respect Regius and Cooke are extremely unusual. In her view, they provide not only a textual means of conferring social capital and legitimacy on building workers but also provide a virtual textual home:

> The "boke[s] of our charges" ... turn masonry into a discourse of celebration and regulation, align the craft production of buildings that is their putative focus with the self-fashioning of artisans, and blur the lines between the artisanal work of masonry and the social work of being a mason. In the process, they provide the mobile masons with a textual space to call home.[34]

Cooper's powerful analysis suggests some new contexts for Regius and Cooke and perhaps helps point towards that instant of articulation which David Wallace has urged us to seek.

Dating and localisation of the MSS

One symptom of the way in which masonic analysis of the Old Charges has become progressively divorced from modern historical discussion since the 19th century is the tendency to ignore modern advances in the dating and localisation of manuscripts and simply to repeat dates assigned by 18th- and 19th-century scholars.

The copy of the Old Charges in the British Library, Lansdowne MS 98, ff.269-272, is generally dated c.1600 in most masonic literature and is thus considered one of the oldest surviving copies of the Old Charges. This dating rests on an opinion given in 1869 by Edward Augustus Bond, Keeper of Manuscripts at the British Museum from 1866 to 1878.[35]

In 1960, Dr. R.A.N. Petrie visited the British Museum to discuss the dating of some recently discovered manuscripts of the Old Charges.[36] He consulted H.R. Aldridge, then Deputy Keeper of Manuscripts at the British Museum, and in the course of their discussions they examined the copy of the Old Charges in Lansdowne MS 98. Aldridge declared that the Lansdowne MS 'is quite clearly of the reign of William III, say 1690-1700'. One reason cited in masonic literature in support of the c.1600 dating for this document was that the Lansdowne MSS include many of the papers of the Elizabethan statesman Lord Burghley who died in 1598. However, the Lansdowne MSS also contain many later papers from other sources, and Aldridge showed Petrie that the copy of the Old Charges in Lansdowne MS 98 were not the only item in the volume clearly dating from after Burghley's death.[37]

Aldridge could not believe that Bond has assigned a date of 1600 to the manuscript, and suggested that Bond, whose handwriting was notoriously bad, had meant to say that the manuscript dated from c.1690. Re-examination of the MS confirms Aldridge's opinion that the writing of the manuscript looks closer to the end of the 17th-century than the beginning, and it seems evident the date of c.1600 should have been abandoned long ago. Petrie reported Aldridge's re-dating of this MS to the Librarian at Freemasons' Hall, but this important information was never communicated further, so that, for example, in 1982 the well-known masonic scholar Colin Dyer repeated the date of c.1600 for the Lansdowne MS (and indeed suggested that it might be slightly earlier), and used this as an important part of his argument that the roots of the development of speculative Freemasonry should be sought in religious tensions in England at the end of 16th century.[38]

The date traditionally cited in masonic literature for Regius rests on more complex but, it turns out, equally shaky foundations. It is generally considered to be earlier than Cooke and is usually dated c.1390. The reason that this dating has become so widespread is that it is given in W.J. Hughan's guide to the Old Charges, first published in 1889, which has been the first port of call for those investigating the history of these documents.[39] However, the chief authority cited by Hughan in support of this dating was David Casley, whose catalogue of the Royal MSS published in 1734 dated the manuscript as 'XIV'. Hughan described Casley as an 'eminent authority', but Casley was working long before the modern study of manuscripts began and his 1734 catalogue is frequently inaccurate in its dating, description and localisation of manuscripts. Hughan declared that 'several experts' had supported Casley's dating. The only one of these experts who can be identified was Halliwell, who declared that Regius was 'written not later than the latter part of the 14th century'.[40] Again, however, Halliwell was writing when the scientific study of medieval hands was in its infancy, and cannot be considered a reliable authority for dating of the hand.

Hughan did not mention that there had been in the 1860s and 1870s a heated debate over the dating of Regius which showed that expert opinion on the dating of the manuscript was by no means firm or settled. The Scottish masonic scholar W.P. Buchan felt dissatisfied with Halliwell's dating. He asked a friend whether he knew anybody at the British Museum who could provide him with an opinion on the dating and he was given a letter of introduction to Edward Augustus Bond (then Keeper of Manuscripts and afterwards Principal Librarian). Bond replied on 8 June 1869 that 'without any hesitation' he dated the hand of Regius to the middle of the 15th century. Cooke was ascribed by Bond to the middle or later part of the 15th century. Bond's authoritative opinion was duly published in the masonic press.[41]

In 1874 the masonic scholar A.F.A. Woodford was criticised for ignoring Bond's opinion and insisting that Regius dated 'unquestionably to AD 1390'.[42] Bond was asked to revisit the matter, but refused to countenance a late 14th-century date for Regius, and insisted that it belonged to the first half of the 15th century. He re-examined both Regius and Cooke and wrote that 'As you seem to desire that I should look at the MSS. again, I have done so, and my judgment upon them is that they are both of the first half of the 15th-century.'[43] Bond's opinion that the manuscript was written in the 15th-century was later confirmed by his distinguished successors G.P. Warner and J.P. Gilson in the *Catalogue of Royal Manuscripts* published in 1921,[44] although they did not hazard a guess as to which part of the century the manuscript was written in.

Woodford remained unhappy about Bond's dating and tried another method to try and prove that the manuscript was written in the late 14th century. One of the assistants in the Department of Manuscripts, Richard Sims (not himself a freemason) prepared for Woodford a version of Regius in modern English.[45] It was perhaps Sims who drew Woodford's attention to similarities between parts of Regius and some texts published by the Early English Text Society, and Woodford duly announced his discovery that Regius incorporated extracts from two Middle English texts, an extract from a work by John Mirk and a poem on etiquette known as *Urbanitatis*.[46] Although as Woodford himself admitted the surviving manuscripts of both texts were much later than 1390, he perversely took his discovery as proof that his insistence on a late 14th-century date for the manuscript was justified, and continued to cling to his belief that Regius was written in about 1390.

In his elaborate facsimile of Regius published in 1889, H.J. Whymper noted that the artist who had prepared the plates, F. Compton Price, himself a pupil of Halliwell's copyist, Joseph Netherclift,[47] disagreed with Bond's dating of Regius. Price also preferred a late 14t-century dating.[48] To demonstrate his point, Price prepared illustrations of Additional MS 15580, a Wycliffite gospels dated by Price as late 14th century and which he considered very similar in appearance to Regius[49] and Arundel MS 38, a presentation copy of Thomas Hoccleve's *Regimen of Princes*, assumed by Price to have been made under the poet's supervision for presentation to King Henry V shortly after the poem was completed in 1411, but which it has recently been suggested may in fact have been made sometime before 1425 for Thomas, 2nd Duke of Mowbray.[50]

Price's facsimiles look convincing. The script of the Wycliffite text is much simpler in character and closer to the appearance of the hand of Regius, whereas the script in the Hoccleve MS is far more elaborate. The implication of Price's juxtaposition of these illustrations is that the simpler script represents an earlier stage of development of the writing of Middle English, suggesting that Regius dates from the earlier period. It was chiefly as a result of Price's facsimiles that a date of 1390 for Regius came to be firmly rooted in masonic literature. Considerable doubt must be felt, however, about the assumptions as to the development of Middle English palaeography which underpin Price's dating.

Price assumed that the Middle English scripts became increasingly florid and elaborate as the 15th century progressed, and that the Hoccleve MS reflects this process. However, the Hoccleve MS was a luxurious compilation intended for presentation to a noble patron, and the more elaborate and time-consuming script of the script simply reflects this fact. It is worth noting that the script of the celebrated Ellesmere MS of the Canterbury Tales, which has recently been identified as the work of Adam Pinkhurst a scribe who worked for Chaucer in the 1380s and 1390s, is also very elaborate in character.[51] Price's assumption that Middle English letter forms went rapidly from fairly set and economical forms to more elaborate ones is not justified; the development was far more complex than his illustrations suggest. He also gave an over-simplified view of the position by providing illustrations of just two manuscripts.

If Price had provided a wider range of comparisons, then Bond's dating of Regius to the first half of the 15th century would have gained much wider currency. The British Library's new digital catalogue of illuminated manuscripts enables us easily to explore some other comparisons to Regius beyond those provided by Price.[52] These support Bond's dating to the first half of the 15th century. This is evident by, for example, comparing the hand of Regius to the Burney MS 30, a Wycliffite gospels recently dated to the middle of the 15th century, and the English rubric in Harley MS 2367, f. 70v, again recently dated to the first half of the 15th century. Particularly telling are comparisons to manuscripts which are explicitly dated to the middle of the 15th century, such as the Arundel MS 327, a collection of saints' lives in English composed by Osbert Bokenham, an Austin friar of Cambridge, and according to a colophon, written down by his son Thomas Burgh in 1447,[53] or Additional MS 36704, a copy of Capgrave's Life of Gilbert of Sempringham, also explicitly dated 1447.[54]

In their edition of Regius, Knoop, Jones and Hamer declared that the dating of the hand of the manuscript to *c*.1390 had been determined by 'the palaeographical experts of the British Museum'. In fact, this dating rests on outmoded judgements by 18th- and early 19th–century scholars such as Casley and Halliwell, on Woodford's perverse determination to maintain a late 14th century dating in the face of Bond's judgement otherwise, and on a very partial selection of illustrative comparisons by Price in the 'Preface' to the 1889 facsimile. The only formally recorded expert opinions on the date of the script, by the three Keepers of Manuscripts at the British Museum Bond, Warner and Gilson, all favoured the 15th century. The only masonic scholar to have given serious consideration to Bond's dating was Gould.[55] If Regius is to be dated on grounds of script alone, then comparisons of the sort listed above suggest that Bond's judgement remains the best, namely that Regius is probably from the first half of the 14th century.

The great 19th-century German masonic scholar Wilhelm Begemann wisely tried to avoid dating Regius on the grounds of its script alone, and placed greater emphasis on its dialect, declaring that its language showed that it was not later than 1410-1415 and indeed probably older than that date. He argued that the dialect of Regius meant that it came from a small area comprising South Worcestershire, Herefordshire and North Gloucestershire.[56] These conclusions were confirmed by Douglas Hamer, who wrote that both Regius and Cooke were

> written in the dialect spoken in the South-West Midland area of England in the later part of the fourteenth century. The Cooke MS., however, contains more Southern forms than the Regius MS. and was probably composed by a man who lived further south, though clearly in a region in contact with the Midlands and West Midlands. The West Midland area of Middle English dialects covers Gloucestershire and West Oxfordshire.[57]

Shortly before his death in 1981, Hamer suggested a firm connection between the manuscript and the Augustinian abbey of Llanthony in Gloucestershire. He pointed out that John Theyer, the former owner of Regius, had acquired over 800 volumes from the last Prior of Llanthony.[58]

Regius was one of the thousands of manuscripts whose linguistic characteristics were analysed minutely in the *Linguistic Atlas of Late Medieval English* (LALME), published in 1986 under the joint-editorship of Angus McIntosh, M.L. Samuels and Michael Benskin.[59] The LALME analysis confirmed that the dialect of the manuscript came from the west of England, but assigned it to a different county to that suggested by Hamer, namely Shropshire. The linguistic profiles of Shropshire manuscripts provided by LALME give a great deal of information which potentially can be used to assist in the dating of Regius. It is not possible here to give such a detailed analysis, but from the point of view of dating Regius, the most significant point is that the manuscript whose linguistic profile in LALME most closely matches Regius is Hand D of Cotton MS Claudius A. ii, ff. 127r-152v, a text of John Mirk's *Instructions for Parish Priests* which has recently been dated to the second quarter of the 15th century.[60] The linguistic evidence of Regius thus tends to suggest a dating of between 1425 and 1450, broadly supporting Bond's opinion of the hand. Unfortunately, Cooke was not included in the LALME analysis, presumably because its compilers were unable to find enough distinctive features in its language to localise it.

The firm localisation of Regius to Shropshire and its possible links to a Mirk manuscript are fascinating, since, as Woodford first pointed out, the concluding section of Regius includes over a hundred lines on behaviour when attending Mass from Mirk's *Instructions for Parish Priests*. Mirk (*fl. c.*1382-*c.*1415) was the Prior of the Augustinian Priory of Lilleshall in Shropshire.[61] He was particularly interested in the education of the everyday clergy, and composed a number of works in English for their use. Mirk's most well-known work was *Festial*, a collection of sermons, written for the help of 'suche mene clerkus as I am myself'. The *Instructions for Priests* is one of two pastoral manuals for priests composed by Mirk, the other being the *Manuale Sacerdotis*. It used to be thought that all these works dated from the end of Mirk's life, but in fact, while the *Manuale* was compiled after Mirk had become Prior, the *Festial* and the *Instructions for Parish Priests* were written while he was still a canon in the 1380s.[62]

Knoop, Jones and Hamer considered, and rejected, the possibility that Regius was composed by Mirk or another canon of Lilleshall.[63] In the light of the LALME analysis of the Regius dialect this possibility needs to be reconsidered, but for the moment the main interest of the extract from Mirk is the extent to which it assists in more firmly dating Regius. Although the *Instructions for Parish Priests* was composed in the 1380s, the earliest surviving manuscripts date from after 1420. The way in which Mirk's lines have been extracted and used in Regius suggests that the *Instructions* were already fairly well known and widely circulated. This makes it unlikely that Regius predates any of the surviving manuscripts. This again tends to suggest a date for Regius of the second quarter of the 15th century.

Regius also contains extracts from two other Middle English texts. The first is a complete copy of *Urbanitatis*, an example of a courtesy book, a form of etiquette manual.[64] *Urbanitatis* may perhaps be identified with the 'booke of vrbanitie' which was used to teach the young knights of King Edward IV's household 'to haue his respectes vnto theyre demenynges, how mannerly they eat and drinke'.[65] As Hamer has observed the exact dating of *Urbanitatis* is obscure,[66] but if it is indeed the book mentioned in the Black Book of the Household of Edward IV, this would show that it was popular in about 1471-2, and would also seem to hint at, if not firmly establish, a 15th-century date for Regius.[67] The third Middle English poem used in Regius is a poem entitled *Merita Missa*.[68] In this case, Regius does not simply transcribe the original lines but summarises and reworks them. *Merita Missa* was ascribed by its first editor to John Lydgate (*c.*1370-1449/50?). However, it was quickly shown that the rhyme scheme was unlikely to have been Lydgate's.[69] The poem occurs in a section of Cotton MS Titus A. xxvi which, as Linne Mooney has recently shown, was probably compiled sometime after 1456.[70] Regius may have drawn on another exemplar, but nevertheless it seems evident that the *Merita Missa* was current in the middle of the 15th-century. While these two other sources of Regius do not firmly establish its dating, it is striking that they are works which occur in manuscripts of the mid 15th century, and seem to point in that direction as far as the dating of Regius is concerned.

To summarise, the conventional dating of Regius to *c.*1390 is based on antiquated appraisals and on Price's limited comparisons. While a late 14th-century date for Regius cannot be completely ruled out, the evidence of its script suggests that it dates from the first half of the 15th century. Analysis of the dialect of Regius and the other poems incorporated in it seem to point towards a dating of *c.*1425-50. Regius can be firmly localised on the grounds of its dialect to Shropshire, and the inclusion of extracts from Mirk's *Instructions for Parish Priests* suggest a link with Lilleshall Priory. Evidence of the continued use and currency of Regius in the late 15th and early 16th centuries is given by some additions in hands of this date on the pastedown at the end of the manuscript, which contain a charm against bleeding and the first verses of Psalms 8 and 18.[71]

The dating of Cooke presents fewer problems. In first publishing the manuscript, Matthew Cooke suggested that it dated from the end of the 15th-century.[72] Bond was again asked to pronounce on its date and in 1869 stated that he considered that it was of the middle or later part of the 15th-century, but rather inclined towards the earlier period. In short, in Bond's view Regius and Cooke come from the same period, with Regius being perhaps slightly earlier. Close comparison of the hand of the two manuscripts, conveniently reproduced in facing plates in Knoop, Jones and Hamer's edition,[73] will show how, while they are clearly the work of different scribes, the differences between them are not sufficiently great to suggest that there was a long gap between the time of their production. They are broadly contemporary. In searching for the moment of historicity that resulted in the production of Regius and Cooke, we are looking for events which occurred at broadly the same time, probably sometime in the second quarter of the 15th-century.

A brief comparison of their contents

Regius contains 794 lines of Middle English verse.[74] It begins by describing how the great clerk Euclid devised geometry and gave it the name of masonry in order to provide employment of the children of great lords and ladies living in Egypt. Euclid ordained that, although there were masters among the masons, they should nevertheless treat each other as equals, 'neither subject nor servant'. It states that masonry came to England in the reign of Æthelstan (presumably Æthelstan the grandson of King Alfred, who reigned from 924 to 939). To regulate the craft, Æthelstan made a series of ordinances, which the poem lists. The themes emphasised by these articles and points include the importance of the general assembly of masons, which all masons were expected to attend, the need for fair pay, and the necessity of masons treating each other as fellows, helping each other in their work, serving each other at meals and avoiding recourse to litigation.

After reiterating that these ordinances were established by Athelstan, Regius recounts the story of the Four Crowned Martyrs, the Christian stonemasons who were martyred by a Roman Emperor. This is probably drawn from a popular hagiographical collection such as Jacob of Voraigne's *Golden Legend*, which was also a major source of Mirk's *Festial*. Regius then returns to the origins of stonemasonry. It describes the destruction of the Tower of Babel because of the pride of its builders. Euclid afterwards revived the art of masonry and devised the system dividing knowledge into the 'Seven Liberal Arts' of grammar, dialectic, rhetoric, music, astronomy and geometry. It concludes with general precepts for good living drawn from three sources. Lines 593-692 consist, as has been seen, of extracts from Mirk's *Instructions for Parish Priests* which are intersected with lines based on the *Merita Missa* poem. Regius ends with the complete transcript of *Urbanitatis*. This 'booke of vrbanitie' shows the mason how to behave well and urges him for example to take off his hat in church, not to speak with a full mouth, and to avoid spitting or sniffing when addressing a lord.

The structure of Cooke's text is simpler than that in Regius. It begins with a history of stonemasonry which considerably expands that in Regius. It opens with an elaborate invocation to God, who had made all things to be subject to man. God had given man knowledge of crafts, including geometry. The 'Seven Liberal Arts' are then listed. Clearly, the author declares, geometry is at the root of them all, since geometry means measurement of the earth, and all tools involve measurement and are made of materials from the earth. All the crafts of the world, he continues, were founded by the sons of Lamach, who were mentioned in Genesis, with Lamach's eldest son Jabal inventing geometry. Lamech's sons wrote their discoveries on two pillars of stone to survive fire or flood. After the flood, Pythagoras found one stone and Hermes the other. Ham, Noah's son, revived the practice of masonry. Nimrod, Ham's son, sent masons to Assyria and gave them charges which, declares Cooke, survive, just as those given by Euclid have survived.

Cooke then repeats the story of Euclid in much the same way as Regius, but with more biblical references and circumstantial information about Egypt. It describes how stonemasonry came to Europe. It states that a king was elected in France called Charles II, who loved masons, and gave them charges which were still in use in France. Shortly afterwards, 'Saint Ad Habelle' came to England and converted St Alban to Christianity. Alban also gave charges to the masons and 'ordained convenient [wages] to pay for their travail'.[75] It then gives a slightly different version of the Æthelstan story. It states that Æthelstan's youngest son himself became proficient in masonry, and gave the masons ordinances. He declared that they should have reasonable pay, and purchased a charter from the King that the masons might hold an assembly at whatever time they thought reasonable. Cooke then repeats the story of Æthelstan's grant in the same terms as Regius, and reiterates the various ordinances. The order of the Articles is slightly different, and some of the more general Articles in Regius are omitted. The effect of the rearrangement is to give greater prominence to the masons' assembly, and Cooke concludes by stressing that any mason who failed to attend the assembly would be arrested by the sheriff ands cast into prison. None of the supplementary material from Mirk, the *Merita Missa* or *Urbanitatis* is included in Cooke.

In taking the legendary history of stonemasonry back to Genesis, Cooke gives references to Bede, Isidore and other authorities, but as Douglas Knoop and Douglas Hamer pointed out these are mostly spurious.[76] For example, it is stated that Pythagoras wrote the Polychronicon,[77] whereas this popular medieval historical encyclopaedia was written by the Chester monk Ranulph Higden, who died in 1361, and translated into English by John de Trevisa in about 1387.[78] It has been generally assumed that both Cooke and Regius are based on a common unknown original which does not survive, and that Cooke represents a much fuller version of this lost original than Regius.[79] This assumption is based partly on a comparison between the Articles and Points in both manuscripts. It also derives from comparisons between Regius, Cooke and much later manuscripts such as the William Watson MS, dated 1687, and the 18th-century Tew MS.[80]

To reach conclusions about the relationship of medieval texts by referring to other manuscripts which are nearly three hundred years later and for which there are no intermediary witnesses is a hazardous critical process, to say the least. Indeed, the whole discussion of the relationship between these texts has been bedevilled by a very odd process whereby late transcripts have been accorded similar status to original texts. It seems absurd to describe Cooke and the two transcripts made in the 1720s as 'the Cooke family'. It is likewise strange to designate Robert Plot's printed description of a manuscript seen by him which apparently no longer survives as the 'Plot MS'. Late transcripts of this kind would not normally be considered in an analysis of medieval texts unless they preserve texts which have disappeared, which is not the case here.

In order to make better sense of the context of the production of Regius and Cooke, it is essential to focus once again on these texts alone, which are after all the only medieval texts of this kind so far identified. A close reading of Regius and Cooke suggests that it is by no means certain that Cooke represents a fuller version of an older original text than Regius. There are other possible interpretations which deserve consideration. For example, there are indications that Cooke may simply be an expansion and amplification of a shorter text similar to, or even identical with, Regius.[81] At several points Cooke appears to be referring to an older set of Charges which it states ascribed the origins of masonry to Euclid. For example, at lines 418-423, it declares that:

Elder masons that were before us had these charges written as we have now in our charges of the story of Euclidus as we have seen them written....

Regius, which ascribes the invention of the craft of masonry to Euclid, would fit this description very well, and it seems likely that the author of Cooke would have considered Regius to represent an earlier and distinct set of Charges rather than a representative of a common textual tradition. Such an interpretation seems to be confirmed by lines 640-642 of Cooke which read:

As is written and taught in the Book of our Charges whereof I leave it at this time.

These lines are clearly intended to introduce the existing Charges, and it is at precisely this point that the section of Cooke which is most closely related to Regius begins. Again, the sense of Cooke is that Regius (or something very like it) represents the existing Charges, of which Cooke was an amplification and development.

Most of the extra material in Cooke is designed to relate the story of masonry to biblical history. As such it provides the craft with an even more ancient lineage than that proposed by Regius. The concern of Cooke to emphasise the Christian character of the story is also evident from the frequent interpretation of false references to the Christian fathers and other respectable sources such as the Polychronicon. Having related to early history of masonry to the bible, Cooke also seeks to provide a more elevated Christian heritage for the appearance of the craft in Britain and to take its story back beyond the time of the 10th-century Anglo-Saxon King Æthelstan. Cooke declares that the proto-martyr St Alban gave the masons in

Britain their first Charges. It also amplifies the story of Æthelstan's involvement. Regius simply ascribes the ordinances to Æthelstan himself, and is content to demonstrate the elevated social status of masons by referring to the invention of the craft by ancient Egyptian nobles. Cooke seeks to show that nobles had also practiced the craft of masonry in England and elsewhere. It therefore introduces into the story an unnamed son of Æthelstan, who it declares became a mason and persuaded his father to make a grant to the masons. The result of the introduction of this story into Cooke is a clumsy double account of the grant to the stone masons by Æthelstan. In the 16th century, this son of Æthelstan came to be identified as Edwin.[82] This identification was to cause confusion when Robert Plot in 1686 pointed out that Æthelstan was not known to have had any sons, although he did have a brother of that name,[83] prompting later masonic historians such as Anderson and the copyists of some 18th-century Charges to try and correct the legend by ascribing the grant of the charter to Æthelstan's brother.

A major objection to an interpretation of Cooke as an amplification of a text similar to Regius is the different treatment in the two manuscripts of the 'Articles' and 'Points' supposedly ordained by Æthelstan. Regius contains more of these ordinances (fifteen Articles and fifteen Points) than Cooke (nine Articles and nine Points, with some unnumbered additions). Table I below provides a comparison between the 'Articles' in Regius and Cooke.

Although Cooke contains fewer Articles, in a number of cases it is clear that the provisions have been strengthened in Cooke in order to address pressing grievances. Thus, while Regius contains a fairly vague Article on the pay of apprentices, in Cooke this is replaced by a more clear-cut provision that 'no master shall pay more to his apprentice during the time of his apprenticeship, whatever profit he may take thereby, than he well knows him to have deserved'. Moreover, in Cooke this Article has been given more prominence by moving it up the list to number four, exchanging positions with the article prohibiting the employment of lame apprentices. A similar refinement by Cooke of a vague provision in Regius is evident in Article 7. Regius enjoins that master masons shall not cloth or feed thieves, lest they bring shame on the craft. Cooke replaces this with a more specific injunction and gives a more practical reason for the rule: no master is to help or sustain a common nightwalker to rob, because such night time activities would prevent them doing a good day's work. Cooke apparently omits some Articles from Regius because they are simply vague injunctions, such as the Article that masters shall not swear false oaths, while others are omitted because they repeat issues covered in earlier Articles, such as the thirteenth and fourteenth Articles in Regius which relate to the training of apprentices, an issue already addressed in the course of some of the earlier Articles.

In general, Cooke seems to represent a shrewd editing of the Regius Articles undertaken in order more effectively to deal with grievances against the master masons. This impression is confirmed by a comparison of the 'Points' in both manuscripts (see Table II below).

The most striking feature of the Cooke Points is that they draw together and considerably strengthen the provisions relating to the assembly of stonemasons, giving them much greater prominence by placing them together at the end of the whole text. As with the Articles, the Points in Cooke seem to represent an intelligent reordering and editing of Regius, so as to remove repetition, deal with more urgent concerns and give greater prominence to central issues, particularly in order to emphasise the authority of the masons' assembly.

It has been seen that Regius and Cooke are probably not far separated in date. Rather than both drawing on a common lost original, it is more likely that Cooke is an amplification and reworking of a text very similar, and perhaps even identical to, that of Regius. Regius emphasised the religious orthodoxy and respectability of the stonemasons by adding to the legendary history and articles a miscellany of material of religious and other material of use to the socially aspiring stonemason. In Cooke, this material has been omitted, and replaced by a new legendary history which takes the story back beyond Euclid and shows how the introduction of stonemasonry to Britain was intimately connected with the arrival of Christianity. However, the compiler of Cooke was not simply concerned to provide these legends of the craft of masonry with a veil of religious respectability. His primary concern was the importance and authority of the assembly of masons, and the text concludes with emphatic claims as to the authority and power of that assembly.

Lay literate culture in the 15th century

In investigating Regius and Cooke, the essential starting point remains the mass of information about medieval stonemasons assembled by the formidable trio of Sheffield scholars, Douglas Knoop, Gwilym Jones and Douglas Hamer, who produced the definitive edition of these texts. Knoop, Jones and Hamer argued that, while Regius and Cooke reflect pride in the stonemason's craft, they were not produced by masons:

> they were written and composed by clerks; but they were composed in large parts of materials current among masons, of customs and perhaps traditions, which had been orally transmitted from generation to generation, much as manorial customs were commonly transmitted before it became convenient or necessary to set them down in writing.[84]

These comments reflect an assumption that literate culture in the 15th century was clerical and that artisan access to it was limited. It was for this reason that Hamer was convinced that Regius was associated with Llanthony Abbey. As has been seen, the LALME analysis of Regius places it instead in Shropshire, which raises the tantalising possibility that it was connected with Lilleshall Priory and the circle of John Mirk. Augustinian Canons were particularly associated with the preparation and dissemination of literary texts in England in the late 14th and early 15th centuries, and an Augustinian connection for Regius would be quite likely. However all this depends on the assumption that a poem such as Regius could only have been compiled in a clerical milieu. This is not a safe assumption. By the 15th century, artisans were owning and apparently using manuscript books. In 1417, the stonemason John Clifford of Southwark , who had been Master of the London Masons' Company in 1386,[85] left to the church of St Olave Southwark his 'principal psalter and another book of gospels in English' for use in the church.[86]   The possibility that a group of stonemasons based in Shropshire would have commissioned a text such as Regius in the middle of the 15th century is not as remote as Hamer suggested. Such a group would doubtless have been aware of a well-known local production such as Mirk's treatise and may well have thought the inclusion of such a text in their manuscript a suitable emblem of respectability.

Society at large became increasingly literate during the 15th century, a process accelerated by the greater use of English in official documents.[87]   Business and government relied on documents and lay people needed to understand what was in them. Already in the early 14th century, some peasants on the manor of Halesowen in Worcestershire were literate and took part in the compilation of manorial records.[88] The rebels in 1381 used letters to communicate with each other,[89] and by 1430 Lollard craftsmen in Somerset and Wiltshire were distributing written criticisms of the church.[90]   Anne Hudson has recently discussed the cases of the leading Lollards Walter Brut and William Swinerby, who were both laymen of apparently humble social positions, but were both literate and displayed a good knowledge of a surprisingly wide range of religious literature.[91]   The emerging literate culture of 15th century urban life has been succinctly described by Susan Reynolds as follows:

> In 1422 the brewers of London decided to keep their records in English because many of them could read English but not Latin or French. Later in the century some city companies required apprentices to be literate, and Sylvia Thrupp estimates that half the laymen (but not the women) could probably read. In 1503 a York glazier left to his apprentice 'all my books that is fit for one prentice of his craft to learn by.[92]

The emergence of this urban literate culture during the 15th-century is reflected in the appearance of a body of literature which, if not actually produced by artisans and craftsmen, shows contact with and sympathy for them. This material provides an important textual context for Regius and Cooke. The American scholar Linne Mooney has recently discovered a treatise in English on the 'Seven Liberal Arts' dating from the late 15th century.[93]   In describing each of the Arts, the treatise gives practical illustrations of their value. Under arithmetic, examples are given of simple mathematical operations, such as how to calculate a square root. Geometry is discussed at great length, with illustrations, apparently drawn from digests of Euclid, of how to measure the length of a field, the depth of a well or the height of a steeple. The importance of geometry in making buildings to protect man from heat and cold and the great craft involved in such operations as erecting steeples was stressed. At the end, the treatise, drawing on the earlier work of Hugh of St Victor, states that the 'Seven Liberal Arts' were complemented by seven special 'sciences' which were practical skills of everyday life, such as agriculture, hunting and medicine. In discussing these special 'sciences', the author attempts to link them to crafts in medieval towns. In this way, in Mooney's words, 'the text expresses a pride in artisanship, the professions and trades that only just falls short of claiming parity with clerical skills'.[94]   This is clearly one milieu in which Regius and Cooke should be placed. Mooney suggests that the manuscript containing this text was prepared for a member of London's mercantile class who was able to commission manuscripts of many popular vernacular works, including Chaucer, Hoccleve and Lydgate.[95]

An even more direct pride in craftsmanship is apparent from another late 15th-century text printed by Edmund Wilson in 1988, *The Debate of the Carpenter's Tools*.[96] This is a lively comic debate between the various tools of the carpenter's trade: the saw, the rule, the plane, the compass and so on. A typical exchange is that between the rule stone and the gouge. The rule stone declares that his master will rule the roost; the gouge says the rule stone was not worth an old shoe: 'You have been an apprentice for seven year, but all you have learnt is how to leer'. Wilson suggests that the *Debate of the Carpenter's Tools* was intended for recitation at a guild feast. The most striking feature of the poem is the technical awareness shown of the various carpenters' tools. If the author was not himself actually a carpenter, he had absorbed a great deal of arcane knowledge of the carpenter's craft. The *Debate* is not unique; it has been pointed out that the presumably clerical author of the shipwrights' play of the Building of Noah's Ark in the 'York Mystery Cycle' also displays similar technical knowledge of the shipwright's craft.[97] In this context, Regius and Cooke appear less unusual. Moreover, it makes it seem less unlikely that the stonemasons themselves played an active part in drawing up the texts in Cooke and Regius.

Guilds were another aspect of this increasing lay literacy. A further major textual context for Regius and Cooke are the returns made by guilds in 1388-9 in response to an inquiry into the nature and property of guilds. More than 450 such returns survive in the National Archives.[98] Most are in Latin or French, but 59 are in English, one of the first times English makes an appearance on such a large scale in the public records. The returns were not necessarily made directly by the guilds themselves. In some cases, guild officials went to Westminster and their Returns were compiled from an oral deposition. In others, guilds used local clerical help. However, some of the returns were doubtless compiled directly by the guilds. This is likely to be the case with many of the English Returns, which are mostly from guilds in London, Norwich and King's Lynn.

Typical of the 1389 guild returns in English are the ordinances of the carpenters in Norwich. The primary purpose of the carpenters' guild was the maintenance of a candle in honour of the Holy Trinity in Norwich Cathedral. An annual meeting was held to ensure the maintenance of this light and the performance of devotions before it. Services were held for members of the guild at their deaths. The guild would assist members who became impoverished, if it was not through their own folly.[99] Surprisingly, there are few references to craft regulations in these returns. There is little to distinguish the Norwich carpenters' return from that of the guild of St Thomas of Canterbury at King's Lynn.[100] This guild had also been established to maintain a light, this time to be placed before a picture of St Thomas in a local church. St Thomas's Guild also offered benefits to its members, and if any member became poor through loss at sea, fire or any other act of God, the guild undertook to assist them. The lack of craft content in the 1389 returns is particularly apparent in the return made by the Fraternity of the Blessed Virgin Mary established by the stonemasons of Lincoln in 1389.[101] Again, this return concentrates on religious observance and mutual benefits for the members of the guild. The only explicit reference to working stonemasons is a regulation that all stonemasons belonging to the fraternity should give forty pence every time they took an apprentice. Likewise, the stonemasons in Norwich had established a fraternity but its main function was again the maintenance of altar candles.[102]

For historians of the generation of Knoop and Jones, the stonemasons' fraternities at Lincoln and Norwich were not true craft guilds but religious fraternities, but recent scholarship has stressed that such firm distinctions were not made in the medieval town.[103] As Elspeth Veale has observed:

> The distinction drawn [by historians of medieval England] between fraternity – an association which concerned itself particularly with religious ceremonies, especially the rites of burial, and with the social activities which its members enjoyed – and organised mistery may well have been drawn too sharply.[104]

Although various fraternities, fellowships, crafts and mysteries (all terms used in medieval documents) were an all-pervading feature of medieval town life, there was no rigid legal categorisation of them – they were loose and flexible organisations. It was from religious associations of this kind that the more trade-oriented fraternities emerged. In London, for example, a fraternity at the church of All Hallows Bread Street was founded by a mercer and a salter.[105] Most subsequent bequests came from salters. Eventually, Salters' Hall was built on land owned by the fraternity and the chapel of the guild became known as the Salters' Chapel. A similar process occurred in York, where during the 15th century the Fraternity of St John the Baptist became associated with the tailors and the guild of Holy Trinity in Fossgate with the mercers.

The chief driving force in the way in which these fraternities with primarily religious and social functions assumed trade responsibilities was the increasing requirement from the late 14th century imposed by royal and civic ordinances for individual crafts to undertake trade regulation. Because the emergence of these guilds was an ad hoc solution to immediate legislative requirements, trade regulation was carried on in a very haphazard fashion. Even more importantly, where such regulation was not required, guilds might not acquire trade regulation functions. Professor Barrie Dobson has recently observed of Durham that

> one is left with the overwhelming impression that, had it not been for the need to impose a procession and sequence of plays on the crafts of the city at their own expense, here would have been no formal guild regulations at all.[106]

In smaller towns such as Grimsby, craft guilds did indeed fail to develop.[107] For historians of the generations of Knoop and Jones, the paucity of references to craft guilds of masons was puzzling, but there is nothing particularly surprising in the available information about masons' guilds – they are much the same as for many other crafts of similar size and status.

A major reason for the assumption of trade regulation responsibilities by various fraternities from the 1360s onwards was the impact of labour legislation. The Black Death had created a labour shortage and this resulted in legislation from 1351 to control wages and regulate terms of service.[108] Between 1351 and 1430 more than a third of the parliaments passed legislation relating to labour. Much of this consisted of attempts to update increasingly elaborate tariffs of wages. The enforcement of this legislation became the responsibility of the JPs. The building trades were a particular problem. The bulk of the surviving prosecutions under the labour legislation concerned carpenters and masons, and a number of the statutes specifically denounce the taking of excessive wages by these trades.[109] Sarah Rees Jones has forcefully argued that increasing urban resentment of the powers of the JPs led to an enactment in 1363 stating that craftsman were to join a single trade and that they were to be regulated by members of their crafts.[110] She suggests that this gave a major impetus to the assumption of regulatory powers by crafts and argues that the emergence of guilds as regulatory authorities fostered the development of oligarchies within the trade. This led to attempts in many trades by journeymen to establish their own guilds, resulting in conflicts which frequently became violent. In 1387, a group of journeymen tailors violently threatened other tailors because they would not join a guild of journeymen tailors they had established at Coventry in opposition to the main tailors' guild.[111]

Considered in these contexts, there is one feature of Regius and Cooke which is particularly surprising. Other than the vague threat that sheriffs would seize those who did not attend the assembly, no penalties for failure to observe Æthelstan's ordinances are specified. In other guild regulations, elaborate penalties are a prominent feature. For example, in ordinances established for carpenters and masons working for the king at Calais in the reign of King Edward IV, breaches are punished by loss of wages, which were to be paid into a common chest, the 'box of St John'.[112] Likewise, those who breached the rules of the masons' fraternity at Lincoln also paid fines to the fraternity. Regius and Cooke rely instead on general injunctions, with an appeal to history, apart from the threat of prison for those not attending the assembly. While many of the provisions of Regius and Cooke can be paralleled in ordinances from other trades, they do not include any of the detailed provision about, for example, working hours or reuse of building materials which can be found in other stonemasons' ordinances, such as those from Calais or York. The only substantive organisational focus of Cooke and Regius is the masons' assembly.

The masons' assemblies contextualised

The search for an assembly of stonemasons in the 15th century has proceeded from the assumption that any such assembly would have the elevated authority and power ascribed to it in Regius and Cooke. Knoop and Jones pointed out that there were many assemblies of crafts in towns, but they were unable to find similar assemblies of the sort described in Regius and Cooke, 'attended not merely by the masters and fellows, but by great lords, knights and squires, as well as by the sheriff of the county, the mayor of the city and the aldermen of the town', and with the authority to order distraint, arrest and imprisonment to enforce its ordinances.[113] Knoop and Jones did not consider the possibility that Regius and Cooke were describing an aspiration rather than a reality, that they were associated with assemblies of doubtful legality which sought to proclaim their legitimacy by claiming an ancient lineage back to Æthelstan and beyond and by insisting that royal officials should be subject to the assembly, rather than suppressing it.

As the responsibilities of guilds for the regulation of particular trades grew in the 15th century, guilds frequently came under the control of elite groups. The humbler journeymen increasingly sought to create their own organisations, both to protect their own position against the masters and presumably also to hold more congenial social gatherings away from the stifling presence of the masters. The resulting tensions could lead to violent conflicts, as was the case in York and other cities during 1381.[114] These journeymen assemblies frequently sought to affirm their power and legitimacy by making ordinances, which were set down in writing.

Thus, in 1396 the Wardens of the Saddlers' Company in London appeared before the Mayor and Aldermen and claimed that for the past thirteen years

> under a certain feigned colour of sanctity, many of the serving men in the trade had influenced the journeymen among them and had formed covins thereon with the object of raising their wages greatly in excess...and further that the serving men aforesaid, according to an ordinance made among themselves, would oftentimes cause the journeymen of the said masters to be summoned by a beadle, thereunto appointed, to attend at the vigils of the dead who were members of the said fraternity...[115]

The six 'governors of the serving men' denied these charges and claimed that the purpose of their association was purely religious and that it had existed time out of mind. Regardless of the exact nature of this organisation, it clearly had a fairly formal structure. It possessed officers, servants, a livery, made ordinances and sought to enforce attendance. The 'feigned colour of sanctity' presumably refers to the claim that the organisation was primarily a religious fraternity, but this may well also have involved some kind of shared legendary history.

Further circumstantial information about the operation of such a journeymen's fraternity is given by another case against a group of London spurriers in 1381.[116] This alleged that for nine years at St Bartholomew's church in Smithfield and elsewhere they had made a 'covin and confederacy to the damage of the common weal'. This fraternity had ordained that no member should make or polish spurs for more than a certain price. They met monthly 'in the church or other places assigned by the captains of their company for the making of new ordinances'. Those who failed to attend the assembly paid a penalty of a pound of wax. The fraternity had established a common box into which each member paid a halfpenny a week, so that it was claimed the fraternity had accumulated over eighteen marks for the maintenance of its ordinances. It was alleged that the fraternity had written ordinances prepared under a notarial seal. The leaders of the fraternity had summoned those who had broken its ordinances for perjury before the Consistory Court of the Bishop of London. It was stipulated that only journeymen should belong to the fraternity. It was also agreed that if any master should employ anybody from outside the city, the journeymen would leave his service until the foreigner had been dismissed. If any member of the fraternity heard an evil work spoken against one of his brethren, he was to immediately inform the society.

The trial showed that the description of the journeymen spurriers' fraternity made in the charges was broadly accurate. One member admitted that he had been involved in the citations before the Consistory Court, had attended monthly meetings and made payments to the common box. Moreover, it turned out the fraternity had held an emergency meeting, apparently in response to the prosecution, despite an order of the Mayor that no congregation should be held. Eventually, the rest of those charged, together with other members of the fraternity who had not been named in the original inquest, appeared in court and were bound over not to engage in any such assemblies.

Journeymen's organisations continued to be a problem in London throughout the 15th century. In 1441, the master bakers petitioned the Mayor and Aldermen that the 'servants of the craft [of bakers]...have on holy days a revelling hall and a drinking thereby which many of them are unable to do good work a day after'.[117] Moreover, they maintained a brotherhood with a distinctive livery, and members of this livery would not work unless they had greater wages than hitherto. They refused to work from Saturday afternoon until Sunday evening. Members of the brotherhood supported each other against the masters if any master criticised them for their work. They threatened to leave the master's service if he sought to correct them, and also declared that they would ordain that none of them should work by night.

The servants of the bakers appeared and vigorously defended themselves. They declared that the revelling hall was nothing new but that 'time out of mind the custom had continued on certain days'. They said that the brotherhood with its distinctive hoods had also existed for a very long time 'to the worship of God and engendering of love and for no manner of confederacy nor to the harm of the craft in any way'. Most of the masters had been members of the brotherhood in their time. They denied that they had absented themselves from their work. As for the claim that they had supported each other when criticised by the masters, this only happened when a master was unreasonable, because 'it is reason that he that so trespasseth above his guilt but not for to slander all servants for the folly of one misdoer'. They declared that as a body they had never entertained the idea that they should refuse to work by night. The representatives of the journeymen sought to demonstrate in detail that their wages had not changed, and complained vociferously about new ordinances of the Bakers' Company which prevented married journeymen going home to their wives. Nevertheless, the Mayor and Aldermen suppressed the journeymen's fraternity and ordered that they should be governed in future by the Bakers' Company.

Similar cases can be found in other towns such as York and Coventry.[118] Clearly organisations such as the fraternity of journeymen bakers had very similar concerns to those expressed by the stonemasons in Regius and Cooke. When challenged, such bodies invariably claimed that they had existed 'time out of mind', and it was a short step from this to alleging that assemblies were authorised by a grant from a primordial figure such as Æthelstan. More powerful guilds were in the process of elaborating such genealogies and this doubtless encouraged the journeymen's fraternities also sought to make such claims. Between 1433 and 1471, the Palmers' Guild of Ludlow donated an elaborate window to St Lawrence's church, showing the granting of a charter to the guild by St Edward the Confessor.[119] There is no evidence that this guild was founded in the 11th century, and the myth that St Edward had incorporated the Ludlow palmers appears to have grown up in the 14th century. One can imagine that the Shropshire stonemasons who worked on the window would have been comforted to know that their fraternities could claim an even more ancient Anglo-Saxon lineage. The appeal to the distant past was a common feature of medieval society, whether a Ludlow guild claiming they had received a charter from Edward the Confessor, monasteries forging charters to show that they had been granted lands by forgotten Kings of the Heptarchy,[120] or the peasants who in the 1370s purchased exemplifications from Domesday Book to show that they were free.[121] The appeal to Æthelstan, Edwin and beyond in Cooke and Regius is simply another expression of this.

In the 1425 Parliament, the Commons presented a petition complaining that the annual congregations and confederacies made by the masons in their general chapters and assemblies were publicly violating and undermining the statutes of labourers. They asked the King and Lords to ordain that the holding and gathering of such chapters should be utterly forbidden and judged a felony, and asked that the JPs should be given authority to enquire into these chapters and assemblies. The King replied that such chapters and congregations should not be held, and those who convene such chapters should be adjudged felons. Any masons who go to such congregations should be imprisoned without fine or ransom at the king's will. A statute to this effect was duly enacted.[122]

Thus, at about the time that Regius and Cooke were being compiled, masons were holding assemblies to try and ensure they got higher wages. The character of these assemblies was presumably similar to those held by the journeymen saddlers, spurriers, bakers and others in London and elsewhere. It seems perverse not to identify the assemblies of masons described in the 1425 statute with those mentioned in Regius and Cooke, but scholars have been reluctant to do so. Salzmann objected that nobody had found evidence of a prosecution under this legislation,[123] but enforcement of the statute was the responsibility of the JPs and only a few Peace Rolls survive from this period.[124] Knoop and Jones were tempted to identify the assemblies of Cooke and Regius with those of the legislation, but hesitated because Regius and Cooke declare that sheriffs and aldermen attended these assemblies.[125] However, if the texts of Regius and Cooke were compiled to authorise the holding of such assemblies, then obviously it would be in their interests to claim that they should be sanctioned by the presence of royal officials. The self-aggrandisement of craft assemblies of this kind was not unusual; in 1299, Walter of Maidstone, a carpenter, was accused of summoning a 'parliament of carpenters at Mile End' to swear an oath not to observe an Ordinance concerning the wages of carpenters.[126]

Another reason for the hesitation of Knoop and Jones in linking the production of Regius and Cooke to the assemblies prohibited in the 1425 statute was that Regius and Cooke refer to the attendance of master masons at the assembly. The assemblies described in the 1425 statute apparently involved journeymen masons only. However, Regius and Cooke do not provide any confirmation that master masons attended the assemblies they describe. Their aim was simply to try and persuade the masters to attend, and they may have been unsuccessful in this. The references to the attendance of masters at the assemblies in Regius and Cooke probably simply indicate that the fraternities which produced these Ordinances wanted greater control over the masters.

There are hints that an oligarchy was emerging among masons similar to that in other crafts.[127] The 1351 statute had awarded the 'mason of free stone' higher wages than other masons. It is perhaps this increasing division which had led to the disputes between the mason hewers and mason setters which led to the London ordinances of 1356. Increasingly in building contracts and elsewhere the freemason appears as a small-scale capitalist entrepreneur.[128] Regius and Cooke react against this trend not only by making demands on such issues as pay, holidays and notice of dismissal, but also by using the legendary history to demonstrate that all masons were equal and the craft of noble origin. The picture given in Regius and Cooke of masons working together as equal fellows are, as Cooper has shown, intended to portray a community of workers, but this community may already have vanished at the time that the texts were composed.

The most persuasive reading of the Regius and Cooke texts is that they are volumes produced in the second quarter of the 15th century recording a legendary history of the craft of stone masonry and ordinances produced by illicit assemblies of journeymen masons of the type recorded in the 1425 legislation, similar in character to the Ordinances made by the journeymen saddlers and spurriers in London. As such, they are a remarkable survival of artisan culture of the 15th century, but the modern masonic heirs of these medieval journeymen have been tempted to read much more into them, and doubtless will continue to do so. Gould argued at length that the legendary history in Regius and Cooke represented an ancient oral tradition of stonemasons. How far is this legendary history true? It will never be possible to establish the roots of the legend with any certainty, but the texts of Regius and Cooke suggest that, like the Palmers' legend of Edward the Confessor in Ludlow, the elaboration of the legend of the stonemasons was relatively recent. It is striking that the stories of the invention of masonry by Euclid was designed to prove that the craft was of noble origins and that there should be no hierarchy among fellow masons. This was clearly an attempt to undermine the hierarchies which, as with other trades at that time, were becoming increasingly evident among masons during the first half of the 15th century.

If Cooke is accepted as an elaboration of an earlier version of the craft legend as recorded in Regius, then the process by which the craft legend was extended and reinforced to support the claims of the journeymen mason becomes more evident. The story of the origins of masonry is extended back to the advent of Christianity in England and is linked to a figure, St Alban, who was commemorated in one of the most imposing ecclesiastical buildings in the country. The introduction of the figure of Æthelstan's son not only reinforces the theme that the craft of stonemasonry was of noble origins, but also adds a vital link in the new extended history of the craft in England. Even small details of the legendary history may have been affected by changes in the masons' trade. For example, the sudden appearance of the French King Charles in Cooke may perhaps be interpreted as reflecting the need to show that the ordinances applied also to masons working in France. The different circumstances of working on fortifications on English possessions in France in the 15th century led to the issue of detailed ordinances governing the masons' working hours, control over material and equipment and victualling arrangements. All these were matters very close to the heart of the fraternities which compiled Regius and Cooke, and it is not surprising to find that they could come up with good historical reasons to show why the customs claimed by stonemasons in England should also be apply when they were working abroad on projects like those described in Edward IV's ordinances for the masons at Calais.

If we are to follow David Wallace's advice and seek that moment of precarious historicity for Regius and Cooke, it lies in that statute of 1425. The most feasible interpretation of Regius and Cooke is that they were written ordinances produced by fraternities of journeymen stonemasons meeting during the 1420s in Shropshire and elsewhere in the West Midlands, similar to the written ordinances prepared by the journeymen spurriers in London in 1381 and by other journeymen's organisations. The legendary history can be seen as an attempt, first, to legitimate the holding of the assemblies notwithstanding legislation forbidding them and, second, to protest against and to subvert the emergence of oligarchies within the craft of stonemasonry by emphasising that all stonemasons were equal in their craft and the craft itself originally devised for noblemen. Like the journeymen bakers in 1441, the stonemasons' assemblies doubtless included a 'revelling hall' and the repetition of these stories would have formed part of the entertainment, just as the carpenters were regaled with the *Debate of the Carpenters' Tools* and the Ludlow palmers were edified by the story of Edward the Confessor's grant to their guild. It is interesting to note that some of the journeymen's assemblies were held in religious houses. The meetings of the London spurriers were held in St Bartholomew's in Smithfield and the journeymen saddlers met in the church of St Vedast in Foster Lane. Possibly the persistent suggestion of a connection between Regius and Lilleshall Priory suggests that the fraternity which produced it met at or near Lilleshall.

It is dangerous to make hard and fast distinctions between literary texts and historical documents. Because they are in Middle English and one is in verse, Regius and Cooke have been regarded primarily as literature, and another reason why these texts have become de-historicised is that they have been viewed chiefly as literary productions. Yet the key to understanding them lies in the petition of 1425, preserved in the parliamentary records, and in labour legislation. We know very little about the enforcement of this labour legislation in the 15th century, but although few justices of the peace records survive, there is information about enforcement of labour legislation dispersed through other legal records such as the rolls of courts such as the King's Bench, Common Pleas and Chancery. If we wish to explore further the context of Regius and Cooke, the next stage lies in these little studied and largely ignored legal records.

Let me conclude by describing briefly one early case from the Chancery dating from 1403-5.[129] Roger Eye, a stonemason, petitioned Henry Beaufort as chancellor, and described how he was apprenticed to learn the specialist craft of mason. At the end of his apprenticeship, Roger had to acquire his own tools, but had no money, so was forced to borrow money from his friends to buy them. Another mason, John Stokes, was jealous that Roger was attempting to establish himself in this prestigious part of the craft. Stokes contrived that he and Roger would work together on a job. At the end of the job, Stokes managed to embezzle the tools and instruments which Roger had secured with such great difficulty. When Roger confronted Stokes and asked for the return of his tools, Stokes threatened to bring a lawsuit against him.

Roger declared that Stokes would have beaten him up if he had not been better defended. Stokes accordingly brought a trespass case against Eye and arranged for friends of his to be empanelled on the jury. He said that he would only withdraw the suit if Eye relinquished his tools to him. Eye requested a writ to bring the case into Chancery.

Stokes's envy of Richard suggests resentment at the increasing specialisations and hierarchies emerging in their shared craft. Richard's petition, presumably drawn up for him by an attorney, echoes the concerns of Regius and Cooke, with their anxiety about emerging hierarchies in the stonemasons' trade. The cost of getting a set of tools, the problems of finding a foothold in a new trade, the envy of other workmen: these were the day-to-day difficulties with which 15th-century artisans struggled and which shaped and bounded their lives.

***

Table I

Regius Articles	Cooke Articles
Master Masons shall pay their fellows fairly	Master Masons shall pay their fellows fairly
All Master Masons must attend the general congregation	All Master Masons must attend the general congregation
Masters shall take apprentices for a term of seven years	Masters shall take apprentices for a term of seven years
Bondmen shall not be made apprentices	Bondmen shall not be made apprentices
Lame men shall not be made apprentices	Apprentices will to receive reasonable pay
Apprentices will be paid less, but receive full pay after their apprenticeship is complete	Lame men shall not be made apprentices
Masters shall not harbour thieves	Masters shall not employ those who plot criminal activities
Masters may exchange deficient workmen for	Masters may exchange deficient

those that are better	workmen for those that are better
Masters not to undertake work that they cannot finish	Masters not to undertake work that they cannot finish
Masters not to poach work from other masters	
Masons shall not work by night	
Masons shall not criticise each other's work	
Masters to give thorough training to their apprentices	
Masters shall ensure that the training of apprentices is complete within their term	
Masters not to swear false oaths	

Table II

Regius Points	Cooke Points
Masons to love God and the Holy Church	Masons to love God and the Holy Church
Masons to do a fair day's work	Masons to do a fair day's work
Apprentices to keep their master's counsel	Apprentices to keep their master's counsel
Masons shall not attack the craft	Masons shall not attack the craft
Masters to give fair warning when masons are laid off	Masons to accept their pay meekly and to take it at the appointed time
Masons to avoid litigation and seek arbitration	Masons to avoid litigation and seek arbitration
Any mason holding an office under the Master to discharge his duties fairly	Masons not to covet the wives or daughters of fellow masons, except for marriage
Stewards to serve drink and victuals fairly; everyone to pay for their own food	Any mason holding an office under the Master to discharge his duties fairly
Masons defaming other masons to be summoned before the assembly of masons	Masons to help each other in their work
Masons to help each other in their work	Masons to attend the assembly when summoned
Ordinances of the assembly to be upheld by all masons	Oath to be sworn by all attending the assembly for the first time
Masons shall not steal	Those who are contumacious of the assembly to be imprisoned
Masons shall swear to observe these ordinances and be loyal to the King. Sheriff to imprison those who break these ordinances.	

NOTES

[1]   D.B. Haycock: *William Stukeley - Science, Religion and Archaeology in Eighteenth-Century England* (Woodbridge, 2002), pp. 224f.

[2]   *Ibid.*, p. 176. Pen trials in the MS (e.g. ff. 39, 39v) suggest that in the 17th- century it was owned by one William Rand. See D. Knoop, G.P. Jones & D. Hamer (eds): *The Two Earliest Masonic MSS.* (Manchester, 1938), p. 54.

[3]   Knoop, Jones & Hamer: *op. cit.*, p. 55, who note that these drawings are now in Stukeley's papers in the Bodleian Library.

[4]   *See* further, p.53.

[5]   Cf. Haycock, *op. cit.*, p. 176.

[6]   *The Constitutions of the Free-Masons* (London, 1723), pp. 38f; cf. Desaguliers's description of Anderson's work in the 'Dedication'.

[7]   Knoop, Jones & Hamer: *op. cit.*, p. 57; Wallace McLeod, 'The Old Charges [The Prestonian Lecture for 1986]', in *AQC* vol. 99 (1986), p. 121.

[8]   These are the MSS now known as the Woodford MS, made by Reid in 1728 for William Cowper, the Clerk of Parliament and afterwards owned by Sir Francis Palgrave, owned by *Quatuor Coronati* Lodge and on loan to the Library and Museum of Freemasonry, and the Supreme Council MS. See Knoop, Jones & Hamer, *op. cit.*, pp. 55ff.

[9]   http://www.jjhc.info/crowerobert1786.htm.

[10]   Knoop, Jones & Hamer: *op. cit.*, p. 54.

[11]   *Ibid.*, p. 55. The note on f. 3, 'The Seven Sciences. A History of Masonry. Its, Articles, Points & c.' is apparently in Fenn's handwriting.

[12]   Madden's diary is in the Bodleian Library, MS. Eng. hist. c. 140-182.

[13]   Madden's memory seems to have been at fault here. The first edition of Halliwell's book was published in 1840.

[14]   Although Halliwell's 'Preface' to the second edition of his book was dated 1843, it was not published until the following year.

[15]   M. Cooke: *The History and Articles of Masonry* (London, 1861).

[16]   The description Cooke gave of himself in the 1861 Census, when he was living at 602 George Street, Marylebone. Cooke, a musician who had been as a boy a chorister in the Chapel Royal, was initiated in the Canonbury Lodge No. 955 (*now* No. 657) in an upper room at the Canonbury Tavern on 18 June 1857. See *The Freemasons' Magazine*, new series, vol. 5 (Jul.- Dec. 1861), pp. 412f. In May 1863 he unsuccessfully proposed the formation of a Lodge to be called the 'Elizabethan Tower Lodge' to meet at the Canonbury Tavern. See Library and Museum of Freemasonry: Rejected Petitions.

[17]   P.R. Harris: *A History of the British Museum Library 1753-1973* (London, 1998), p. 230. Cooke was also a friend of Halliwell.

[18]   In revenge, Cooke started his own periodical, *The Masonic Press*, and described his argument with Smith as follows: '"The Scientific Press" coolly took eighteen months to print this book of one hundred and eighty pages. Subscribers died and others repudiated their orders during such a lapse of time.' Cooke did not receive any indication of the cost of printing until two weeks after the book was delivered. The bill when it arrived proved to be 'so monstrous in amount that we felt it could only be settled by putting witnesses into a box to prove it was more than twice as much as a fair and reasonable printer would claim'. *See The Masonic Press*, vol. 1 (1 January 1866), pp. 6ff.

[19] Halliwell married in 1842 the daughter of the bibliophile Sir Thomas Phillipps whose huge collection of manuscripts included three 17th-century copies of the 'Old Charges' of the masons. Phillipps opposed the match and in his will forbad Halliwell and his wife access to his library. Halliwell took his wife's name after her death.

[20] M. Spevack: *James Orchard Halliwell-Phillipps - the life and works of the Shakespearian scholar and bookman* (Delaware and London, 2001), pp. 124-40.

[21] Halliwell's 'Collections on the History of Mathematics. Principally from the Books and Manuscripts in the British Museum', compiled in 1837-8 is now in the British Library, Add. MS 14061. Unfortunately, there is no description of Royal MS 17 A. I in these collections.

[22] The description is by David Casley, whose 1734 catalogue of the Royal MSS was at that time the working catalogue for them. See Knoop, Jones & Hamer: *op. cit.*, p. 53.

[23] He dedicated his *Reliquiae Antiquae*, published in 1841, to Charles Purton Cooper, the notorious Secretary of the Second Record Commission, who was afterwards Provincial Grand Master of Kent. Halliwell's close friend and associate, the Shakespearean forger John Payne Collier, was also a freemason, prompting the masonic press to rally to his defence when his forgeries were exposed in 1860. *See The Freemasons' Magazine*, ns vol. 2 (Jan.-Jul. 1860), pp. 243-247, 351, 392 & 434. Spaek, *op. cit.*, p. 27, states that the first edition of *The Early History of Freemasonry* was dedicated to Collier which, if true, would suggest that Collier had played some part in helping Halliwell appreciate the significance of his discovery. However, the copy of the first edition of Halliwell's book in the Library and Museum of Freemasonry is dedicated to Samuel Charles, a close friend from Trinity College. It should also be noted that the annual Returns of the Scientific Lodge No. 88 meeting in Cambridge show that a very large number of students from Trinity College were initiated in the Lodge from 1830.

[24] J. Halliwell: 'On the Antiquity of Free Masonry in England', in *Archaeologia* vol. 28 (1840), pp. 444-47. Among the contributors to this volume of the transactions of the Society of Antiquaries was the Anglo-Saxon scholar John Mitchell Kemble, who was Initiated, Passed and Raised in 1833 while still a student at Halliwell's old college, Trinity, in the Scientific Lodge No. 88 at Cambridge: Library and Museum of Freemasonry, Lodge Returns.

[25] *The Early History of Freemasonry in England* (London, 1840).

[26] Knoop, Jones & Hamer: *op. cit.*, pp. 52f.

[27] R.F. Gould: *A Commentary on the Masonic Poem, Urbanitatis and Instructions for a Parish Priest*, *QCA* vol. 1, pt. 3 (1889), p. lv.

[28] McLeod: *op. cit.*, pp. 121, 139-42.

[29] H. Cam: *Liberties and Communities in Medieval England: Collected Studies in Local Administration and Topography* (London, 1963), pp. ix-xiv.

[30] The most useful introduction to this bibliography is in McLeod: *op. cit.*, p. 142.

[31] E. Akenhead: 'The George Grey Manuscript of the Old Charges (E.d.24)', in *AQC* vol. 112 (1999), pp. 127-37.

[32] D. Wallace: *Chaucerian Polity: Absolutist Lineages and Associational Forms in England and Italy* (Stanford, 1997), p. 3.

[33] L.H. Cooper: 'The "Boke of Oure Charges": Constructing Community in the Masons' Constitutions', in *Journal of the Early Book Society* vol. 6 (2003), pp. 1-39.

[34] *Ibid.*, p. 23.

35 W. P. Buchan: 'Masonic MSS in the British Museum', in *Freemasons' Magazine and Masonic Mirror*, n. s. 21 (Jul.-Dec. 1869), p. 29, printing letter by Bond dated 8 Jun. 1869; W.J. Hughan, *The Old Charges of the British Freemasons* (2nd. ed., London, 1895), pp. 43-4. Hughan notes that the 19th century masonic scholar A.F.A. Woodford suggested an even earlier date of c. 1560.

36 For the following, see the letter of R. Petrie dated 8 April 1960 on the subject file 'Old Charges – Various MSS.' in the Library and Museum of Freemasonry. Petrie was urged by the Librarian at Freemasons' Hall to report Aldridge's re-dating of the 'Old Charge' MS in Lansdowne MS. 98 in *AQC*, but it seems he never did. Aldridge's datings of the Hadfield and Wakefield MSS. are reported in McLeod, 'Additions to the List of Old Charges', *op. cit.*, pp. 103, 106.

37 Lansdowne MS 98 includes a large number of Elizabethan papers, but also contains a copy of a prophecy dated 1661-2 (ff. 208-9), 'Maxims and Instructions for Ministers of State', composed towards the end of Queen Anne's reign (ff. 223-246) and a biblical chronology also apparently dating from the early 15th-century (f. 268). Sewing holes are clearly visible in the copy of the 'Old Charges' in Lansdowne MS. 98, and it was evidently at one time stored separately as a paper roll. The statement by Richard Sims noted in the commentary to the engraved facsimile of Lansdowne MS. 98 in *QCA* vol. 2 that this MS never formed a roll means that the document never formed part of the separate collection in the British Museum known as the Lansdowne Rolls. The evidence of the sewing holes is conclusive that at some earlier stage in its history this document formed a roll.

38 C. Dyer: 'Some Thoughts on the Origins of Speculative Masonry', in *AQC* vol. 95 (1982), pp. 126, 168.

39 Hughan: *op. cit.*, p. 16. In general, the second edition of Hughan's work, published in 1895, should always be consulted, as it contains substantial additions and corrections.

40 Halliwell: *op. cit.*, pp. 7f.

41 Buchan: *op. cit.*, p. 29. Bond also provided dates as follows for a number of other masonic manuscripts which are now in the British Library: Harley MS 2054, middle of the 17th century; Harley MS 1942, beginning of the 17th century; Sloane MS 3848, f. 213 (179 present pagination): dated 1646; Sloane MS 3323, f. 195, latter part of the 17th century; Sloane MS 3329, f. 102, probably beginning of the 18th century; Lansdowne MS 98, art. 48, about the year 1600 [but cf. p. 48 above]. See Gould: *op. cit.*, p. lv; and [H. J. Whymper], *Constituciones Artis Gemetriæ Secundum Euclydem* (London and Boston, 1889), p. 5 where it is claimed that Bond had suggested that the manuscript was mid 15th century.

42 J. Norton: 'The Difficulties of Ascertaining the Age of Old Masonic MSS', in *Masonic Magazine* vol. 1 (1874-5), p. 83.

43 'Masonic Archaeology No. IV', in *Masonic Magazine* vol. 2 (1874-5), pp. 76ff.

44 G.F. Warner & J.P. Gilson: *Catalogue of Western Manuscripts in the Old Royal and King's Collections* (London, 1921), vol. 2, p. 213.

45 'The Old Masonic Poem', in *Masonic Magazine* vol. 1 (1873-4), pp. 339f, & 371f. See also *Masonic Magazine* vol. 2 (1874-5), pp. 13f, 40f, 68ff, & 119. Sims also provided a detailed description of Regius and of two MSS in the Cotton Collection containing the Mirk poem and 'Urbanitatis': *Masonic Magazine* vol. 2 (1874-5), pp. 258-61. On Sims, see further A. Prescott, 'What's In A Number? The Physical Organisation of the Manuscript Collections of the British Library' in N. Doane & K. Wolff (eds.): *Beatus Vir: Studies in Memory of Phillip Pulsiano* (MRTS, forthcoming). Sims was also cited as a MS expert in the inquiry into the authenticity of the Mahatma letters. See V. Harrison: *H.P. Blavatsky and the SPR: an examination of the Hodgson Report of 1885* (Pasadena, 1997), available on-line at: http://www.theosociety.org/pasadena/hpb-spr/hpbspr-h.htm. Joseph Netherclift, Halliwell's copyist, also played a central part in this debate.

46 A.F.A. Woodford: 'The Age of Ancient Masonic Manuscripts', in *Masonic Magazine* vol. 2 (1874-5), pp. 98ff; and his 'Our Masonic MSS': *ibid.*, pp. 130, 163ff, & 194

[47] Netherclift was a well-known lithographic artist who corresponded with Francis Fox Talbot. He was used by Halliwell in his folio edition of Shakespeare. *See* Spevack: *op. cit.*, p. 218.

[48] Whymper: *op. cit.*, p. 5.

[49] The most recent analysis of these Wycliffite texts has confirmed that they were probably compiled sometime before 1408. *See* A. Hudson: *The Premature Reformation: Wycliffite Texts and Lollard History* (Oxford, 1988), pp. 238-49.

[50] K. Scott: *Later Gothic Manuscripts 1390-1490* (London, 1996), vol. 2, pp. 158ff.

[51] L. Mooney: 'Chaucer's Scribe: New Evidence of the Identification of the Scribe of the Hengwrt and Ellesmere Manuscripts of Chaucer's *Canterbury Tales*', in *Speculum*, forthcoming.

[52] http://www.bl.uk/catalogues/illuminatedmanuscripts/welcome.htm.

[53] A. Watson: *Catalogue of Dated and Datable Manuscripts, c.700-1600 in the Department of Manuscripts, the British Library* (London, 1979), no. 46, plate 488.

[54] *Ibid.*, no. 376, pl. 515.

[55] Gould: *op. cit.*, p. iv. Gould, however, also reproduces Price's plates from Add. MS 15580 and Arundel MS 38 on p. 55.

[56] W. Begemann: *Vorgeschichte und Anfänge der Freimaurerei in England* (Berlin, 1909), vol. 2, pp. 108-9; G.W. Speth: 'Begemann on the Regius Poem' in *AQC* vol. 7 (1894), p. 34.

[57] Knoop, Jones & Hamer: *op. cit.*, p. 63.

[58] D. Hamer: 'Further Consideration of the Regius MS', in *AQC* vol. 94 (1981), pp. 166-9.

[59] A. McIntosh, M.I. Samuels & M. Benskin: *A Linguistic Atlas of Late Mediaeval English* (Aberdeen, 1986), vol. 1, pp. 115, 233ff; vol. 2, pp. 424-38.

[60] G. Kristensson: *John Mirk's Instructions for Parish Priests* (Lund, 1974), pp. 13-15.

[61] S. Powell: article on 'John Mirk', in *Oxford Dictionary of National Biography* ed. H. Matthew & B. Harrison (Oxford, 2004), vol. 38, pp. 368-9.

[62] Powell: *op. cit.*, p. 368. *See also* S. Powell: 'A New Dating of John Mirk's *Festial*', in *Notes and Queries* vol. 227 (1982), pp. 487ff.

[63] Knoop, Jones & Hamer: *op. cit.*, p. 7.

[64] J. Nicholls: *The Matter of Courtesy: Medieval Courtesy Books and the Gawain Poet* (Woodbridge, 1985), pp. 69-74 & 194.

[65] A.R. Myers: *The Household of Edward IV: the Black Book and the Ordinance of 1478* (Manchester, 1959), pp. 126f.

[66] Hamer: *op. cit.*, p. 168.

[67] See also the cautionary remarks of Nicholls, *op. cit.*, p. 70. Nicholls' discussion however relies on Knoop, Jones and Hamer's dating of Regius to *c.*1390.

[68] Printed in T. Simmons (ed.): *The Lay Folks Mass Book*, Early English Text Society vol. 71 (1879), pp. 148-54 from Cotton MS Titus A xxvi, ff. 156-8. The parallels with Regius are noted in Knoop, Jones & Hamer: *op. cit.*, pp. 186 & 188f.

[69] *The Minor Poems of John Lydgate* ed by H.M. MacCracken, EETS - extra series, vol. 107 (1911), p. xlvi.

[70] L. Mooney: 'John Shirley's Heirs', in *Yearbook of English Studies* vol. 33 (2003), pp. 195f.

[71] f. 33. These additions are not included in any of the facsimiles of the MS.

[72] Cooke: *op. cit.*, p. v.

[73] Knoop, Jones & Hamer: *op. cit.*, pp. 66f.

[74] The best edition of the texts of Regius and Cooke remains Knoop, Jones & Hamer, *op. cit.*, and the following is based on their edition.

[75] Knoop, Jones & Hamer: *op. cit.*, p. 103.

[76] *Ibid.*, pp. 8ff.

[77] *Ibid.*, p. 81.

[78] On Higden and his work, see J. Taylor: *The Universal Chronicle of Ranulf Higden* (Oxford, 1966).

[79] See, for example, H. Poole & F.R. Worts (eds.): *The "Yorkshire" Old Charges of Masons* (Leeds, 1935), pp. 26-9.

[80] See, for example, Knoop, Jones & Hamer: *op. cit.*, p. 59; McLeod: 'The Old Charges', *op. cit.*, p. 125; Poole & Worts: *op. cit.*, pp. 26-9. On the Watson and Tew MSS, see further in Poole & Worts: *op. cit.*, pp. 42-69.

[81] In considering the relationship between the two texts, the summary tabulation in Knoop, Jones & Hamer: *op. cit.*, pp. 4-6, is very helpful.

[82] This identification is apparently given for the first time in Grand Lodge MS 1, dated 1583 in the Library and Museum of Freemasonry.

[83] Hughan: *op. cit.*, p. 33. The statement that Edwin was Æthelstan's brother apparently occurs for the first time in the William Watson MS, dated 1687, one year after the publication of Plot's criticisms of the masonic legend. In the 1723 edition of the *Book of Constitutions*, Anderson dealt with the problem of Edwin's status by simply providing a transcription of a version of the story from a copy of the 'Old Charges'. In the second 1738 edition, however, he directly identified Edwin as Æthelstan's brother and proposed a date of 926 for the grant of the Constitutions. For a convenient presentation of the relevant texts, see further in A. Horne: *The York Legend in the Old Charges* (London, 1978), pp. 13-52.

[84] Knoop, Jones & Hamer: *op. cit.*, p. 1.

[85] R. Sharpe: *Calendar of Letter Books ... of the City of London - Letter Book H* (London, 1907), p. 274.

[86] National Archives: PROB 11/2B f. 108. I owe this reference to Prof. S. Lindenbaum.

[87] See, for example, S. Lindenbaum: 'London Texts and Literate Practice' in *The Cambridge History of Medieval English Literature*, ed. by D. Wallace (Cambridge, 1999), pp. 284-309.

[88] Zvi Razi & R.M. Smith: 'The Origins of the English Manorial Court Rolls as a Written Record: A Puzzle', in Zvi Razi & Richard Smith (eds.): *Medieval Society and the Manor Court* (Oxford, 1996), pp. 60-7.

[89] S. Justice: *Writing and Rebellion - England in 1381* (Berkeley, 1994), pp. 13-66.

[90] National Archives: KB 9/227/2, mm. 1-2.

[91] A. Hudson: '*Laicus litteratus*: the paradox of Lollardy', in *Heresy and Literacy, 1000-1530* ed. by P. Biller & A. Hudson (Cambridge, 1994), pp. 222-36.

[92] S. Reynolds: *An Introduction to the History of English Medieval Towns* (Oxford, 1977), p. 169.

[93] L. Mooney: 'A Middle English Text on the Liberal Arts', in *Speculum* vol. 68 (1993), pp. 1027-52.

[94] *Ibid.*, p. 1036.

[95] *Ibid.*, pp. 1036-7.

[96] E. Wilson: 'The Debate of the Carpenter's Tools', in *Review of English Studies* n.s., vol. 152 (1987), pp. 445-70.

[97] *Ibid.*, p. 453.

[98] A number of the 1389 returns are printed in *English Gilds*, ed. by S. Toulmin & L. Smith, and others are summarised in H. F. Westlake: *The Parish Gilds of Mediæval England* (London, 1919), pp. 137-238. On the context of their production, see J. Gerchow: 'Gilds and Fourteenth-Century Bureaucracy: the Case of 1388-9', in *Nottingham Medieval Studies* vol. 40 (1996), pp. 109-47 and C. Barron & L. Wright: 'The London Middle English Guild Certificates of 1388-9', in *Nottingham Medieval Studies* vol. 39 (1995), pp. 108-45.

[99] Smith: *op. cit.*, pp. 25f.

[100] *Ibid.*, pp. 80ff.

[101] National Archives: C 47/41/154, ed. & trans. in W. J. Williams: 'Gild of Masons at Lincoln', in *AQC* vol. 54 (1941), pp. 108ff.

[102] Smith: *op. cit.*, p. 82.

[103] E. Veale: 'The "Great Twelve": Mistery and Fraternity in Thirteenth-Century London', in *Historical Research* vol. 64 (1991), pp. 237-63; S. Reynolds: *op. cit*, pp. 164-8; C.M. Barron: *London in the Later Middle Ages: Government and People, 1200-1500* (Oxford, 2004), pp. 199-216; C.M. Barron: 'The Parish Fraternities of Medieval London', in *The Church in Pre-Reformation Society: Essays in Honour of F. R. H. Du Boulay*, ed. by C.M. Barron & C. Harper-Bill (Woodbridge, 1985), pp. 13-37; S. R. Jones: 'Household, Work and the Problem of Mobile Labour: the Regulation of Labour in Medieval English Towns', in *The Problem of Labour in Fourteenth-Century England*, ed. by J Bothwell, P. Goldberg & W.M. Ormrod (York, 2000), pp. 133-53; R.B. Dobson: 'Craft Guilds and City: the Historical Origins of the York Mystery Plays Reassessed', in *The Stage as Mirror: Civic Theatre in Late Medieval Europe* ed. by Alan E. Knight (Cambridge, 1997), pp. 91-106; G. Rosser: 'Going to the Fraternity Feast: Commensality and Social Relations in Late Medieval England', in *Journal of British Studies* 33 (1994), pp. 430-46; G. Rosser, 'Communities of parish and guild in the late Middle Ages', in *Parish, church and people : local studies in lay religion, 1350-1750* , ed. S.J. Wright (London, 1988) , pp. 29-55; G. Rosser, 'Crafts, guilds and the negotiation of work in the medieval town', in *Past and Present* vol. 154 (1997), pp. 3-31; H. Swanson: 'The Illusion of Economic Structure: Craft Guilds in Late Medieval English Towns', in *Past and Present* vol. 121 (Nov. 1988), pp. 29-48.

[104] Veale: *op. cit.*, p. 263.

[105] Barron: 'Parish Fraternities', pp. 14-17.

[106] Dobson: *op. cit.*, p. 100.

[107] S.H. Rigby: *Medieval Grimsby: Growth and Decline* (Hull, 1993), p. 67.

[108] C. Given-Wilson: 'The Problem of Labour in the Context of English Government, *c.*1350-1450' in Bothwell, Goldberg & Ormrod: *op. cit.*, pp. 85-100; 'Service, Serfdom and English Labour Legislation, 1350-1500', in *Concepts and Patterns of Service in the Later Middle Ages*, ed. by A. Curry & E. Matthew (Woodbridge, 2000), pp. 21-37..

[109] D. Knoop & G. Jones: *The Mediaeval Mason* (Manchester, 1933), pp. 183f.

[110] Rees Jones: *op. cit.*, pp. 146-53.

[111] E. Kimball: *Rolls of the Warwickshire and Coventry Sessions of the Peace, 1377-97*, in Dugdale Society vol. 16 (1939), p. 63.

[112] National Archives: E 101/198/6.

[113] Knoop & Jones: *op. cit.*, pp. 178-84.

[114] R.B. Dobson: 'The Risings in York, Beverley and Scarborough', in *The English Risings of 1381*, ed. by R. Hilton & T. Aston (Cambridge, 1984), pp. 112-42.

[115] H.T. Riley: *Memorials of London and London Life in the XIIIth, XIVth and XVth Centuries* (London, 1868), pp. 542ff.

[116] A.H. Thomas: *Calendar of Plea and Memoranda Rolls ... of the City of London..., 1364-1381* (Cambridge, 1929), pp. 291-4.

[117] R. Sharpe: *Calendar of Letter Books ... of the City of London: Letter Book K* (London, 1911), pp. 263-6; S. Thrupp: *A Short History of the Worshipful Company of Bakers of London* (London., 1933), pp. 110f.

[118] *See*, for example, *The Coventry Leet Book or Mayor's Register*, ed. by M. D. Harris, in Early English Text Society vol. 134 (1907), pp. 91-6, 180-4 & 418f; Kimball: *op. cit.*, pp. lxxix-lxxxiii; H. Swanson: *Medieval Artisans - An Urban Class in Late Medieval England* (Oxford, 1989), pp. 114f.

[119] C. Luddy: 'The Palmers' Guild Window, St Lawrence's Church, Ludlow: A Study of the Construction of Guild Identity in Medieval Stained Glass', in *Shropshire History and Archaeology* vol. 72 (1997), pp. 26-35.

[120] *See*, for example, P. H. Sawyer: *Anglo-Saxon Charters* (London, 1968), nos. 2-6, 43-5, 54-5, 64-6.

[121] E.M. Hallam: *Domesday Book Through Nine Centuries* (London, 1986), pp. 99-109.

[122] Knoop & Jones: *Mediaeval Mason*, op. cit., p. 183. The original petition of the Commons against the assemblies of masons is London is in National Archives, SC 8/24/1196.

[123] L.F. Salzman: *Building in England down to 1540 - A Documentary History* (Oxford, 1952), p. 42.

[124] A. Prescott: 'Labourers Lives: prosecutions of artisans in the fifteenth century', in *Fifteenth-Century Studies* (forthcoming).

[125] Knoop & Jones: *The Mediaeval Mason, op. cit.*, p. 184.

[126] A.H. Thomas: *Calendar of the Early Mayor's Court Rolls...of the City of London... 1298-1307* (Cambridge, 1924), p. 25.

[127] Cf. Salzman: *op. cit.*, pp. 30-44.

[128] This is suggested by a number of 15th-century lawsuits relating to building contracts in the Early Chancery Proceedings in the National Archives, such as: C 1/7/104, C1/64/780, C 1/66/411. *See also* Salzman: *op. cit.*, pp. 495f, 505-9, 556-9 & 561ff.

[129] National Archives: C1/66/164.

5

Redivivus: the Russian masonic revival

by

Lauren G. Leighton

The earliest years

he most prominent distinctive feature of Russian Freemasonry is that its history was shaped more by repression than is typical of other nations. A correlative of this national experience is that periods of repression have been followed by energetic devotion to the Craft. Interest in the Craft was first shown in the 1730s. Interest developed into commitment in the 1760s and 1770s when enthusiastic Russians rushed to found Orders and open lodges from the Baltic through Siberia. Relations were established with prominent masonic bodies abroad, primarily with the Order of York in Berlin and the Grand Lodge of England. The Ancient English, Swedish and Zinnendorf systems competed with French and German Rosicrucianism, Templarism and authorizations by a variety of French, German, English, and Swedish Orients and Orders. Much of this activity was generated more by the enticements of novelty and secrecy than by readiness for serious work, but Freemasonry was not a passing Russian fancy. Both practical and speculative Freemasonry flourished, most notably among the intellectuals organized around the poet and publicist Ivan Novikov. These freemasons were not a bit troubled by devoting themselves simultaneously to the development of the remarkable Russian Enlightenment that flourished into the 1790s and to the creation of a literature steeped in esoteric masonic symbolism. Nor were the political ramifications of Freemasonry left unattended. In 1790 Aleksandr N. Radishchev (1749-1807), a freemason of the Enlightenment, published his social, political and philosophical views in the form of his *Journey from Petersburg to Moscow* (*Puteshestvie iz Peterburga v Moskvu*)[1].

Left to themselves and their great expectations, it is probable that the Russian freemasons might have achieved a state of high development. All the more so in that the Craft was welcomed into Russia by the Enlightened Autocrat Catherine the Great. Newly initiated adepts read and studied the works of Helvetius, Pope, Voltaire, Swift, Gibbon, Goethe, and Schiller.[2] By the 1780s more than a hundred lodges were at work. Among their members were some of the best poets and writers of the 18th-century, including several who wrote works shaped by masonic teachings and ideals. Novikov, who believed fervently in the masonic virtue of self-perfection as the basis of the masonic quest, advocated his beliefs in his journals *Morning Light (Utrennii svet,* 1777-80), *Moscow Monthly Press (Moskovskoe ezhemesiachnoe izdanie,* 1781), *Evening Sunset (Vecherniaia zaria,* 1782-83) and *The Hard-Working Man at Leisure (Pokaiushchiisia trudoliubets,* 1784-85). Nor is it easy to underestimate the efforts of Novikov and his followers to develop Freemasonry in Russia in publications of the Moscow University Press while Novikov was its director (1779-89) and the Typographical Company he helped found in 1784.[3]

As the title of Radishchev's work indicates, the Russians treated the masonic quest as prescribed - an allegorical journey, a journey to the East, to the light, to the temple, to knowledge and self-knowledge ('Know thyself'). In his verse epic *Vladimir Reborn (Vladimir vozrozhdennyi,* 1785) the prolific poet Mikhail M. Kheraskov (1733-1807) followed the masonic plot outline to perfection: a young man wonders the path of truth, is subjected to temptations, falls into the darkness, finally gains control of his passions and finds the path to truth. In his second masonic work, his allegorical novel *Cadmus and Harmonia (Kadm i Garmoniia,* 1789), Kheraskov again followed the masonic plot: a young man is regenerated by the Masonic journey from blindness to insight, and from ignorance to moral knowledge. Similarly, in his 'Ode to Those Seeking Wisdom' ('Oda ishchuschim mudrosti', 1778) the poet and satirist Vasily I. Maikov (1728-1778) entreats freemasons to seek truth in Nature and themselves. Ignorance leads to gloom, knowledge to happiness. Freemasons should follow the path to self-perfection. In the poetry of the dramatist and journalist Alekandsr P. Sumarokov (1718-1777) - specifically in his 'On the Vanity of Man' (*Na suetu cheloveka,* 1759) and 'Ode on the Vanity of the World' (*Oda na suetu mira,* 1763) - the reader is assured that true happiness is internal and spiritual, not the fleeting pleasure of the external world. In the 'Anacreontic Verses' (*Stikhi anakreonticheskie,* 1784) by 'S. I. G.' (probably the prominent freemason S.I. Gamalia) the poetry of this genre, usually devoted to Eros, is transformed into a devotion to Divine Love. Here successful struggle with the passions leads to love of light and hatred of darkness. However tolerant the Empress Catherine the Great may have been, or pretended to be, by the late 1780s her growing concern turned to suspicion. In 1794 she banned the Craft; the ban was continued by Tsar Paul I. This does not mean that 18th-century Freemasonry became less than a major aspect of Russian culture of the time. Quite the contrary for studies of 18th-century Russia include several important papers on the subject.[4]

19th-century developments

Nor was Catherine the only autocrat to encourage and then put an end to periods of vital activity. In 1803 the 'liberal' new Tsar Alexander I encouraged the reopening of the Lodges and in 1809 lent Imperial approval to the Craft. In 1815 the disbanded Grand Directorial Lodge, first constituted in the 1760s, was reconstituted as the Grand Provincial Lodge and then as the Directorial Lodge. In the same year, under the heady influence of the flourishing of the modernized Free and Accepted Rites, the Grand Lodge of Astraea was founded and authorized to work in accordance with the Ancient English System. By 1820 Astraea was the dominant force in Russian Freemasonry with twenty-five lodges in its obedience.[5] By this time, however, Tsar Alexander had fallen under the influence of mystic religionists who convinced him that Freemasonry was a threat, and in 1822 he ordered the lodges closed again. In 1826, following the death of Alexander and the ensuing Revolt of 14 December 1825, Tsar Nicholas I reaffirmed the ban. Although Freemasonry did not assert significant influence on Russian culture for the remainder of the 19th-century, freemasons who continued to work 'in silence' were more active than has been appreciated. Of interest here is the novel 'The Masons' *(Masony,* 1878-80) by Aleksey Pisemsky (1821-1881), devoted to those who continued to work. Interesting, too, is that recent research has uncovered more than a few indications of active work throughout the 19th-century and on into the following century.[6]

In the 20th-century

Russian Freemasonry continued its history of starts and stops in the 20th-century. In the early century membership in a Lodge became an active ingredient of the Modernist movement, and it began to seem that the Craft would flourish anew. Not unexpectedly, *avant garde* poets and artists were attracted to speculative Freemasonry and esotericism.[7]

Political Freemasonry also made its reappearance when, following the 1905 Revolution, between 1906 and 1909, practical lodges were opened by freemasons with political interests, in particular Anglophile liberals of the Cadet Party (Constitutional Democrats) in the short-lived Duma (Parliament). Much has been made of a reputed masonic influence on the events of 1917, especially during and after the February Revolution.[8] A 'February Revolution conspiracy' has been taken seriously by some recent Russian specialists, but although some Cadets (Constitutional Democrats) and members of the Provisional Government were educated at Oxford and Cambridge and initiated into the Craft there, most historians do not take seriously accusations that they were behind the events of 1917.[9] Similarly, although present-day extreme right activists are convinced that freemasons were active as members of the Craft in the Duma prior to World War I, organized the February Revolution, brought down Tsar Nicholas II, and controlled the Provisional Government, serious scholars have concluded that masonic influence *per se* was so negligible as to be insignificant.[10]

After 1917 Russian Freemasonry flourished in the First Wave of the Emigration, especially in Paris, but this ended with the Nazi occupation. It would seem inconceivable that Freemasonry survived in any way, shape or form during Soviet power, but documents found in the archives of the OGPU (predecessor of the KGB) show that 'occult Masonry' experienced a 'Renaissance' in the 1920s and that in the 1930s members of a United Brotherhood of Labour ('Red Masons') offered their services to Stalin (and were promptly executed).[11]

Some masonic victims

The ups and downs of the history of Russian Freemasonry are sharply marked by a record number of victims of political repression. Novikov was imprisoned in 1792 and released only after the death of Catherine in 1794, never again to play an active role in Russian affairs. For daring to publish his *Journey from Petersburg to Moscow* Radishchev was imprisoned, sentenced to death by Catherine in a mock trial, exiled to Siberia, and so cruelly tormented after his return to Russia that he committed suicide in 1802. Most of the members of the revolt of 14 December 1825 known as the Decembrists left the Craft in the early 1820s because the lodges proved to be poor vehicles for revolution, but some remained active, including the two leaders Kondraty F. Ryleyev (1795-1826), a serious freemason, and Pavel I. Pestel (1793-1826), an opportunist. They and three other chief participants in the movement were hanged in 1826.

And this is to say nothing of the actual and fancied freemasons who shared the fate of the millions of victims Stalin's purges and the many more sent to a Gulag. Or for that matter, of the Jews and freemasons hunted down by the Nazis in the Second World War. Nor did Russian Freemasonry avoid the fate of freemasons everywhere, namely to be blamed for every untoward national event. Not only the Decembrist Revolt, but the assassination of Tsar Paul I in 1801, the sudden and never fully explained death of Tsar Alexander I in 1825, the Polish Rebellion of 1830, the revolutions of 1905 and 1917, the Civil War of the 1920s. In the 1990s radical nationalists blamed *glasnost* and the accession of the democrats to power on nefarious foreign freemasons. And yes, of course, in the 1990s the ubiquitous Jewish-Masonic conspiracy reappeared as the source of all evil to befall 'pure Russians'. Well known in this connection is the vile work of V.F. Ivanov, first published in China in 1934 and republished in the 1990s. In his view, Russian Freemasonry is synonymous with the 'despicable' intelligentsia class as a whole. Every crime in Russia against the autocracy, the Russian Orthodox Church, and the long-suffering Russian people is traceable to freemasons. In the West, where these and other crimes supposedly originated, 'atheistic', 'internationalist' freemasons were behind every 'catastrophe', from the Reformation and Humanism to the American and French Revolutions to the principle of separation of church from state to the intention to subordinate all countries to the League of Nations.[12] One of the most powerful anti-masonic weapons has been legend that Russia's beloved national poet Alexander Pushkin was murdered by Masonic conspirators.[13] According to M. D. Filin, Freemasonry is anti-national, anti-Church and 'not Russian'. The participation of freemasons -foreign as well as Russian - in the events that led to Pushkin's death in a duel cannot be taken for a 'Masonic conspiracy', but 'nevertheless, after all, their participation cannot be doubted'. Study of the events has for too long been left to 'liberal and cosmopolitan' points of view. It is time to reconsider those events 'from the point of view of Russian national traditions and interests'.[14]

The appeal of membership of the Craft to Russian intellectuals

A distinctive feature of Russian Freemasonry is that it has appealed to intellectuals more strongly than elsewhere, and perhaps less strongly to merchants and craftsmen. Just as the Novikov group was a vehicle of the Russian Enlightenment, so also was the Sentimental interlude significantly shaped by the masonic ideals of the poet, writer and national historian Nikolai M. Karamzin (1766-1826). Karamzin soon became disillusioned, and under his influence his principal successor, the early Romantic poet-translator Vasily A. Zhukovsky (1880-1922), eschewed the Craft. But there is little doubt that Karamzin was significantly influenced by his active participation, however brief, and Zhukovsky's high morality originated in the masonic ideals on which his education at the Moscow Pension of the Nobility was based.

Not just a few of the other so-called Karamzinian 'sentimental-elegiac' poets and writers of the early romantic period were influenced by masonic teachings. Especially influential during the period when the Grand Lodge of Astraea flourished was the Lodge *Izbrannyi Mikhail* [Michael the Elect], noted for its poets, writers, artists and musicians. The membership lists of the lodges obedient to Astraea are a virtual honour roll of the early 19th-century Russian intelligentsia.[15]

Aleksandr S. Pushkin (1799-1837) was not a serious freemason, but his stature as Russia's national poet ensured that the revival of Freemasonry in the 1990s reached its peak during the bicentennial Pushkin celebration of 1999. Surprisingly, despite reports that the masonic revival during *glasnost* and since was the work of the new businessmen, O.F. Solov'ev reported that at a prominent masonic ceremony he attended in 1994 there were no representatives of the new political and financial elite present. The majority of participants were scholars and intellectuals.[16]

And at present...

As for the present state of Russian Freemasonry, it has proved to be as attractive as ever in the past. This was first demonstrated anew in the 1970s when emigrés of the Third Wave rushed to be initiated and found lodges of their own in Europe, North America, and Israel. Russians did not wait for the Soviet Union to fall before launching their revival in the homeland. In 1990 contact was established between Russians in Moscow and the *Grand Orient Française*, and in 1991 the first five Russians were initiated in a ceremony held somewhere outside Moscow. Several lodges were opened under the obedience of the Grand Orient in 1991-92; in 1992 they went over to the *Grand Loge National Française*. A Grand Lodge of Russia was constituted by the Grand Loge on 24 June 1995, and its obedience on the entire territory of the Russian Federation has been recognized by over seventy Grand Lodges. At present nine 'workshops' are active under the auspices of the Grand Lodge: Harmony, Lotus, Aurora, The Four Crowned Ones, Northern Light, Brotherly Love and A.S. Pushkin in Moscow, Astraea in Saint Petersburg, and the Inter-Regional Lodge of Jupiter. One Lodge – Aurora - works in English.

Brethren visiting Russia from abroad are welcome to participate and contact may be facilitated through the Grand Secretary (Freemasonry@Freemasonry.ru/contacts_e. html). The numbers of freemasons working under other auspices are not known, but lodges are at work in Orients all the way to Vladivostok. According to V.S. Brachev (*Russian Masonry of the 20th Century*) Grand Lodges and subordinate lodges have been opened in other former Soviet republics, including Armenia, the three Baltic countries, and Ukraine.

***

NOTES

[1] *A Journey from St. Petersburg to Moscow* [translated by L. Wiener, ed. with Introduction & Notes by R.P. Thaler], (Cambridge, Mass., 1958).

[2] For my knowledge of 18th-century Russian Freemasonry I am grateful to the late S. Baehr: 'The Masonic Component in Eighteenth-Century Russian Literature', in *Russian Literature in the Age of Catherine the Great* (Oxford: Willem A. Meeuws, 1976), pp. 121-39; 'Masonry in Russian Literature: Eighteenth Century', in *Modern Encyclopedia of Russian and Soviet Literature* (Gulf Breeze, Florida: Academic International Press, 1987), vol. 3, pp. 30-36; and *The Paradise Myth in Eighteenth-Century Russia - Utopian Patterns in Early Secular Russian Literature and Culture* (Stanford, California: Stanford Univ. P, 1991).

[3] A reliable study is G.W. Jones: *Nikolay Novikov, Enlightener of Russia* (Cambridge & New York: CUP, 1984).

[4] *See* R. Lauer: Russische Freimaurerdichtung in 18.jahrhundert', in *Beforderer der Aufklarung in Mittel- und Osteuropa: Freimaurer, Gesellschaften, Clubs* (Berlin: Camen, 1979 & Essen: Reimar Hobbing, 1987); D. Smith: *Working the Rough Stone: Freemasonry and Society in Eighteenth-Century Russia* (Dekalb, Ilinois: Northern Illinois Univ. P, 1999); A. Levitsky: 'Masonic Elements in Russian Eighteenth Century Religious Poetry', in *Russia and the World of the Eighteenth Century* (Columbus, Ohio: Slavica, 1988), pp. 419-36; and a recent collection ed. by V.I. Sakharov: *Masonstvo i russkaia kul'tura XVIII-nachala XIX vv.* [Masonry and Russian Culture of the Eighteenth and Early Nineteenth Centuries (Moscow: URSS, 2000).

[5] L.G. Leighton: 'Freemasonry in Russia: The Grand Lodge of Astraea, 1815-1822', in *Slavonic and East European Review,* vol. 60 (April, 1982), pp. 244-61.

[6] *See* A.I. Serkov: *Istoriia russkogo masonstva XIX veta* [The History of Russian Masonry in the XIX Century] (Saint Petersburg: lzd. imeni N. I. Novocova, 2000), has found evidence of more activity than was previously realized. Serkov, an archivist who zealously guards his monopoly of the Masonic archives in Moscow, has also published a second bibliographic survey, *Istoriia russkogo masonstva, 1845-1945* [The History of Russian Masonry...] (Saint Petersburg: lzd. imeni N. 1. Noyjkova, 1997).

[7] N.A. Bogomolov: *Russkaia literatura nachala XX veka i okkul'tizm* [Russian Literature of the Early 20th Century and Occultism] (Moscow: Novoe literaturnoe obozrenie, 1999).

[8] For a study of this and other controversial questions *see* G. Katkov: *Russia,1917 - The February Revolution* (New York: Harper and Row, 1967), pp. 163-73.

[9] For a substantive study of the question pro and con *see* V.S. Brachev: *Russkoe masonstvo XX veka* [Russian Masonry of the 20th Century] (Saint Petersburg: Stomma, 2000), pp. 6-23. Serious new studies of Russian Freemasonry in the 20th century and before have also been provided by S.P. Karpachev: *Masonskaia intelligentsiia kontsa XIX nachala XX veka* [The Masonic Intelligentsia of the Late 19th - Early 20th Centuries] (Moscow: Tsentr gumanitarnogo obrazovaniia, 1998); and O.F. Solov'ev: *Russkoe masonstvo: 1730-1917* [Russian Masonry. . .] (Moscow: MGOU, 1993).

[10] E.g., A. la. Avrekh: *Masony i revoliutsiia* [The Masons and Revolution] (Moscow: Politicheskaia literature, 1990).

[11] Brachev: *Russian Masonry of the XXth Century*, pp. 197-230.

[12] *Russkaia intelligentsiia i masonstvo ot Petra I do nashikh dnei* [The Russian Intelligentsia from Peter I to our Time] (Moscow: Auspices of the journal *Moskva*, 1997). The word for the particularly Russian class known as the 'intelligentsia' did in fact originate with the freemasons - a link which has proved fortuitous for extremists who use both terms to denote a curse on the Russian people. Anti-

Masonry was, of course, an inevitable consequence of the movement. A 'Psalm on the Unmasking of the Freemason' was included in Nikolai Kurganov's 'Russian Universal Grammar' *(Rossiiskaia universal naia grammatika,* 1769). The great 18th-century poet Gavriila Derzhavin praised Catherine the Great for her opposition to Freemasonry in his 1782 poem 'Felitsa' which he dedicated to her and in his 'Ode on Fortune' (*Na schast'e,* 1789) in which he mocked the Martinists with a play on the similarly sounding word *martyshka* ('monkey'). Catherine herself wrote three anti-Masonic comedies and a satirical tract titled 'The Secret of the Anti-Absurd Society' (*Taina protivonelepogo obshchestva,* 1780).

[13] For a more thorough treatment of this subject *see* my previous study 'The Masonic Revival in Russia: The Poet Pushkin at Issue', in *Freemasonry on Both Sides of the Atlantic,* ed. by. W. Weisberger, W. McLeod & S.B. Morris. (Boulder, Colorado: East European Monographs - distributed by Columbia U. P., New York, 2002), pp. 449-67.

[14] 'Dve perchatki v grobu. "Masonskii sled" v sud'be Pushkina' ['Two Gloves in a Coffin - A "Masonic Clue" to Pushkin's Fate'], in *Moskovskii pushkinist: Ezhegodnyi sbornik* [Moscow Pushkinist: Annual Collection], vyp. H. (Moscow: Nasledie, 1996), pp. 244-51.

[15] *See* Leighton: *op. cit.,* pp. 259ff.

[16] *Masonstvo v mirovoi politike XX veka* [Masonry in Twentieth-Century World Politics] (Moscow: Rosspen, 1998), pp. 29 & 210.

*****

6

The muse of Freemasonry:
masonic songs, marches, odes, cantatas, oratorios and operas, 1730–1812

by

Malcolm Davies

Introduction

usic, the sixth Liberal Art, held an immensely important place in 18th-century Freemasonry. By the time the *Masonic Miscellanies in Poetry and Prose in three parts* was published in 1797 it could boast that the first part, 'The Muse of Masonry', contained 'nearly 200 masonic songs' chiefly adapted to familiar tunes: Cantatas, duets, catches, glees, oratorios, anthems, eulogies, odes, sonnets, prologues and epilogues, with appropriate Toasts and Sentiments. In fact this catalogue is a little optimistic: there is but one glee, one oratorio (*Solomon*), one catch, two cantatas etc., and there are ninety-two songs. But this corpus does demonstrate the important and ambitious place music and song held in Freemasonry at the turn of the century. This paper will outline the exciting variety of music and lyrics written by freemasons; an immense amount of creative effort mostly to be used behind closed doors. After briefly reviewing songs I shall discuss masonic marches, funeral music, odes, cantatas, oratorios and operas.

Countless musicians have been drawn to Freemasonry. It is well known that Wolfgang Amadeus Mozart was a freemason and it is fairly common knowledge that his father, Leopold, and the composer, Joseph Haydn, were also freemasons. The signatures of many well-known composers like Abt, Arne, Abel, J.C. Bach, Boyce, Cherubini, Dalayrac, Gossec, Liszt, Meyerbeer, Méhul, Piccini, Pleyel, Puccini, Spohr, Sibelius, Sousa, Sullivan, and Pijper are on lodge records, to name but a few.

Masonic musicians often banded together. The famous violinist and composer, Francesco Geminiani,[1] helped to found and became 'musical dictator' of a special London society for freemason musicians and other creative gentlemen, named *Philo-musicae et architecturae Societas Apollini* in 1725.[2] The Society only lasted two years, but during that time it formed an orchestra and amassed a substantial library of music.

The celebrated French chess player and successful opera composer François André Danican Philidor, who had the first performance of his *Carmen Saeculare* at Freemasons' Hall, London in 1779,[3] was a member of the Parisian Lodge *Les Neuf Soeurs*, which had an allied society for musicians and artists, the *Société Apollonienne*. There were special lodges for performing artists (musicians and, to a lesser degree, actors and dancers) in The Hague, such as *L'Egalité des Frères, Les*

Neuf Soeurs and *Les Coeurs Unis*. In 1784 another masonic-based society, *Les Concerts de la Loge Olympique* in Paris, commissioned six symphonies from Haydn. The figures are quite startling for the Parisian Lodges from 1775 to 1790, during which somewhere in the region of 200 professional musicians were members.[4]

Songs

The 1723 *Constitutions of the Free-Masons* by James Anderson included four songs[5] and more songs were added to the 1738 edition. The lyrics range from doggerel to an approach to real poetry and the content varies from the mythopoeic masonic history to the expression of a serious attempt to attain virtue. Anderson himself, who came up with lines like *'But Samson's blot /Is ne'er forgot /He blabb'd his secrets to his wife...'* ranks with the worst poets. An example of one of the more serious contributions is the 'Ode to masonry' by Bro Banks[6] which also has one of the earliest English masonic references to Astraea:

> Then may our Vows to *Virtue* move
> To *Virtue* own'd in all her Parts
> Come *Candour*, *Innocence* and *Love*,
> Come and possess our faithful Hearts:
> *Mercy*, who feeds the hungry Poor
> And *Silence*, Guardian of the Door
>
> And thou ASTRÆA (tho' from Earth,
> When Men on Men began to prey
> Thou fled'st to claim celestial Birth)
> Down from *Olympus* wing thy Way;
> And mindful of thy ancient Seal
> Be present still where MASONS meet.

In Britain masonic songs were printed in masonic and non-masonic collections and the mix of sacred and profane continued. The 1751 edition of *The Ancient Constitutions and Charges of the Free-Masons*, published in London by Bro Benjamin Cole, is not alone in exhibiting a rich mixture of low- and high-minded masonic and religious thought. A speech by Bro John Entick refers to

> the *Wisdom* by which *Masons* contrive and conduct their Lord's Work [...] descends from Heaven, and is first *pure*, then *peaceable*, gentle and easy to be intreated, full of Mercy and good Fruits, without Partiality and without Hypocracy.[7]

The words of the 'Magnificat' are quoted: 'he scattereth the proud in the imagination of their hearts', and much of the language is prayer book or biblical in character though the main subject is the masonic triad of Wisdom, Strength and Beauty.

However, the songs which were claimed to be by 'celebrated masters', are hardly as refined as Entick's speech. References to virtue are few and far between. 'Wine, women and song' dominate. The 'FREE-MASON'S Health' is no exception with its:

Let malicious People censure:
     They're not worth a Mason's Answer.
     While we drink and sing
     With no Conscience sting
Let their evil Genius plague'em
And for Mollies Devil take 'em
     We'll be free and merry
     Drinking Port and Sherry
Till the Stars at Midnight shine...

The *Ahiman Rezon or Help to a Brother*, published from 1756, contains more than sixty songs. The compiler of this *Book of Constitutions* for the Antients, Lawrence Dermott, apparently enjoyed singing himself. In 1752, as Secretary to the Grand Committee, he is said to have 'actually sung and lectured the Brethren out of their senses.'[8] Although many doggerel songs were subsequently reprinted by the 1813 edition there were rather more serious songs such as:

Hail Masonry, thou source divine
     Of pure and solid pleasure
With friendship's chain, our hearts entwine
     Thus prove our joy and treasure

The route by which masonic songs and songbooks spread throughout Europe is fascinating. Although they developed differently there was one single source and that was the London 'French Union Lodge' formed by French Huguenots in 1732.[9] Several of its members went on to establish lodges in various other countries which were the first on the Continent to publish songs. Vincint la Chapelle at The Hague in 1735, John Coustos[10] (together with the professional musician Jacques Christophe Naudot) in France in 1737 and Louis-François de la Tierce in Frankfort in 1742.

The Master of the French Union Lodge, Lewis Mercy, was himself a professional musician in the service of James Brydges, Marquess of Caernarvon (*later* 3rd Duke of Chandos [1771]), (GM premier GL 1754-56). Mercy wrote some music for *The Fellow-craft's Song*, the words of which were published in Anderson's 1723 *Constitutions*.[11] Apparently Anderson presented him with an autographed copy which was used to be in the Library and Museum of Freemasonry in London bound together with an autograph copy of Mercy's music. The original has not been located but a copy of Mercy's music was transcribed by Dunstan in 1921 and is reproduced here for the first time (fig. 7).[12] Another member of the French Union Lodge, Thomas Lansa, is mentioned in the *Chansons originaires des Francs-Maçons* published in The Hague in 1744 and 1749. This French-language volume is associated with the names of La Chapelle, Lansa and De la Tierce. The connections go even further; Lansa visited The Netherlands with Danican Philidor to meet and arrange a tour with Geminiani in 1745.[13] This tour was cancelled after the death of Lansa's daughter who was a harpsichord-playing prodigy.[14]

Although the first collections in France, Germany and the Netherlands were all in French and had a common heritage they soon went their own way. During the century French remained important as the language of Lodges in most European countries and their colonies. However, lodges increasingly added songs in their own native language. The largest 18th-century collection of masonic songs *La Lire Maçonne* was published in The Hague in 1763 (figure 2).[15] The 1787 edition contained an astounding 270 songs, 219 in French and 51 in Dutch and included many songs of a more serious nature. The 'lodge' increasingly became a 'temple'. A song by one of the co-editors, De Vignoles says:

> *Quel éclatant spectacle*
> *Vient s'offrir à mes yeux!*
> *C'est le plus beau miracle*
> *De la bonté des cieux.*
> *Un immense Edifice,*
> *Par l'amour habité,*
> *Fondé par la justice*
> *Qui fait sa beauté.*
> *Temple de la raison,*
> *L'asyle du Maçon.*[16]

[Trans.- What shining spectacle comes to offer itself to my eyes! It is the most beautiful miracle of the goodness of the heavens. It is an immense edifice inhabited by love and founded by justice who makes it beautiful. Temple of reason, sanctuary of the mason.]

The lodge was also seen as a temple of virtue. There were attempts to define what was meant by 'virtue'. In *La Lire Maçonne* 'virtue' is depicted as being rather vague but highly desirable: '*La vertu fait nos délices, C'est l'objet de nos desirs.*' It was understood as being an amalgam of all the various masonic qualities, such as honesty, being receptive to learning, supporting the Brother or widow of a Brother who has come upon hard times and so on.[17] A Dutch song says:

> *Gy, die den Broeder ziet in nood,*
> *Weeduw en wees in armoê weenen;*
> *Nog uit uw mond niet spaart wat brood,*
> *Maar voor hen u hart laat versteenen;*
> *Weg, weg, want gy niet waardig bent,*
> *Voor Metzelaars te zyn erkent.*

[Trans. You, who see a Brother in need, widow and orphan weeping in poverty, but do not spare some bread from your own table, but allow your heart to turn to stone against them, go away, go away, for you are not worthy to be recognised as freemasons.]

The Dutch collection of 1806 the *Gezangboek voor Vrijmetselaaren* considered Freemasonry to be at the focus point of a new world order with politics, morals, science, music, literature and humanitarianism in the ascendant, unparalleled by – and an improvement on – all previous epochs. All this has been made possible because of the Enlightenment.

Marches

The Minutes of the first few meetings of the Coustos-Villeroy Lodge provide us with the oldest extant lodge records in France.[18] Jacques-Christophe Naudot was present at the first meeting and within three months other musicians had joined. The virtuoso violinist and composer, Jean-Pierre Guignon; the organist and composer, Louis-Nicolas Clérambault; the celebrated tenor and counter-tenor, Pierre Jelyotte; and finally Naudot's own son were initiated one after another. On 9 May 1737, Naudot performed a 'Freemasons' March' which he had composed. Then, after the other musicians had been consulted, by unanimous agreement the care for the well-being of the music in the Lodge was handed over to him.[19]

The same year his short collection of songs, the *Chansons Notées de la très vénérable Confrerie des Francs Maçons*[20] was published in Paris and soon an extended collection was issued with a supplement *Recueil de Chansons nouvelles de la maçonnerie.*[21] There are two instrumental pieces, both masonic marches by Naudot. Both marches are in D major and in rondo form (ABACA) with *Cors de chasse, ou autres instruments* (horns or other instruments) specified for the A section, and *Flûtes et hautbois* (flutes or recorders and oboes) given for the B and C sections (Fig. 3). These must surely constitute the earliest examples of instrumental music written specifically for use in the lodge. In the same book there is a 'parody' or poem added to the tune by Godenèche based on the French habit of using military terms for glass (canon), wine (powder) and so on during 'Table Lodges'.

Naudot was not the only French composer to write masonic marches. Michel Blavet (1700–1768) wrote a March for the Grand Lodge. A virtuoso flautist, he was the superintendent of music to Louis de Bourbon-Condé, Count of Clérmont, who became Grand Master in 1743. Henri-Joseph Taskin (1779–1852) wrote a masonic funeral march. Funeral music has a special place in Freemasonry (see below).

The Minutes of the Lodge *La Bien Aimée,* one of several Amsterdam lodges to have an orchestra of professional musicians, refer time and time again to '*Accourez Tous Maçons*' as the Lodge's 'usual march'. This was very similar in character to the marches of Naudot and can be traced to a collection published in 1752 at 'Jerusalem' (which could indicate Paris, Amsterdam or elsewhere).[22] It was played or sung at meetings of *La Bien Aimée* as a kind of anthem from about 1754 when it was published in a lodge song book. It was included in other collections and was sung in other lodges. There is an interesting reference to this march in 1795 after the Netherlands had been 'liberated' from the tyranny of the *stadholder* by the French. The Secretary wrote in large letters right across the page in the Minute Book '*Vryhyd, Gelykhyd, Broederschap*' (Freedom, Equality, Brotherhood) and at the drinking of toasts *de Marseillaansche Marsch.* On this occasion the *Marseillaise* took precedence the normal march, '*Accourez Tous Maçons*'.

In a set of MS orchestra part books for the same Lodge from about 1785 as well as Minuets, Gigues, Prestos, Andantes and other pieces, twenty-seven out of the fifty items are marches. The composer and original context is known for only a few of these pieces. Two marches come from operas, one is specially composed by P. Dahmen, a well-known virtuoso who was a member of the professional lodge orchestra.[23] A set of parts written about 1820 by Jacob Rauscher, the musical director of the Amsterdam Lodge, *Willem Fredrik*, still begins with the march '*Accourez Tous Maçons*'.[24]

Marches were also a part of the repertoire of American lodges. One of the earliest is the 'Free Mason's March'. It was composed by William Dubois and was published in keyboard and instrumental versions in Philadelphia sometime between 1798 and 1804.[25] The melody of another march is in the Bellamy Band Book (1799) in the Library of Congress, Washington.

Marches were not the only form of ritual non-vocal music. Johann Gottlieb Naumann (1741–1801), the *Oberkappellmeister* of the Elector of Saxony's musicians in Dresden, successful opera composer and member of the *Zum goldenen Apfel* Lodge, added two pieces for keyboard to his *Vierzig Fremäurerlieder* (Berlin 1784). The *forte* and *piano* markings would make it most suitable for piano or organ though some lodges may still have used harpsichords. The first is '*Beym Eintritt in die Loge*' (for use when entering the lodge). The predominant rhythm is two semiquaver, one quaver rhythm (two sixteenths followed by an eighth note) which spell out the rhythm of echoing ritual knocks (o o —, o o —, o o —). This ritual rhythm, used at various points in lodge proceedings, has varied from time to time and from place to place. This particular rhythm is the same as one used in one of the best known rituals of the 18th century, proposed at the Convent of Wilhelmsbad in 1782.[26] Naumann's other piece, '*Die Kette*', was almost certainly for use during the enactment of the Chain of Union. This displays the musical symbolism of suspensions (a consonant interval becomes a dissonance and is then resolved) which is often used by Germanic composers to represent chains.

Funeral music

One of the most extended compositions written for a masonic occasion was written by the Superintendent of the King's Music, François Giroust, in 1784. The words are by the poet and Past Master Félix Nogaret. Both were from the Lodge *Le Patriotisme* (at the court of Versailles) the membership of which was in the hundreds and this included about forty singers and instrumentalists from among the royal and regimental musicians. It is more than a cantata; it is a whole funeral ritual with music and song called '*Le Déluge*' (The Flood) lasting about half an hour. The music is of a high quality and contains some of the most beautiful music written for a masonic occasion. The solos choruses and trios are a versification of an existing and widely used ritual called the '*tenues de deuil*' (order of mourning or 'Lodge of Sorrows'). It begins with a muted roll on the tympani, the orchestra then play three, almost terrifying, minor chords like the sad beating of the Master's mallet. Then the music represents the chaos that could result from the idea of total destruction. *Choryphée*, a bass soloist puts the apocalyptical description into words. Man in anguish is confronted with the majesty of the Grand Architect of the Universe. At one point the orchestra strikes twelve, midnight, the hour when a freemason lays down his tools. Then the piece becomes quieter and more reflective. There is a silence in the ritual as the Master leaves his chair to go to the urn which symbolically contains the ashes of the departed Brother. During quiet symphonic music the brethren approach the urn in turn pronouncing a ritual word and giving the urn a fraternal kiss. A solo cellist accompanied by strings expresses great sadness and, at the same time, great peace. The Chain of Union is formed around the urn. The Master and the Senior Warden touch the urn; the departed Brother remains part of the masonic 'chain'. After the music has finished, the 'Chain' is broken and the ritual closes.[27]

This was not the only music written for masonic funeral occasions. The 'Funeral March' written by Henri-Joseph Taskin is effective in portraying a solemn, somewhat agitated, slightly heroic mood. A manuscript copy of an elegy on the death of HG the Duke of Cumberland in 1765, 'O'er William's Tomb', by the celebrated tenor and composer Thomas Norris (1741–1790) is preserved in Ralph Dunstan's manuscript collection.[28] And, of course, the best known is Mozart's *Masonic Funeral Music*, written to commemorate the deaths of Brethren Mecklenburg and Esterházy. It was first performed at a Lodge of Sorrows at Lodge *Zur gekrönte Hoffnung* on 17 November 1785. Once again it displays all the elements of mourning, the minor key, the feeling of wandering in darkness. The sacred character is underlined by the use of plainchant. This is the tone that the Roman Catholic Mozart would recognise from the chanting of the 'Lamentations of Jeremiah' on Good Friday and Holy Saturday. The major chord at the end represents 'resurrection' and 'hope'.

Odes, cantatas and an oratorio

In this age of Handel, and later Haydn, brethren wanted masonic odes, cantatas, oratorios and operas. There are odes in many masonic collections of songs and poetry in various languages. The ode was often similar to a short cantata with recitatives, arias and choruses. Thomas Hale's *Social Harmony* of 1763, was a general songbook which contained some masonic songs including the 'Ode sacred to Masonry', words by Bro Jackson and music by the Oxford Professor of Music, composer and conductor Bro Dr Hayes. It is scored for soloists, two tenors and bass, four part choir and continuo (i.e., a keyboard instrument with the lowest notes doubled by a bass instrument, for example a harpsichord with a cello). In a first verse Comus and all loud, wanton and vain people are sent away. The pensive science with good, just, merciful, truthful and innocent qualities is invited to replace them. A one-line recitative forms a bridge 'But chiefly thou, fair friendship, welcome guest'. Then follows the chorus:

> And harmony to crown the Mason's feast
> Hail! Masonry thou faithful, Kind
> Instructor of the human mind.
> Thy social influence extends
> Beyond the narrow sphere of friends.
> Thy harmony and truth improve
> On earth our universal love.[29]

When the new Freemasons' Hall was dedicated on 23 May 1776 specially composed and arranged music was provided by soloists, choir and orchestra. As well as variations on 'Rule Britannia' (used more often in a masonic context), the anthem *Zadok the Pries'* by Handel, a march and other orchestral music, a new anthem and an extensive ode, provided by the violinist and composer John Abraham Fisher (1744–1806), were performed. The manuscript score and parts for orchestra and choir are preserved in the Library and Museum of Freemasonry in London. The text of the ode was provided by an unnamed member of the Alfred Lodge at Oxford University.[30]

A cantata is a dramatic poetical and musical work in which the action is told in recitatives and states of mind are portrayed in solos, duets etc. and choruses. *Les Francs-Maçons* by Louis-Nicolas Clérambault and published in 1743 was one of the earliest masonic cantatas. This well-written and attractive cantata consists of three recitatives alternating with three arias. It is scored for baritone solo, violin and continuo. The first section addresses the envy and misconceptions the wider world has of the Order whose laws were dictated by Virtue from the empyrean celestial realms above. The divine Astraea will appear among us for a second time. The second section, reflecting on the arrests of several freemasons, including Naudot, is angry and regretful: What do I see, are they going to close our temples and wreck our altars? Black calumny, barbarous fury, you rise up from the infernal regions. The third section talks of the menace of the jealous imaginations of fair sex. This is the most cruel cut of all. Ladies, please be assured that the laws which demand mystery form tender, loving hearts.[31]

Renowned for his operas, Luigi Cherubini wrote the cantata *L'Allience de la Musique á la Maçonnerie* for the 'loge and society', *The Olympic*, in Paris in 1786. Scored for soloist, four-voice choir, two flutes, two oboes, two bassoons, two horns, two trumpets and strings,[32] the poetry was very second rate. The main activity of this Lodge was music. In this year it counted sixty-six professional musicians (including Danican-Philidor) amongst its members and eighty by 1788. It commissioned works from several composers. Haydn's Paris Symphonies (nos. 82 to 87, composed 1785-1786) were commissioned by this Lodge.[33]

In his time Haydn was seen as being the first composer to consciously make 'musical poetry and paintings'.[34] His oratorios *Die Schöpfung* and *Die Jahreszeiten* with words translated and adapted by the freemason Gottfried Baron von Swieten[34] were translated and performed in Amsterdam by freemasons. The overture and beginning of *Die Schöpfung* especially, would seem to have masonic overtones. Such was the popularity of Haydn's works that they were imitated on a smaller scale in Jacob Rauscher's manuscript music for the numerous cantatas which are printed in the *Gezangboek voor Vrijmetselaaren* of 1806.[36]

A work of an impressively high quality – which should be revived and recorded at the earliest opportunity – is the cantata written for a St John's feast *Kantate für die Hohe Johannes-Feyer* by Johann Philip Degen (Copenhagen, 1779).[37] The highly professional music forms a work in two acts concluding with a song of praise and chorus. It tells the story of an non-mason who overhears the happy and peaceful sounds of a masonic choir as it sings. The musical forces are varied, solo, trio, quartet and choir. Act I concludes with a conversation between the non-mason and a freemason. As Act II begins the newcomer is welcomed, shown the light and becomes overjoyed. An older brother sings and then the last word is given to the Master. After an extended responsorial choir and soloist 'Lobesang' the work ends with a Schlusschor:

> Heil dem dreymal grossen Orden
> der das Glück der Welt geworden
> Schalle laut durch dreymal drey
> Preis der edlen Maurerey.

The cantatas which are still occasionally performed today are those by Mozart. A rare list of music performed during a masonic concert at the Lodge 'Newly Crowned Hope' and several sister lodges in Vienna on or near 15 December 1785 has been preserved.[38] It includes symphonies by Wranizky, a concerto and for two basset horns, a wind sextet (with great 8ve bassoon) by Bro Stadler, a piano concerto played by the Hon Brother Mozart, Fantasies by the Hon Brother Mozart and a cantata in honour of the very Hon Brother Born with music by the Hon Brother Mozart sung by the Hon Brother Adamberger.[39] This would have been *Die Maurerfreude* KV 471 (with words by Franz Petran) which was written as a homage from the Lodge to the mineralogist Bro. Ignaz von Born. The cantata is for tenor solo, male-voiced choir and an orchestra. The beginning is joyful and powerful. Von Born had discovered a way of improving mine safety and had been made an imperial knight by the Emperor Joseph II. The message of the poem is: the natural scientist penetrates the wonder of Creation and perceives how the world is ordered. This divine knowledge fills his heart with virtue. His activity makes him wise and earns him the crown of St. Joseph, the first worker.

The *Kleine Freimaurer-Kantate: 'Laut verkünde unsere Freude'* (KV 623), was first performed on 18 November 1791 at the consecration of a new temple for Lodge *Zur neugekrönten Hoffnung*. This 'small' cantata is Mozart's longest and lasts about 12 minutes. After a joyful chorus the Temple is described as the seat of Wisdom and Virtue, devoted to the task of unravelling the great Mystery. Charity, the queen of all virtues, rules in quiet glory. Brethren should live in harmony and love.

Mozart composed music for some seven masonic pieces if we do not count others which have masonic overtones. As well as the two cantatas there are three songs for tenor soloist, male-voiced choir and keyboard (piano or organ – KV 148, 483, 484) and one song for tenor and keyboard (KV 468). Mozart's masonic funeral music (KV 477) has already been mentioned.

An oratorio is like an extended cantata with recitatives, arias and choruses. Often a complete story is portrayed in the music. Unlike opera it would be performed in a concert setting without any acting. *Ahiman Rezon's* 'choice collection of mason's songs', from the first edition of 1756 to that of 1813, contains the oratorio *Solomon's Temple*. The oratorio was first performed on 15 May 1753 at 'the Philharmonic-Room in Fishamble Street, Dublin, for the benefit of sick and distressed Free-Masons'. The words were by Mr. James Eyre Weeks. The music composed by Mr. Richard Broadway, Organist of St. Patrick's Cathedral, seems to be lost. It was not the first time an oratorio had been performed in Fishamble Street. Handel's *Messiah* had received its first performance in the New Music Hall there almost exactly eleven years earlier. However, any comparison between the two works ends there. Solomon's Temple is in three short Acts. In Act I they meet to build the temple. Some masonic history going back to Adam is repeated. Now Solomon will oversee the raising of a structure that will make all men wonder and angels gaze. 'By Art divine it shall be rear'd, / Nor shall the Hammer's Noise be heard'. Uriel recognises Hiram from his masonic dress and trowel. The building work begins. In Act II Sheba suddenly arrives. She kneels in front of Solomon in admiration of his wisdom. She is received as a queen. There is a concert celebrating her beauty. Act III opens on a view of the Temple. The domed temple is built and it is ready for Sheba to see it so that she can report its glory on her return to the South. Solomon and Sheba sing a duet in praise of each other. Hiram remarks that in this way Wisdom and Beauty combine. The oratorio ends with a chorus:

> Give to Masonry the Prise,
> Where the Fairest chuse the Wise;
> Beauty still shou'd Wisdom love,
> Beauty and Order reign above.

Operas and other dramatic works

Perhaps the earliest masonic opera is the three-act *The Generous Freemason* with words by William Rufus Chetwood. The music consists mostly of well- known tunes with some newly composed music by Henry Carey, Richard Clarke and John Steeples. It was first performed in 1730 and published the following year. The title refers to a moor, Mirza, who, after recognising a masonic cry for help, rescues the hero (Sebastian) and the heroine (Maria) from a dungeon in Tunisia. Mirza, it seems, is also a freemason.

Another opera, *Les Franc-Maçonnes*, was first performed at the *Théâtre de la Foire* S. Laurent on 28 August 1754. The anonymous libretto and selection of well-known vaudeville tunes is based on the 'Amazones' act from the *Fêtes de l'Amour et de Himen*. Three new tunes for the dances have been printed at the end of the libretto. The story is told in eight scenes. A lodge, looking forward to an Initiation followed by a good banquet, is threatened by thirty women. The leader is the beautiful Hortense, whom the Master secretly loves. Why, he argues, is it that women are excluded from Freemasonry? The lodge opens with the usual ceremonies. The new Candidate brought in by the *orateur* and placed in the centre. The Master sings: 'You are about to discover the famous secret, the profound mystery; it is...' and at this point there is a great noise. The ladies are trying to force their way in and refuse to leave. There is a furious argument between the freemasons and the women. Gradually the Master and the heroine Hortense find themselves alone. They reason with each other falling more and more in love as they do so. Hortense's girls return with flowers. The angry freemasons return ready to punish the women. Instead they are decorated with sweet-smelling flowers and knotted ribbons. All except the Senior Warden are won over. He is told that if he does not soften his attitude he will be excluded from the banquet. This is too much, he also gives in. The freemasons and women have formed an alliance. After this, the whole story is repeated in a carefully choreographed ballet. When the point is reached where the men and women are reconciled the *corps de ballet* form the best known masonic symbols.

The *Harlequin Freemason* of 1780 with words and music by Charles Dibdin (1745-1814) was a pantomime.[40] The public and most newspapers loved it. It was a great success with 63 performances being put on at Covent Garden during the following year and 24 more performances in 1789 and 1793. The 'songs, duettos, glees and catches' all contributed to a story of a stone figure turned into Harlequin – with a masonic apron and a magic trowel – by Hiram Abbiff (the Grand Warden to Solomon and his assistant in building the Temple). Harlequin glimpses Colombine while he is talking to her father who wants a house to be built. The trowel completes the job at a single touch. Then he builds a temple to Bacchus for a group of peasants in the Alps. There are many other wonders and scenes, a frost scene in Holland, a stormy sea, a Court of Justice, the Market at Billingsgate. Eventually Hiram Abbiff manages to gain the consent of Colombine's father for Harlequin to marry her. Then it seems it is necessary to attend a Grand Lodge to install a new Grand Master of the Ancient and Noble Order of Free and Accepted Masons. This introduces a procession of all the principle Grand Masters from Enoch to the present time. Thus 'the Antiquity, Advancement, and Dignity of Masonry are illustrated in a pleasing and instructive Manner'. The only discordant note was sounded by the reporter from the *Morning Post* who, for some reason, found the whole thing absurd.

One masonic opera which is known to have existed is *Osiris* by Johann Gottlieb Naumann. It was first performed in 1781 in Dresden. The libretto was by

Naumann himself with the help of Lorenzo da Ponte, who was later to become Mozart's librettist. The opera had an Initiation ceremony, a choir of priests and portrayed the opposition of good and evil forces.[41]

This is not the place to discuss the masonic or alchemical implications of *The Magic Flute*, first performed on 30 September 1791, just two months before Mozart's death. There are obvious masonic allusions from the masonic knocks rhythm in the overture (o – –, o – –, o – –) through to the last chorus: *Strength* has triumphed and rewarded *Beauty* and *Wisdom* with an eternal crown! There are many articles and whole books devoted to searching out the masonic, alchemistic and mystical implications of Emanuel Schikaneder's words and Mozart's music.

It is worth mentioning the discovery in 1997 by Professor David Buch of Mozart's connection with the fairy-tale opera from 1790, *Der Stein der Weisen oder Die Zauberinsel* ('The Philosopher's Stone, or the Enchanted Isle'). The libretto is by Schikaneder and the music is by a team of composers: Mozart, Johann Baptist Henneberg, Benedikt Schack, Franz Xavier Gerl and Emanuel Schikaneder. Both operas, 'The Magic Flute' and 'The Philosopher's Stone', were written for Schikaneder's *Theater auf der Wieden*. There are many musical parallels between the two works which were essentially written for the same cast of singers to perform. It would be surprising if, with such a title, there were no alchemistic implications, though no masonic symbolism is immediately apparent.

Conclusion

The use of song to unite members of an Order was not unusual. Each Order, and there were very many in the 18th century, had its own song book. One particular book even tried to provide for many different Orders: *Fraternal Melody, Consisting of original odes, cantatas, and songs for the use of The Most Ancient and Honourable Fraternity of Free and Accepted Masons. The most Noble Order of Bucks. The Honorable order of Select Albions. The Honorable Lumber Troop. The Ancient Corporation of Stroud-Green. The Ancient Family of Leeches. The Worthy Court of Do-right. The Free and Easy Counsellors of the Cauliflower, &c., &c., Adapted to the most celebrated ballad tunes; and illustrated with Annotations, and Anecdotes of some of the Orders. To which is added an ode. In Honor of the laudable Institution of the Protestant Charity-Schools* by William Riley, Member of the several societies. London: Printed by the author, 1773. The 'Noble Order of the Bucks' had their 'Odes to Nimrod', their Cantata entitled 'Venison and Claret' and their other songs with music composed by respected church organists. The same could be said of the 'Order of Felicity or the Order of Fendeurs' ('Forest Masons') in France or the 'Order of St Peter', 'The Knights of the Five Daggers, or Infantry of the Five Sabres' in The Netherlands. These all have their books of songs, mainly toasts, drinking songs and mythopoeic history. There might have been a danger that Freemasonry could have been equally meaningless, but instead Freemasonry matured during the 18th century into an organisation of social significance. In the Netherlands, for example, by 1806 the philosophy represented in the words of the songs is a mixture of Calvin and Kant. Within the holy masonic Temple tears are shed for the poor and needy. In addition Freemasonry has attracted renowned poets, composers and musicians. The typical 18th-century freemason musician was young, itinerant and living in an uncertain, fast-changing world. When the blindfold was removed, darkness and chaos gave way to light and order. The lodge revealed to him was a meeting place and a sanctuary; a place of conviviality and harmony. It was a place of liberty, equality and brotherhood. The lodge was part of a world-wide international, visionary and idealistic movement. To be a musician in a lodge was to be part of the dynamo powering the changes to society. In writing and performing music for use in the lodge and as freemasons Mozart, Giroust, Naudot, Naumann, Philidor and their colleagues were giving musical expression to the Enlightenment.

* * * *

Being the first verse with the chorus by L=m=y

Hail Mas- on- ry! Thou Craft di- vine! Glo- ry of earth from Heav'n re- veal'd Which dost with jew- els prec- ious shine, From all but Mas- sons' eyes con- ceal'd Thy prais- es due who can re- hearse,

Fig. 7: The Fellow-craft's Song, with music by Lewis Mercy.

LA LIRE MAÇONNE,
OU
RECUEIL
DE
CHANSONS
DES
ꞌFRANCS-MAÇONS.

Revu, corrigé, mis dans un nouvel ordre, &
augmenté de quantité de Chanſons qui
n'avoient point encore paru;

PAR LES FRERES

DE VIGNOLES ET DU BOIS.

Avec les AIRS NOTÉS, *mis ſur la bonne
Clef, tant pour le* CHANT *que pour
le* VIOLON *& la* FLUTE.

NOUVELLE EDITION.

Revuë, corrigée & augmen·te,

A LA HAYE,

Chez R. VAN LAAK, Libraire;
M. DCC. LXXXVII.
Avec Approbation.

Fig. 8: Title page of *La Lire Maçonne*, a large collection of French and Dutch masonic songs published in The Hague.

Fig. 9: The Freemasons' March by Jacques-Christophe Naudot.

NOTES

1. He was initiated on 1 February 1724.

2. February 1724 (os). Before the English Parliament adopted the Gregorian calendar in 1751, the year began on 25 March. The masonic year continued to begin in March.

3. R. Cotte: *La Musique Maçonnique* (Paris, 1987), pp. 90 – 95. G. Gefen : *Les musiciens et la franc-maçonnerie* (Paris, 1993), pp. 131 – 132.

4. *See* G. Gefen: *op. cit.*, p. 63 ff.

5. 'The Master's Song' – a 'history' recounted in 28 long verses by Anderson. 'The Warden's Song or another history of Masonry' (this time in only 13 verses) also by Anderson. Two shorter songs: 'The Fellow-Craft's Song' by Charles Delafaye and 'The Enter'd 'Prentice's Song' by 'Mr Matthew Birkhead, deceas'd'.

6. *Book of Constitutions* (1783), vv. 7 – 8, p. 214. It was set to music by the celebrated composer and church musician Dr. W. Boyce and published in the *London Magazine*, January 1748. Another version with music is in *Broadley's Masonic Miscellanea* with music by Mr C. Vincent (melody and bass). Also, without music, in *Ahiman Rezon,* 1756, pp. 142–143.

7. *The Ancient Constitutions and Charges of the Free-Masons with a true representation of their Noble Art in Several Lectures or Speeches to which are added Prologues and Epilogues and A compleat Collection of Songs and Odes by the most Celebrated Masters.* London, 1751. This begins with 'A true representation of Free Masonry in a Lecture, delivered at the King's-Head Lodge in the Poultry, London on March 20, 1751, by Brother ENTICK, M.A.' The quotation is from p. 2. John Entick (c.1703 – 1773) was commissioned to revise Anderson's *Constitutions* to produce a third edition which was published in 1756. The next issue of 1767 also has his name on the title page as Anderson's successor though this was produced with further revisions by a Grand Lodge committee.

8. Of 224 pages the second edition of 1764 more than half, 118 pages contain poetry and songs. In the 1813 edition which has 234 pages, pp. 135–234, contain song and verse: 66 songs, a hymn, 2 anthems, 4 odes, 1 oratorio, spoken prologues and epilogues. There is no music given, however, some tunes are suggested.

9. The Lodge first met at the Prince Eugene's Head. A few months later, between the two Grand Lodge meetings of 21 November 1732 and 29 May 1733, the new Lodge changed its meeting place to The Duke of Lorraine's Head (the location of these Lodges was within easy walking distance of the French Church at Spring Gardens). The 1730 membership-list of this French Lodge is in *QCA* vol. X, *The Minutes of the Grand Lodge of Freemasons of England 1727–1739* (London, 1913) pp. 192 – 193. By coincidence Prince Eugène of Savoy had been one of the great military leaders in the war of Spanish Succession (1702–1713). He had spent some time at The Hague before going to Vienna, and his circle of friends there had included freethinkers and radicals. Francis, Duke of Lorraine (later Holy Roman Emperor) was initiated at the British Embassy in The Hague.

10. John Coustos, a Swiss by birth but naturalized an Englishman, by trade a diamond-cutter, by religion a Protestant. He was also at the first Lodge at the residence of the British Ambassador in Portugal. He was arrested and examined by the Inquisition c.1742. He survived months of examination, torture, dungeon, prison and a period as a galley-slave from 1743 until October 1744. This was an experience that one of his friends did not survive. He escaped from Portugal on a Dutch boat and by December of the same year he had returned to London; in 1746 he published a book *The Unparalleled Sufferings of John Coustos* (Rep. London/Dundee c.1950).

11. W. Wonnacott: 'The Rite of Seven Degrees in London', in *AQC* vol. 39 (1928), pp. 63–98. Mercy was well known in his own day as a fine recorder player and composer for the instrument. Hawkins described him as 'a celebrated player on the *flute à bec* and an excellent composer for that instrument'.

Worried about the recorder's decline in popularity he worked together with the renounced instrument-maker Stanesby on developing a new system, which could rival the transverse flute and violin. He published three sets of sonatas, of which the set for 'special' recorder, Op. 2, has been lost.

12. R. Dunstan: *The Masonic Muse*, manuscript, 1921 in Library & Museum of Freemasonry, p. 28. Another contemporary tune by J.F. Lampe is extant. For a facsimile of this see H. Poole: 'Masonic Song and Verse of the Eighteenth Century', in *AQC* vol. 40 (1928), p. 10.

13. *See* G. Allen: *The Life of Philidor, Musician and Chess-player. Supplementary essay by Tassilo von Heydebrand und der Lasa* (Philadelphia, London, Paris & Leipzig, 1863) [Facsimile: Da Capo Press, New York 1971].

14. *See* M. Davies: *The Masonic Music, Songs, Music and Musicians Associated with Dutch Freemasonry: 1730–1806* (The Hague, 2002), chapter 2.

15. *La Lire Maçonne ou recueil de chansons des Francs Maçons. Revu, corr, mis dans un nouvel ordre et augm. de quantité de chansons, qui n'avoient point encore paru. Avec les aires notés, mis sur la bonne clef tant pour le chant que pour le violon et la flute. Avec approbation.* De Vignoles and Du Bois, The Hague. Editions from 1763–1787.

16. His two songs for the Hague and Amsterdam Lodges to the tune *Carillon de Dunquerque* (Davies numbers: F 222a and F 222b) begin in this way.

17. Verse 6 of *Laten wy voor 't onkundig Wust, / Asschetsen 't Taf'reel van ons leeven;...* (Davies number D 78), only in the 1787 version of *La Lire Maçonne*.

18. G. Gefen: *op. cit.*, pp. 39 – 41. However, the conclusion that this is the same John Coustos as the member of the London French Union Lodge is mine.

19. '*Ce jourd'hui 9 mai 1737 [...] le v.m. Cousteau a proposé aux freres de la part du t.v.m. duc de Villeroy de nommer le frere naudot surintendant de la musique de la loge et ledit frere naudot ayant executé la marche des massons qu'il a composé tous les freres ont donné leur voix pour lui confier le soin de notre musique. Les freres musiciens ont été consultés*' (quoted from G. Gefan : *op. cit.*, p. 40).

20. *Chansons Notées De la très vénérable Confrerie des Francs Maçons; Précédées de quelques Pieces de Poësie Convenables au sujet, et d'une Marche. Le tout recueilli et mis en ordre par Fr^{re} Naudot.*

21. The revised edition was in one single volume containing 90 pages of words and music, which were through-numbered. The first poem is on p. 3. The index follows on p. 91. Then follows a second instrumental March by Naudot (the first is on p. 12).

22. *Recueil de la Très Vénérable Confrairie des Francs-Maçons* ('Jérusalem', 1752).

23. *See* M. Davies: *op. cit.*, pp. 297 – 300.

24. *Ibid*, pp. 167 – 168.

25. In: *Masonic Music, Selected and Composed for the installation of Merrymack Lodge, Haverhill, Massachusetts, by Samual Holyoke*, and *The Instrumental Assistant* (volume 2, 1807) also collected by Holyoke.

26. P.A. Autexier: *La Lyre Maçonne* (Paris, 1997), pp. 179 – 180.

27. R. Cotte: *op. cit.*, pp. 95ff.

28. Dunstan: *op. cit.* pp. 302–303. He took it from 'an interesting volume of music, property of the Apollo University Lodge, Oxford. Originally from the Lodge of Alfred in the University of Oxford (ceased formally in 1790).

29. Quoted in A. Poth: *De ontwikkelingsgang van het Maçonnieke Lied* (The Hague, 1956), p. 21.

30. *See also* S. McVeigh: 'Freemasonry and Musical Life in London in the Late Eighteenth Century', in *Music in Eighteenth-Century Britain*, ed. by D.W. Jones (Aldershot, 2000), pp. 83 – 85.

31. Quoted in R. Cotte: *op. cit.,* pp. 82f. For the full text listen to track 8, CD2 of *Musiques Maçonniques*, (compilation of music recorded 1958 – 1990 digitally remastered in 1996) EMI classics 7243 5 69567 2 8.

32. P.A. Autexier : *La colonne d'harmonie* (Detrad - Paris, 1995), p. 51. For more about *L'Olympique* see his *La Lyre Maçonne* (Detrad - Paris, 1997), pp. 47f.

33. P.A. Autexier : *op. cit.*, p. 40.

34. This was the view of the celebrated Dutch author Johannes Kinker. See A.J.A.M. Hanou: *Sluiers van Isis, Johannes Kinker als voorvechte van de Verlichting, in de vrijmetselarij en andere Nederlandse genootschappen 1790-1845* (Deventer, 1988), pp. 511 – 515 for a detailed account of Kinker's views on Haydn.

35. Born in Leiden in 1734, died in Vienna, 29 March 1803.

36. *See* M. Davies: *op. cit.*, p. 164–165.

37. Library & Museum of Freemasonry (London), M/18.

38. *See* P.A. Autexier: *op. cit.*, pp. 88f. The announcement and invitation was made on 9 December, the concert was planned for the 15th and was mentioned in the press on 17 December.

39. O. E. Deutsch: *Mozart - A Documentary Biography* (London, 1965), pp. 256f.

40. W.B. Hextall: 'A Masonic Pantomime and Some Other Plays' in *AQC* vol. 21 (1908), pp 138–160.

41. Lenhoff-Posner: *Inernationales Freimaurerlexicon*, (1932), col. 1099

*****

'His Prints we Read':
Jacobitism in William Hogarth's Masonic Narratives and Edgar Allan Poe's *The Cask of Amontillado*

by

Marie Mulvey-Roberts

Introduction

C harles Lamb famously said of William Hogarth: 'Other Pictures we look at, - his Prints we read'.[1] As a literary artist and satirist, Hogarth broke down the bifurcation between word and image with visual ironies, puns and literalised metaphors to produce multi-layered visual narratives, encoding the secret signs and symbols relating to Freemasonry, its ritual punishments and subversive links with the Jacobites.[2] In common with Hogarth, Edgar Allan Poe uses a masonic penal narrative for his short story *The Cask of Amontillado* (1846), where he also makes concrete the figurative with specific reference to Freemasonry. Deciphering such clues planted by artist and writer reveals layers of masonic sub-texts and inter-textuality, particularly in relation to the third degree, a ritual centred around the search for the lost word.

Hogarth identified with literary writers. His self-portrait (1745) is a picture within a picture resting on three volumes by Shakespeare, Milton and Swift next to his artist's palette, upon which is drawn an S-curved line, denoting the Hogarthian Line of Beauty and Grace, central to his treatise *The Analysis of Beauty* (1753).[3] Ronald Paulson has suggested that 'Freemasonry...may have been the ultimate source of [Hogarth's] serpentine Line of Beauty'.[4] In *The Analysis of Beauty*, Hogarth draws attention to the purpose of secret symbolism:

> It has been ever observed, that the ancients made their doctrines mysterious to the vulgar, and kept them secret from those who were not of their particular sects, and societies, by means of symbols, and hieroglyphics.[5]

Here he also records his disappointment at not finding the 'grand secret' of the ancients in a certain book on aesthetics, where he had hoped to find it.[6]

By becoming a freemason, Hogarth became part of a tradition that had embraced clandestine esoteric knowledge.[7] In the self portrait, Paulson suggests that Hogarth may be juxtaposing the Serpentine Line of Beauty and Grace with his pug[8] dog, Trump, because dogs had associations with the 'higher secrets and the higher degrees of Masonry',[9] and pugs were used as an emblem of secrecy among the Jacobite faction of freemasons.[10] The secretive organisations of freemasons and Jacobites converge in a number of Hogarth's works. For freemasons, the obligation to preserve certain secrets was reinforced by the threat of gruesome ritual punishment, even though this was intended to be purely rhetorical. By contrast, Jacobites discovered plotting to restore the Stuart line risked being executed for treason.

The Mystery of the Masons... (1724)

Hogarth linked the freemasons and the Jacobites in his earliest known masonic engraving, the satiric *The Mystery of the Masons brought to light by the Gormogons* (1724). The Gormogons were a Jacobite faction of freemasons,[11] led by the former Grand Master, Philip Duke of Wharton, who had met the Old Pretender, James Stuart.[12] After Wharton's election in June 1722, as Grand Master, the Jacobite anthem, *Let the King enjoy His Own again*, was played at the Annual Feast. The Brethren, who welcomed the song, were reprimanded by 'a Person of Great Gravity and Science',[13] who appears to have been John Theophilus Desaguliers. A former Grand Master, Desaguliers was elected as Wharton's Deputy.[14] The two were at loggerheads. Wharton marked his subsequent departure by burning his leather apron and gloves, an appropriate gesture for the founder of the club of the Hell-Fires.[15] He went on to found another society, the Gormogons, which was lampooned in a hoax press notice for 3 September 1724 as 'the truly Ancient and Noble Order of the GORMOGONS'.[16] Here there is a reference to the visit of a hoax founder, the first Emperor of China, Chin-Quaw-Ky-Po, identified in Hogarth's engraving as the first Wise Man. This is probably a satiric reference to James Stuart, the Old Pretender, who visited Scotland in 1715.[17]

Hanoverian Whig freemasons hijacked Freemasonry in order to distance themselves from Scottish and Jacobite elements, following the formation of the Grand Lodge of England in 1717.[18] Anderson, who was a Scottish Presbyterian Mason, colluded in this process by playing down the Scottish presence within masonic history in his rewriting of the Society's *Constitutions* (1723). The open book (which metaphorically Freemasonry was not) positioned above his head in Hogarth's engraving (fig. 10), could refer to this text, particularly as, in the frontispiece, Wharton is shown being presented with it by the previous Grand Master, John Duke of Montagu.[19] Wharton appointed Anderson his Grand Warden and, John Theophilus Desaguliers his Deputy.[20] The old woman riding the donkey is said to be a portrait of Desaguliers.[21] Exposure is Hogarth's satiric purpose, as symbolised by the old woman's bare buttocks, which are in close proximity to the upturned face of the sycophantic Anderson[22] in an evocation of an obscene literalised metaphor, reinforced in the accompanying verse: 'But Mark[23] Free Masonry! What a farce is this? How wild their Mystery! What a Bum they Kiss'.[24] Another concrete trope is the ape in the foreground of the engraving wearing a mason's apron and glove. But who is aping the true freemasons: the Jacobite Gormogons or the new Hanoverian freemasons?

This mock nativity procession is heralding the birth of a new age of Freemasonry. Yet the old Woman is representing the older masonic traditions for, as Paulson suggests, Hogarth used a satiric epistolary sub-text that refers to a mock punishment of Anderson and Desaguliers for having 'deflower'd a venerable OLD Gentlewoman, under the notion of making her a European HIRAMITE'.[25] Like the Hanoverians, the newly formed

Freemasons had assimilated older traditions and fabricated 'a far-fetch'd Antiquity'[26] being 'mere *Pretenders* to nothing more than Labour and Mechanicks, who boast so much of their Hod-man-ship'.[27] In his letter, the head of the Order, Hang Chi, (Wharton), who is identified in Hogarth's engraving as the <u>fourth Wise Man</u>, defends the Gormogons with the ironic quip: 'nor dare I render it cheap and contemptible, by admitting every *Pretender*'.[28]

Night ... (1738)

In 1738, Sir Robert Walpole told the House of Commons 'I am not ashamed to say I am in fear of the Pretender!'[29] In the same year, Hogarth's masonic Jacobite print *Night* (1738) appeared with its suitably tenebrous backdrop cloaking subversion and intrigue (fig. 11).[30] It is set on the night of 29 May, the anniversary of Charles II, who evaded capture by hiding in an oak tree.[31] The fire and smoke in the background are reminiscent of the Jacobite riots, taking place during the 1730s on Restoration Night.[32] Commemorative oak leaves are worn in the hats of Hogarth's freemasons and around the barber's pole. Looming in the background is Le Sueur's equestrian statue of King Charles I, who was executed.[33] The legendary founder of Freemasonry, Hiram Abif, King Solomon's builder and architect, has also been seen as a martyr for a cause when he was killed for refusing to divulge his building secrets.

One of the two freemasons in the foreground is Colonel Thomas De Veil, a past Master of Hogarth's lodge, who may have emerged from the Rummer situated on the left of the print, where a lodge met.[34] (The Rummer and Grapes was the meeting place for one of the four London lodges that amalgamated to form the premier Grand Lodge of England.) In *Night*, a bunch of grapes hangs next to the sign for the Rummer, which had an unsavoury reputation.[35] Grapes carry Dionysian symbolism, and De Veil was a drunkard and debauchee, who visited prostitutes. Brothel-signs appear on each side of the street.[36] De Veil was also a corrupt magistrate, in charge of enforcing the Gin Act of 1736,[37] which restricted the sale of the spirit, seen by the government as the poisonous purveyor of foreign influence. Wide populist opposition to the Act became a rallying point for Jacobite sympathy. In 1736, several months into prohibition, while the King was out of the country, a crowd mobbed the carriage of his consort Queen Caroline with the words 'No gin, No King'.[38] She put her head out of the window and reassured them that they would see the return of both by the next Session.[39] Is she being represented as the portly woman being attacked in the carriage in the engraving? Illegal sellers of gin, in common with the freemasons and Jacobites, were known to use cryptic codes, signs and pass-words. The phrase '*Ecce Signum*', the Latin for 'Behold the Sign',[40] may refer to this clandestine sub-culture,[41] since it appears redundantly on a barber-surgeon's sign.[42] In addition, gin could be the liquid being poured into the barrel in the background. Gin-inebriated Londoners, sleeping on the street were familiar sights, like the man and woman snoozing under the very nose of the drunken De Veil.

The chamber pot contents being poured over his head may be related to the Pass Word in the second degree, 'Shibboleth', which is commonly used to refer to a test word or phrase as used by a partisan group. The original Hebrew translates as 'a stream of water'[43] as well as 'an ear of grain', which, in terms of Hogarthian word-play, could be a reference to 'a-corn'.[44] This has connotation of oak, while 'grain' or 'corn' was used to distil gin.[45] According to the Fellow Craft degree Tracing Board Lecture, an army of Ephraimites crossed the river Jordan to attack Jephthah, the Gileaditish general. Their intention was to seize the booty, which the general had commandeered from his exploits in the Ammonitish war. In response to their threat to kill him and burn down his house, the General and his men took up arms. They successfully vanquished their enemies, many of whom tried to flee back to their own country. Those who were captured, attempted to pass themselves off as Gileaditish soldiers. The easiest way of distinguishing friend from foe was to ask them to utter the word 'Shibboleth'.[46] Those, who mispronounced it, were exposed as Ephraimites and killed instantly.[47] Like the general, De Veil was a military man, whose house in Frith Street, Soho was threatened by a 'tumultuous Assembly'. One agitator encouraged 500 of them to pull it down and to kill two informers inside, who had been used by De Veil to enforce the Gin Act.[48]

Supporting the Colonel is Andrew Montgomerie,[49] a member of the Lodge which met then at the Mourning Bush Tavern, which had Jacobite associations.[50] Freemasons' plant of mourning was cassia, a sprig of which had been used to mark the grave of the murdered Hiram Abif.[51] Cassia was seen by some to have Jacobite implications since it is derived from 'Cas' - the Gaelic for 'a branch of a tree' and also for a 'young man, a lad'. The name was changed to 'Acacia' in 1745, the year when the Young Pretender, Charles Edward Stuart (Bonnie Prince Charlie), landed in Scotland and marched south into England.[52] Hogarth shows the English troops departing for battle in his *March to Finchley* (1749), which he dedicated to King Frederick II of Prussia, a fellow freemason.[53] The defeat of the Jacobites at the Battle of Culloden marked the last serious challenge to Hanoverian sovereignty. One of their leaders, executed for rallying the Highland clans on behalf of the Stuart cause, was Simon Fraser 11th Lord Lovat, another freemason. At St Albans, *en route* to his trial, his portrait was painted by Hogarth,[54] whom he greeted with 'kiss fraternal'.[55] Lovat was the last person in Britain to be beheaded on Tower Hill, yet he was not the only one to die that day. Wooden grandstands, set up for Londoners to witness the execution, collapsed, killing several spectators before Lovat was hung from the gallows.

Reward of Cruelty... (1751)

The punishment for traitors was decapitation until 1820, and hanging and disembowelment up to the 1790s.[56] Hogarth's representation of state retribution as spectacle in his *Reward of Cruelty* (1751) was produced a few years after the 'decapitations, disembowelings and displays of spiked heads on Temple Bar' in the wake of the Jacobite risings in 1745 (fig. 12).[57] Hogarth's engraving depicts another form of punishment for certain executed prisoners, which was to be anatomised on the surgeon's table. Prior to the Anatomy Act of 1832, only the bodies of murderers could be requisitioned for dissection. Since these were not numerous enough to meet the needs of the anatomists, the trade in body snatching thrived.

A satire of the Company of Surgeons dissecting a corpse is the subject of the last engraving in the series of Hogarth's *The Four Stages of Cruelty* (1751). The narrative's anti-hero is Tom Nero, who has been executed for the murder of a serving girl he got pregnant. The iconography simultaneously parodies the punishment metered out by the state for treason and the masonic penalty for perjury.[58] The masonic candidate agrees that his tongue be torn out and his heart taken from beneath his left breast should he reveal the secrets of Freemasonry. The terms of the oath had themselves been revealed in a pamphlet called *Masonry Dissected* (1730) by Samuel Prichard, which provides a masonic sub-text for this engraving. According to Prichard's exposé, during the initiation for Entered Apprentice, the initiate is asked 'What are the secrets of a mason?' to which he replies 'Signs, tokens and many words'. The answer to the next question 'Where do you keep those secrets?' is 'Under my left breast'.[59] In the engraving, Tom Nero's left breast is being probed by a freemason[60] surgeon called John Freke, who was the innovator for a new method of dissection.[61] Here the innermost secrets of his body are being exposed as a public spectacle, at the same time, as the innermost secrets of Freemasonry are revealed through an engraving, distributed within the public domain.

The first full exposé of the tri-gradal system was, in fact, Prichard's pamphlet. It has been suggested that it was a deliberate leak by Grand Lodge to establish the new third degree, which had been grafted onto the bi-gradal structure.[62] The ritual focuses upon the murder of Hiram Abif, believed by some masonic historians to have a Jacobite significance.[63] The rumour in 1746 that Prichard's heart and tongue had been torn out in open lodge, as punishment for perjury, may have been circulated in another exposé to reinforce the credibility of his revelations.[64] In a retaliatory pamphlet entitled *The Perjur'd Freemason Detected* (1730), the author (said to be Daniel Defoe) suggests that Prichard should be renamed as 'The Free Mason Dissected'. Hogarth's retributionalist print may be read as making this metaphor literal. The corpse looks as if it were about to rise, which relates to the raising of the Master Mason in the third degree from death to life. This was a re-enactment of the murder of Hiram Abif,[65] who was killed by three assassins, for refusing to reveal his masonry secrets. These assailants were executed and their bodies mutilated for the crime along the lines of the freemason's oath. This may be the explanation for the three skulls boiling in the pot.

Five years before the print appeared, an English freemason, living in Portugal, published his account of how he was tortured for his refusal to divulge the secrets of Freemasonry. Eventually he was released with the help of the British government.[66] This was John Coustos, who was imprisoned by the Roman Inquisition as a result of Pope Clement XII's Bull of 1738 denouncing Freemasonry. A number of brutal contraptions, ropes and winches (which appear in Hogarth's engraving,[67] published in the year of another papal encyclical against Freemasonry[68]) were used to torture him over many months, during which time he was imprisoned in a dungeon.

The Cask of Amontillado

Another incarcerated freemason who, like Coustos was interested in precious stones, is the subject of Edgar Allan Poe's *The Cask of Amontillado*.[69] In this short story, a freemason called Montresor murders Fortunato,[70] also a freemason, by walling him up alive in his family's catacombs. Like De Veil in Hogarth's *Night,* whose drunkenness marks his downfall, Fortunato is drunk and is lured to his doom by Montresor's promise of a fine bottle of wine in his vaults. The old adage that 'Wine ye masons makes you free./Bacchus the father is of Liberty',[71] rings hollow for Fortunato, who will soon become a prisoner.

Once his murderous task is completed, the narrator describes how: 'Against the new masonry I re-erected the old rampart of bones'.[72] In terms of this allegory, Montresor represents the 'Antients', who were the rival body of freemasons who formed a London Grand Lodge.[73] In America, this was replayed later in 1730, followed by a counter movement of working-class men intent on taking over lodges in Philadelphia and Boston.[74] In England in 1751, the same year that Hogarth's dissection print appeared, the masonic body was disrupted by a dispute between the 'Antients' (whose precursors, it is claimed, were the Gormogons) and the 'Moderns'.[75] According to Robert Con Davis-Undiano, this conflict is dramatised in Poe's story. For example, Montresor fails to understand Fortunato's masonic sign, but declares that he, too, is a freemason. When Fortunato asks for a sign, Montresor produces his operative tool, a trowel.[76] The significance of this working tool is explained by William Morgan in his *Illustrations of Freemasonry* (1827), an exposé of the Craft, which would have been accessible to non-masons like Poe:

> The working tools of a Master Mason are all the implements of Masonry indiscriminately, but more especially the trowel. The trowel is an instrument made use of by operative masons to spread the cement which unites a building into one mass, but we, as Free and Accepted Masons, are taught to make use of it for the more noble and glorious purpose of spreading the cement of brotherly love and affection.[77]

Instead, Montresor uses the trowel to cement Fortunato's fate, when he walls him up alive. This can be seen to parallel the horrors of the imprisonment of John Coustos.[78] Fortunato's ordeal is a gruesome parody of the rite of initiation for the first degree of Entered Apprentice, over which the Master presides. The proselyte is blindfolded to symbolise how he is being brought from darkness into the light of Freemasonry. Neophytes for the degrees of Entered Apprentice, Fellow Craft and Master Mason identify themselves, through catechistic replies, as seekers of light. Traditionally, the candidate for the first degree sits in a dark closet, situated outside the lodge room, where he contemplates his own mortality. In some workings, the candidate for the degree of Master Mason would lie in a coffin or grave meditating upon death. But in Poe's tale, the underlying ritual re-enactment of the murder of Hiram Abif, goes beyond representation into reality. (Death and the mason have allegorical resonance through the ancient ritual of the interment of the builder, along with consecrated wine, in the foundations of the building he had erected.)[79]

Just as Hogarth appears to be referring to the alleged murder of Samuel Prichard for revealing masonic secrets, so does Poe seem to be alluding to the supposed murder in 1826, of the American freemason, William Morgan, for his revelations in his *Illustrations of Freemasonry* (1827).[80] At the back of this book is a woodcut of the abducted Morgan, chained in a dark niche. This image may have inspired Poe with his idea of having Montresor fetter Fortunato in a niche (fig. 13). Several Freemasons were indicted and convicted for the murder, but the token sentences they received prompted rumours of a masonic conspiracy.[81] The American Antimasonic Party, which formed in 1826 in response to the Morgan case, continued up to 1843, three years before Poe published his story.

Revenge is the leitmotif of 'The Cask of Amontillado', yet the nature of the 'thousand injuries' which Montresor has supposedly inflicted upon Fortunato remain unspecified. Vengeance lies in Montresor's ancestry since his Latin family motto was: *Nemo me impune lacessit* ('No one injures (attacks) me with impunity'). These words were used on the coins of James VI of Scotland (James I of England), claimed by some to have been a freemason, and credited with bringing Freemasonry to London.[82] Poe may have heard this apocryphal story from his Scottish foster father, John Allan, who, like Fortunato, was a wealthy freemason, also interested in wines.[83] Poe could also have read about King James's connection with Freemasonry in *The Sufferings of John Coustos* (1746).[84]

Was Montresor exacting revenge for the way in which the ancient traditions of Freemasonry and its Scottish character, along with much religious content, had been written out of masonic history? This may account for Montresor's enigmatic response to Fortunato's plea for his life. Just as the macabre masonry reaches its completion, he exclaims: 'For the Love of God, Montresor!' to which Montresor replies: 'Yes...for the love of God!' before placing the last stone into position.[85] Davis-Undiano has argued that this enclosure represents the sacred space of the lodge.[86] If this be so, then the closure of this story can be read as a horrifying pastiche of the ceremonial closing of the Lodge. The ending can also be seen as an ironic and literal re-enactment of the symbolic burial of a lost masonic history, whose deliberate and careful interment was carried out by freemasons themselves.

***

Fig. 10 Hogarth's *The Mystery of the Masons*, 1724
(with permission of the Library & Museum of Freemasonry, London)

Fig. 11 Hogarth's *Night...*(1738)
(with permission of the Library & Museum of Freemasonry, London)

Fig. 12 Hogarth's *Reward of Cruelty* (1751)
(with permission of the Library & Museum of Freemasonry, London)

***

NOTES

I would like to thank Professors Benjamin Fisher, Andrew Prescott, Wallace McLeod and David Stevenson; Dr Steve Poole, Robert Con Davis-Undiano, Alec Bac, and the library staff at Freemasons' Hall in London, for their assistance with this paper. I am especially indebted to Matthew Scanlan for his invaluable help. All errors are my own.

[1] C. Lamb: 'On the Genius and Character of Hogarth', in *The Complete Works in Prose and Verse of Charles Lamb*, ed. by R.H. Shepherd (London: Chatto & Windus, 1875), p. 295.

[2] The Jacobites were the supporters of the Catholic Stuarts, James the Old Pretender, son of the deposed James II of England, and his own son, the Young Pretender Bonnie Prince Charlie, who had laid a claim to the English throne, which was being occupied by Hanoverians. In 1603, King James VI of Scotland united England and Scotland when he ascended the English throne as James I. On his death in 1625, his son Charles became king but was beheaded in 1649 during the Civil War. His son, Charles II, regained the throne and was succeeded by his brother James II, who supported the Catholic faith. Since his son, also named James, was Catholic, to prevent his succession, James II was deposed in favour of his Protestant cousin Mary and her husband William, in what was known as the Glorious Revolution of 1688. James died in exile in 1701. After the reign of Queen Ann, Mary's sister, the crown passed in 1714 to the Hanoverian Protestant, George I. Because of support for the Stuart cause, there were Jacobite uprisings in 1715, and then in 1745, when the Jacobites were defeated at the Battle of Culloden.

[3] The words 'and GRACE' were originally painted out but now show through the painting. See R. Paulson: *Hogarth - High Art and Low, 1732-1750* (New Brunswick, New Jersey: Rutgers University Press, 1992), vol. 2, p. 263.

[4] W. Hogarth: *The Analysis of Beauty* (1753), ed. by R. Paulson (New Haven and London: Yale University Press, 1997), p. xxxv.

[5] *Ibid.*, pp.10-1.

[6] Hogarth wrote: ' I was in hopes from the title of the book [*The Beau Ideal* by Lambert Hermanson Ten Kate (1732)] (and the assurance of the translator, that the author had by his great learning discover'd the secret of the ancients) to have met with something there that might have assisted, or confirm'd the scheme I had in hand; but was much disappointed in finding nothing of that sort....I have given the reader a specimen, in his own words, how far the author has discover'd this grand secret of the ancients, or *great key of knowledge*, as the translator calls it.' *Ibid.*, p. 8.

[7] Details of his Initiation are not known. He is listed as having attending the Lodge that met at the Hand and Appletree Tavern in Little Queen Street, in 1725, though Paulson surmises that he probably joined the masons earlier. *See* Paulson: *Hogarth*, vol. 2, p. 56. This Lodge later moved to the Vine Tavern in Holborn, by which time Hogarth appears to have left, being no longer listed. In 1731, Hogarth was a member of the Lodge that met at the Bear and Harrow tavern, known later as the 'Corner Stone' Lodge. In 1735, he was honoured with the office of Grand Steward, which led to his membership of the Steward's Lodge. According to tradition, Hogarth designed the Grand Steward's jewel known as Hogarth's jewel, which was in use up to 1835.

[8] The 'masonic' Society of Mopses, were associated with the pug, representing fidelity. Two pugs are included in a Dresden porcelain statuette, *Femme aux Mopses* of 1750.

[9] *See* Paulson: *op. cit.*, vol. 2, p. 262. Implicated in the invention of the 'higher' Degrees during the 18th-century is Chevalier Michael Ramsay, the Jacobite and Roman Catholic tutor to Prince Charles Edward, who aimed to use Freemasonry to help restore the Stuart fortunes.

[10] *See* Paulson: *loc cit.* He points out here that if the Jacobite interpretation of the pug still 'carried any currency a self-portrait with a Jacobite pug would have been a rash gesture in the year of the Forty-Five.' Three years later, Hogarth engraved the headpiece to Henry Fielding's burlesque *Jacobite's Journal* (1747-1748), which was a virulently anti-Stuart response to the Jacobite uprising of 1745. The journal was intended to support the still unpopular Hanoverian monarchy and the Pelham Whig ministry in the face of Jacobite opposition. Henry Pelham succeeded Walpole as First Minister in 1743.

[11] *See* R.F. Gould: 'Masonic Celebrities, No. VI — The Duke of Wharton, G.M., 1722-23; with which is combined the true history of the Gormogons', in *AQC* vol. 8 (1895) [referred to hereinafter referred to as 'The Duke of Wharton and the Gormogons'], p. 143.

[12] Wharton had met with the 'Old Pretender' at Avignon in 1716. After he was made a Duke, he contrived for his supporters to elect him Grand Master. His title was useful in giving credibility and respectability to the freemasons. Yet Wharton was far from respectable. He was a drunken, coarse and dissolute womanizer and, it is not beyond possibility, that he was involved with spying and Jacobite intrigue while Grand Master. In Hogarth's engraving, Gould identifies the 'Mad Duke of Wharton' with the 'Crazy Knight of La Mancha', *ibid.*, p. 140. In 1726, two months before he departed to Spain on the instructions of the Pretender, Wharton compared himself to Cervantes's anti-hero in a letter to John Graeme where he wrote: 'I, like my renowned predecessor Don Quixote.' *See* M. Blackett-Ord: *Hell Fire Duke - The Life of the Duke of Wharton* (Shooter's Lodge, Windsor Forest, Berks: The Kensal Press, 1982), p. 154. Hogarth copied the figure of Don Quixote, amongst others in his engraving, from Charles-Antoine Coypel's *Don Quixote Demolishing the Puppet Show* (1725), published earlier in 1724, in Paris.

[13] D. Knoop, G.P. Jones & D. Hamer (eds.): *Early Masonic Pamphlets* (Manchester: Manchester University Press, 1945 - rpt edn., 1978), p. 109. (*See also* note 71). Desaguliers was a Newtonian scientist who was said to be of 'forbidding aspect'. See F. L. Pick and G. N. Knight: *The Pocket History of Freemasonry* (London: Frederick Muller Ltd, 1953, rev. edn., 1977) p. 73. The feast took place at the Stationers' Hall in London. *See* Blackett-Ord: *op.cit.*, p. 89.

[14] Desaguliers was the third Grand Master. He held office from 1719 until 1721, when he was succeeded by John, Duke of Montagu. Desaguliers was elected Wharton's Deputy in 1722 and the following year was re-elected by one vote as Deputy to Wharton's successor, the Whig Earl of Dalkeith. Wharton, who had reached the end of his one year in office, and had originally refused to nominate a successor, disliked Desaguliers and was displeased with this election result. Shortly afterwards, he left the Craft unceremoniously and for good.

[15] *The British Journal* of December 12, 1724 reported that 'a Peer of the first Rank, a noted Member of the Society of Free-Masons, hath suffered himself to be degraded as a member of that Society, and his Leather Apron and Gloves to be burnt, and thereupon enter'd himself as a Member of the Society of Gormogons, at the Castle-Tavern in Fleet Street', p. 126. *See* Gould: 'The Duke of Wharton and the Gormogons', p. 126. Wharton founded the Hell Fire Club in 1719 to challenge orthodox morality and thought, and was said to have been the President. This claim was incorrect, as the President was claimed to be the Devil.

[16] *See* Knoop, Jones & Hamer: *op. cit.*, p. 143.

[17] Kloss suggested that the Œcumenical Volgee, who figures in Hogarth's engraving as the third Wise Man, is the Jacobite Chevalier Michael Ramsay (see note 9). *See* Gould: 'The Duke of Wharton and the Gormogons', p. 125. Gould, however, identified him with Pope Benedict XIII. *See ibid.*, p. 143. Matthew Scanlan suggests that the Old Woman is a parody of the Pope. *See* note 22. This would indeed be tongue in cheek in view of the positioning in the engraving of Anderson, who equated Popery with slavery and had warned against Catholics and Jacobites in a published sermon. *See* D. Stevenson: 'James Anderson (1679-1739): Man and Mason', in *Freemasonry on both sides of the Atlantic: Essays concerning the Craft in the British Isles, Europe, the United States and Mexico*, ed. by R.W. Weisberger, W. McLeod & S. Brent Morris (Boulder, Colo.: East European Monographs, 2002), p. 203. Gould believed it very likely that Wharton was being caricatured, not just as Don Quixote, but also as the Mandarin Hang Chi, the fourth

Wise Man in the print, who, according to a contemporary satire Hogarth is drawing on, is about to leave for Rome. *See note 25, ibid.*, p.141 and Knoop, Jones & Hamer: *op. cit.*, p. 143.

[18] This involved the amalgamation of the four Lodges that met at the Goose and Gridiron Ale-house in St Paul's Church Yard, the Crown Ale-house in Parker's Lane, the Apple-Tree Tavern in Convent Garden and the Rummer and Grapes Tavern in Channel-Row, Westminster. Their purpose was more economic and social than political in 1717, as M. Scanlan proposes to reveal in a forthcoming book.

[19] The book is represented in the form of a scroll with the word 'Constitutions' written on it, thereby alluding to its antiquity and absorption of the older 'Gothick' Constitutions. The book was published near the end of Wharton's year as Grand Master and pays homage to him in *The Warden's Song*: 'To Wharton, noble Duke our Master Grand/He rules the Freeborn sons of Art/By love and friendship, hand and heart', quoted by Gould: 'The Duke of Wharton and the Gormogons', p. 119. This verse was omitted in the 1738 edition of the *Book of Constitutions*. Gould, however, identifies the book in the engraving as *The Grand Mystery of the Free Masons Discover'd* (1724), to which were appended letters satirising the Gormogons, that form such an obvious sub-text to this engraving. See note 25 and Gould: 'The Duke of Wharton and the Gormogons', p. 139. Gould had considered the book to be Samuel Prichard's exposé *Masonry Dissected* (London: J. Wilford, 1730), while wrongly assuming that the print was issued in 1730, *ibid.*, pp.140-141.

[20] *See* note 14.

[21] E. Ward saw a closer resemblance between the nose of the Old Woman and Hans Hysing's portraiture of Desaguliers, than that appearing in Coypel's engraving of *Don Quixote Demolishing the Puppet Show.* See his 'William Hogarth and his Fraternity', in *AQC*, vol. 77 (1964), p. 18.

[22] *See* Gould: 'The Duke of Wharton and the Gormogons', p. 140. As Ward points out, the engraving is based on Coypel's engraving, and the only principal figure which does not have a counterpart in Coypel, is the portrait of Anderson. *See* Ward: 'William Hogarth and his Fraternity', p. 18. This posturing is suggestive of Anderson's subservience to Desaguliers, who appears to have been the driving force behind the Whig take-over of Freemasonry. In the anonymous *The Free Masons: An Hudibrastick Poem*, (1722/3), the letter of dedication declares: 'Sir, Having had the Honour, not long since, when I was admitted into the Society of Masons, of Kissing your Posteriors, (an Honour superior to Kissing the Pope's Toe) I am fully determin'd to make you only the Deserving Patron of these my Labours', in Knoop, Jones & Hamer: *op. cit.*, p. 85. There are much ruder relevant sections of the poem which have not been included by Knoop, Jones and Hamer and appear in the full version edited by W. McLeod. *See* his 'The Hudibrastic Poem of 1723', in *AQC*, vol. 107 (1994), pp. 9-52. The mocking of Anderson may also have sexual nuances. He was said to have been a libertine and was accused of having contracted the Pox. M. Scanlan has suggested that Wharton is the author, not only of the Gormogon satires, being the 'true' Verus Commodus, but also of this bawdy poem, which was in keeping with his particular brand of wit and crude humour. McLeod thinks that it was probably written by a non-mason, which would rule out Wharton.

[23] This is a pun relating to the marks inscribed by stone-masons on buildings. These relate to a Mark degree which predates the earliest record of Mark Masonry in a speculative body of 1 September 1769 - see F.L. Pick & G.N. Knight: *op. cit.*, p. 214.

[24] Contained in *The Freemasons* poem is the rhyming couplet: "Tho' he's not worth a single Farthing,/Who'll not endure a strong Bumbarding", Knoop, Jones & Hamer: *op. cit.*, p. 90.

[25] Knoop, Jones & Hamer: *op. cit.*, p. 148. This is a Gormogon satire attached to the second edition of *The Grand Mystery of Freemasons Discovered* (1724), written by the pseudonymous 'Verus Commodus' in the form of letters. *See Hogarth: 'The 'Modern Moral Subject', 1697-1732* (New Brunswick and London: Rutgers University Press, 1991), vol. 1, pp. 117-118. 'Commodus' derived much of the material from *The Plain Dealer*, which appeared a month earlier in September. From August until October, when Verus Commodus's letters were published, a variety of newspaper reports appeared about the Gormogons.

[26] *Ibid.*, p.150.

[27] *Loc.cit.* My italics are in the quotation.

[28] *Ibid.*, p. 134. My italics are in the quotation.

[29] P. Dillon: *The Much-Lamented Death of Madame Geneva - The Eighteenth-Century Gin Craze* (London: Review, 2002), p. 131. Robert Walpole's position as the Whig Prime or First Minister was assured by his response to a Jacobite plot uncovered in April, 1722, known as the Atterbury plot after Francis Atterbury, the Tory bishop of Rochester. After its failure, one conspirator was executed and Atterbury was exiled for life. Walpole used the victory to brand all Tories as Jacobites, which won public support and was a factor in keeping them out of office until 1770. Wharton was a great supporter of Atterbury for, as Gould explains: 'A bill of pains and penalties was introduced into Parliament, and it passed the Commons with little difficulty. In the Lords the contest was sharp. The young Duke of Wharton, distinguished by his parts, his dissoluteness, and his versatility, spoke for Atterbury with great effect', *see* his 'The Duke of Wharton and the Gormogons, p. 120. Wharton's speech in support of Atterbury was in May 1723 while he was still Grand Master.

[30] 'Night' is the last in Hogarth's series *The Four Times of Day* (1738) and was exhibited along with 'Evening' in Vauxhall Gardens, which functioned, in this respect, as an early public art gallery in London. The painting was situated in the fourth pavilion behind the orchestra.

[31] According to Paulson, 'the contiguity of George I's birthday and the Jacobite anniversary of Charles II's restoration (as well as Charles's I's martyrdom) allowed for the anti-Hanoverian crows to celebrate in a subversive way'. *See* his *Hogarth*, vol. 2, p. 133.

[32] Three years before this engraving appeared on 30 January 1735, there was a noisy celebration at a London tavern. This was the carousing of a group of the Dilettanti Club to which the Duke of Wharton had belonged. That night was the anniversary of King Charles I's execution and the revellers were mistaken for the Calves Head Club of the Restoration with their king-killing oaths. As a result, a mob carrying calves' heads on stakes hurled stones at them and stormed the inn for two hours. Hogarth was a founding member of the Sublime Society of Beefsteaks in 1735. The title of Hogarth's engraving, *The Gate of Calais. Or The Roast Beef of Old England* (1748) may be a reference to the club. *See* Paulson: *op. cit.,* vol. 2, p. 62.

[33] James Anderson in the 1723 edition of the *Book of Constitutions* claims that King Charles I was a freemason and that Charles II was an 'Accepted Free-Mason as every one allows he was a great Encourager of the Craftsmen', *The Constitutions of the Free-Masons in the Year of Masonry 5723 and The New Book of Constitutions of the Antient and Honourable Fraternity of Free and Accepted Masons in the Vulgar Year of Masonry 5738* (London: *Quatuor Coronati* Lodge, facsimile edn., 1976), pp. 40-41. Stevenson refers to a masonic reviewer of *The Book of Constitutions*, who notes that Anderson expressed uncertainty about whether Charles II was a mason. *See* Stevenson: 'James Anderson', p. 225.

[34] The engraving is set in Hartshorn Lane, Charing Cross, which opened onto Trafalgar Square and, was later renamed Northumberland Street, and then Northumberland Avenue. According to Jacob Hugo Tatsch: 'a Lodge, constituted 18 August, 1732 and erased in 1746, met at the 'Rummer, Charing Cross' but removed in 1733'. Another sign, to the right of the engraving is that of the 'Earl of Cardigan's Head'. Tatsch points out that: 'from 1739-42, a Lodge which was constituted 15th April, 1728, and erased in 1743, held its meetings at the Earl of Cardigan's Head, Charing Cross'. Tatsch: 'William Hogarth - A Brief Sketch of his Life and Masonic Works', in *The Builder: A Journal for Freemasons*, IX, no 3 (March, 1923), p. 69.

[35] Walpole had made this inference. *See loc.cit.*

[36] The barber shaving the customer looks like a woman with a comb in her hair. S. Poole has suggested that the 'New Bagnio' may have connotations of homosexuality.

[37] The First Gin Act was in 1729 then followed by Acts in 1736, 1743, and 1751, 1757 and 1760. *See* Dillon: *op. cit.*, pp. 68-78, 117-23, 219 - 231, 260 - 262, 280 - 283 & 283 – 286.

[38] *Ibid.*, p.160.

[39] Lord Egmont recorded that 'She put forth her head and told them that if they had patience till the next Session they should have again both their gin and their King.' *Loc.cit.*

[40] I have interpreted this as the freemasons' penal sign. *See* my 'Hogarth on the Square', in *British Journal of Eighteenth-Century Studies* vol. 26, no 2 (Autumn, 2003), p. 261.

[41] Some of the surviving Jacobite codes have remained unbroken to this day. In regard to Freemasonry, there were layers of secrecy within different degrees, which were beginning to proliferate on the Continent. New passwords made it more difficult for Hanoverian spies, for example, to infiltrate Lodges with suspected Jacobite members.

[42] The barber's shop could be that of Captain Tom the Barber, who was a ring-leader for organising riots against Irish pubs, which combined with protests against the Gin Act in 1736. *See* Dillon: *op. cit.*, pp. 133-34. Walpole wrote to his brother that 'the Jacobites are blending with all other discontents, endeavouring to stir up the distillers and gin retailers, and to avail themselves of the spirit and fury of the people', *Ibid.*, p.135.

[43] In view of De Veil's hiring of spies, the liquid being poured from the chamber pot could be an allusion to the expression 'it rains', which was used to identify the approach of a male cowan or Lodge spy. A female cowan was indicated by the more drastic weather condition of 'it snows'. These signals are on record in the 'irregular prints' of the mid 18th-century according to B.E. Jones: *Freemasons' Guide and Compendium* (London: Harrap, 1950, rev. edn., 1977), p.424. See my 'Hogarth on the Square', pp. 259-61.

[44] W.B. Hextall drops these cryptic clues without revealing the Password or the wider context of the Lodge Lecture. *See* his 'William Hogarth and Freemasonry', in *Leicester Lodge of Research Transactions*, (1908-9), p. 112.

[45] *See* chapter six on 'Corn' in Dillon: *op. cit.*, pp. 79-92.

[46] *See Shibboleth: Or Every Man a Free-Mason* (Dublin: William Steater, 1765).

[47] Shibboleth (spelt 'Schiboleth') was used in 1748 in France, according to an anti-masonic exposé. See H. Carr (ed.): *Early French Exposures* (London: The *Quatuor Coronati* Lodge, 1971), p. 415. (I am indebted to Matthew Scanlan for drawing my attention to this source.)

[48] This took place in January 1737/38. De Veil read the Riot Act, which instead of dispersing the 1,000 strong crowd, exacerbated the situation. This led to Roger Allen inciting half of them to destroy De Veil's property and kill two of his paid spies. Hogarth issued a new advertisement for a subscription of *The Four Times of Day* on the day of Allen's trial which, as Paulson points out, could not have been a coincidence. *See* Paulson: *op. cit.*, vol. 2, pp. 132-3. In relation to De Veil's espionage system, the word for someone spying on a lodge meeting is a 'cowan'. If discovered the ritual punishment for a cowan was to stand below the eaves of a house in rainy weather until water poured out of his or her shoes hence the word 'eavesdropper'. *See* S. Prichard: *Masonry Dissected*, p. 7. This punishment is parodied in the engraving by the chamber pot pouring a stream of urine over De Veil. *See* my 'Hogarth on the Square', p. 259.

[49] The resemblance can be clearly seen in his portrait by A.F.V. Meulen, which was engraved by A.V. Haecken in 1738, the year that Hogarth's *Night* appeared and is reproduced in Jones: *op. cit.*, plate opposite p. 65.

[50] This was in Alders Gate Street and the Lodge met there between 1735-1765. Originally, it was called the 'Bush' after an ivy bush hanging up by the door. It was changed to 'Mourning Bush' when the landlord was so incensed by the death of King Charles I, that he painted the sign black for mourning. (I am indebted to Matthew Scanlan for this point.)

[51] The cassia plant, known now as acacia, was at one time used at masonic funerals.

[52] In Prichard's *Masonry Dissected*, p. 13 cassia is given as the name of a Master Mason. This ties in with a sprig of cassia being placed at the head of the grave of Hiram Abif, whom the Master Mason is said to emulate. *See also* Jones: *op. cit.*, pp. 189f.

[53] It had originally been dedicated to the King George II, but he was so displeased by the way in which the troops had been depicted that Hogarth withdrew the dedication. Hogarth's engraving *The Gate of Calais or The Roast Beef of Old England* (1748), portrays a defeated kilted Jacobite hidden crouching in the corner in the dark. The link with Freemasonry is the friar, who is a portrait of Hogarth's friend, John Pine the masonic illustrator. Hogarth, also appears in the engraving, drawing the scene. This is a reminder of the time when he was arrested for spying by the French, after he was seen sketching the Calais fortifications.

[54] Hogarth told his friends that his portrait shows Lovat counting on his fingers the number of rebel troops or clans. *See* Paulson: *op. cit.*, vol. 2, p. 276.

[55] *See* J. Uglow: *Hogarth - A Life and a World* (London: Faber, 1997), p. 417. She quotes from J. Nichols: *Biographical Anecdotes of William Hogarth with a Catalogue of his Works* (London: J. Nichols, 1781, 1782 & 1785), re-issue ed. & intro. by R.W. Lightbown, (1971), p. 283. Nichols denies that the two men were already acquainted which Paulson regards as a denial of 'the Scottish connection for which there was considerable evidence'. *See* Paulson: *op. cit.*, vol. 2, p. 276.

[56] *See* V.A.C. Gatrell: *The Hanging Tree - Execution and the English People, 1770-1868* (Oxford: Oxford University Press, 1994), p. 281.

[57] *Ibid.*, p. 15. The retribution works on a symbolic level, since the treason threatening to destroy the political body is punished by the hanging, drawing and quartering of the traitor's body as a mirror of the crime against the state.

[58] The caption below reads 'torn from the root thy wicked tongue', which is a punishment for lying or perjury rather than for murder. Christian iconography of martyrdom can also be read into the print and that could be another parallel with the third degree. *See* note 63.

[59] Prichard: *Masonry Dissected*, p. 7.

[60] *See The Minutes of the Grand Lodge of Freemasons of England 1723-1739*, ed. by W. J. Songhurst, *QCA*, vol. 10 (London: *Quatuor Coronati Lodge*, 1913), p. 34.

[61] In his 'An Essay on the Art of Healing' (1748), Freke, who has associations with Hogarth, discusses the hazards of breast surgery for the removal of cancerous tumours. His surgical method was to use a knife to divide the skin and muscles and then to penetrate the pleura with his finger and insert a canula in the wound. The figure presiding over the procedure might be a caricature of William Hunter (1718-1783), the eminent surgeon, who performed public anatomies during the 1740s and 1750s. The portrait of Hunter by Allan Ramsay, (*c.*1760) at the Hunterian Art Gallery in Glasgow, and the engraving (*c.*1764) by an unknown engraver after the Ramsey portrait, housed in the National Portrait Gallery, portray him with a thinner face and finer feature than that of the anatomist in the engraving, though both men have a squarish jaw. Hunter reported that Hogarth was 'amazingly pleased' by witnessing a dissection he carried out in front of him and that he 'very well expressed it' in a drawing. *See* Martin Hopkinson: 'William Hunter, William Hogarth and the *Anatomy of the Human Gravid Uterus*, in *Burlington Magazine*, vol. CXXVI, (1984), p. 10. Hunter's first uterine specimen was dissected in 1750, which was the year before Hogarth's

print appeared. Hunter subscribed to *The Analysis of Beauty* and *Four Prints of an Election. See* Uglow: *op. cit.*, p. 738. *See* W.F. Dynum & R. Porter (eds.). *William Hunter and the Eighteenth-Century Medical World* (Cambridge: Cambridge University Press, 1985). *The Analysis of Beauty* contains references to dissection. See *op. cit.*, p. 53

[62] H. Bogdan, *From Darkness to Light: Western Esoteric Ritual of Initiation* (Ph.D. thesis: Göteberg University, Department of Religious Studies, 2003) claims that originally there had been one Degree with two stages: Entered Apprentice and Fellow Craft. The latter was originally the equivalent of the later Master's degree, though this did not necessarily correlate to being the Master of the Lodge. The Fellow Craft ritual also included a meditation upon death, the vestiges of which may have found their way into the new Third Degree, which was an innovation of Grand Lodge Masonry. According to 'Verus Commodus', the Old Woman was made into 'an European HIRAMITE'. It is tempting to surmise from this an early reference to the third degree and the Hanoverians, but this can be in no way conclusive.

[63] *See* W.W. Covey Crump: *The Hiramic Tradition - Hypotheses Concerning It* (London: Masonic Record, 1935). The Jacobites invented a new substitute word for the third degree: 'Macbenac'. The Gaelic word 'Mac' means 'son' and 'bena' means 'blessed son' which the Jacobites applied to James. It resembles the Master Mason's lost word 'Machbenah' (denoting 'the builder is smitten'), for which Hiram Abiff was murdered, as explained in the ritual of the Third Degree. *See* S. Prichard: *Masonry Dissected*, pp. 12-14. The search for this lost word became an important feature of the Master Mason's degree. The ritual reply to 'Machbenah' is YHVH meaning 'the flesh falls from the bone'. *See* Bogdan: *op. cit.*, p. 112. This is what has already happened in Hogarth's engraving as we can see from the central figure of the skeleton. The protruded forefinger from which the flesh has fallen could relate to the expression, 'it stinks', which was when a freemason tried to raise the corpse of Hiram Abiff by the finger and the flesh came off. This is re-enacted in the ritual of Master Mason and is referred to as 'giving the slip' which has also been interpreted as an allegory for circumcision. Crump notes that 'a bare possibility does remain that the Hiramic tradition had in some way a Jacobite application, and that it was with the object of concealing that connection from Anderson, that the famous holocaust [*sic*] of masonic documents was effected in 1720.' *Ibid.*, p. 99. Parallels can also be seen with the Resurrection of Christ as well as with earlier rituals of raising Noah from the grave.

[64] *See Abbé* Larudan [Gabriel Lois Calabre Perau]: *Les Francs-Maçons Écrasés: suite du livre intitulé, 'L'Ordre des Francs-Maçons trahi, traduit du Latin* (Amsterdam: no publisher given, 1747**)**, pp. 57 - 60 & 103 - 106.

[65] Freke also published in 1748 *An Essay to show the Cause of Electricity and why some things are non-Electricable, in which is also considered its Influence in the Blasts on Human Bodies etc....* Georgian surgeons used electricity for therapeutic purposes. *See* D. Porter & R. Porter: *Patient's Progress: Doctors and Doctoring in Eighteenth-Century England* (Cambridge, Polity Press, 1989). Certainly experiments in galvanism were carried out on the hanged corpses of felons by 1803, when Luigi Galvani's nephew, Luigi Aldini, conducted an experiment. Hogarth's skeleton looks as though it has been electrified into 'life'.

[66] *See* J. Coustos: *The Sufferings of John Coustos for Freemasonry, and for refusing to turn Roman Catholic, in the Inquisition at Lisbon* (London, 1746) introduction by W. McLeod (Bloomington: Illinois: The Masonic Book Club, 1979). Coustos was born in Switzerland and moved to England in 1716, where he became a naturalised citizen. According to the inquisitor's records, at the sight of the instruments of torture, Coustos revealed the secrets of Freemasonry.

[67] Hogarth appears to be using a Freemason's lewis to winch Tom Nero's body in the engraving as a parody of the freemason, being represented as a finished stone or ashlar, being winched up at death to take his place as a 'living stone' in a heavenly King Solomon's Temple. Since Nero's body was that of a murderer, he would not be a candidate for Heaven anyway. Also, according to common Christian belief, his body could not rise on the Last Day of Judgement, since it had been mutilated. *See* my *Hogarth on the Square*, pp. 265-66.

[68] In 1751, when Hogarth's engraving appeared, another papal bull condemning Freemasonry was issued, this time by Pope Benedict XIV. These must have been problematic for Catholic Jacobite freemasons.

[69] Poe tells us that 'In painting and gemmary Fortunato, like his countrymen, was a quack', (The Cask of Amontillado', in *The Complete Tales and Poems of Edgar Allen Poe* (London: Penguin books, 1982), p. 274. Coustos was arrested by the Inquisition on the pretext of his having been involved in the theft of a stolen diamond.

[70] The name 'Montresore' means 'my treasure' in French [*mon trésor*] while Fortunato relates to 'fortune'. Perhaps this is some word-play here relating to Coustos's trade in precious stones and the masonic mythologizing of stones, which range from the building blocks of the stonemasons' trade to the symbolic perfect stone or ashlar, to which all freemasons aspired.

[71] This jingle is from a book entitled *Ebrietatis Encomium* or: *The Praise of Drunkenness* (1723), which is a translation of Henri Albert de Sallengre, *L'Eloge de l'Yvresse* (1714) thought to be by Robert Samber. The rhyming couplet is taken from Chapter XV 'Of Free Masons and other learned Men, that used to get Drunk' where there is a description of the Annual Feast of freemasons, where the Jacobite song mentioned above was played. *See* Knoop, Jones & Hamer: *op. cit.*, p. 109.

[72] E.A. Poe: *op. cit.*, p. 279.

[73] This split has often been seen in terms of a division between operative and speculative or symbolic Freemasons, which is a misleading distinction. Within operative lodges, there were building secrets, ceremonial aspects and rituals, yet conversely, purely symbolic and ceremonial freemasons did not have the skills of the operative craftsmen.

[74] *See* R.C. Davis-Undiano: 'Poe and the American Affiliation with Freemasonry' in *Symploke* vol. 7/1-2 (1999), pp. 138-99.

[75] The Antients formed a rival Grand Lodge in 1751. G. Kloss, however, conjectured that 'in the Gormogons we meet with the precursors of the Schismatic Masons, or "ancients" ' *see* Gould: 'The Duke of Wharton and the Gormogons', p. 125.

[76] *See* P.J. Sorenson: 'William Morgan, Freemasonry and "The Cask of Amontillado" ', in *Poe Studies* vol. 22, 2 (December, 1989), p. 45.

[77] '...that cement which unites us into one sacred band or society of friends and brothers, among whom no contention should ever exist but that noble contention, or, rather, emulation, of who can best work or best agree' - *see* W. Morgan: *Illustrations of Masonry by one of the Fraternity with an account of the kidnapping of the author* (New York printed for the Author, 3rd edn.,1827), p. 56.

[78] ' 'Twas then', wrote Coustos, '.... that, struck with the Horrors of a Place, of which I had heard and read such baleful Descriptions, I plunged at once into the blackest Melancholy; especially when I reflected on the dire Consequences with which my Confinement might very possibly be attended", *op. cit.*, p. 20. After being interrogated, Coustos was taken to an even deeper dungeon 'the design of which', he said, 'I suppose was to terrify me completely, and here I continued seven weeks', *op. cit.,* p. 32.

[79] Besides wine there was also consecrated oil and corn.

[80] An American anti-masonic book states: 'Freemasonry is an inhuman institution because it is founded upon a law requiring murder; moreover, it is unlawful and immoral for any man to swear away his life by making it forfeit as Masonic oath requires'. J.G. [Lazier] Stearns: *An Inquiry into the Nature and Tendency of Speculative Free-Masonry* (Utica: Northway and Bennett, 3rd edn., 1827), p. 117. I am grateful to the late Mark Madoff for directing me to this material.

[81] The prosecutors and many of jurors - and even the Governor of New York, Governor Clinton - were freemasons.

[82] There is no evidence that King James VI was actually a freemason. Anderson represents him as 'the mason king of Scotland'. *See* Stevenson: 'James Anderson', p. 218.

[83] *See* K. Silverman: *Edgar A Poe - Mournful and Never-ending Remembrance* (New York: HarperCollins, 1991), p. 317. Silverman points out that the name of Allan is contained in 'The Cask of Amontillado' (*loc cit.*)

[84] Six editions of the text were published throughout the nineteenth century in America. Three of these were published in Massachusetts: in 1800 in Brookfield, in 1803 in Boston and in 1817. The latest American edition before Poe's story was written was published in 1821 in Enfield, Connecticut. *See* W. McLeod: 'Editions of Coustos's Book', in *AQC* vol. 92 (1979), pp. 130-136. Was Fortunato's imprisonment to do with him being a Freemason? Coustos eventually realised that this was the reason for his incarceration: 'From that instant I was firmly persuaded, that I had been imprisoned solely on Account of Masonry. They [the Inquisition] afterwards ask'd, "What were the Constitutions of this Society?" I then set before them, as well as I could, the antient Traditions relating to this noble Art, of which (I told them) James VI, King of *Scotland*, had declared himself the Protector, and encouraged his subjects to enter among the Free-Masons: That it appeared, from authentic Manuscripts, that the kings of *Scotland* had so great a Regard for this Honourable society ... that monarchs established the custom among the Brethren, of saying whenever they drank, <u>God preserve the King and the Brotherhood</u>: That this Example was soon followed by the Scotch Nobility and the Clergy, who had so high an Esteem for the Brotherhood, that most of them entered into the society. That it appeared from other traditions, that the Kings of <u>Scotland</u> had frequently been Grand-Masters of the Free-Masons.' *See* Coustos: *op. cit.*, p. 28.

[85] Poe: *op. cit.*, p. 179.

[86] *See* Davis-Undiano: *op. cit.*, pp. 126-32.

*****

8

Why was James Boswell a freemason? An old question revisited

by

David Stevenson

I n 1966 two well known historians of Freemasonry, J.R. Clarke and G.P. Jones, published an article in *Ars Quatuor Coronatorum* titled 'Why was James Boswell a freemason?'[1] This is unusual wording for the title of an essay on the career of an individual freemason. There are plenty of articles on masonic careers, but usually presented straight, without a question mark. They do not have a 'why', because freemasons accept that it is quite ordinary, reasonable, indeed virtuous, to be a freemason. So, why the 'why'? Clarke and Jones were considering Boswell in the framework of a proposed wider inquiry into why men became freemasons in the 18th century, and Boswell was central to seeking an answer to this question because, so far as I know, no British diarist, journal keeper or letter writer wrote more on their masonic activities than he did. But, though Clarke and Jones were slow to admit it, there was I think an underlying reason why the question 'why' was being asked of Boswell in particular. In a many respects Boswell was a man whom it was difficult, for 20th century English freemasons like Clarke[2] to believe should ever have been admitted to the Craft. In the '*Why* was Boswell a freemason' I there is a think a trace of a stifled cry of anguish.

Why was James Boswell seen as such an unlikely and unsuitable freemason? Because one side of his reputation lies in drunkenness and sexual excess, and he kept detailed journals for much of his life recording his conduct. Some have been lost, and in those that survive some of what were regarded as the most explicit descriptions of debauched behaviour have been torn out. But the surviving material alone records a life of frantic, compulsive, sexual activity. His papers record encounters with well over sixty prostitutes in many European cities. In addition, he kept (over time) a number of lower-class mistresses, and had less commercial relationships with women of higher status. He was treated at least seventeen times after becoming infected with gonorrhoea.[3] It becomes apparent why Clarke and Jones were uneasy at the idea of such a man being a 'Brother' in a movement which believed in high ideals of morality.

Boswell kept most of his secrets for a long time after his death. For nearly two centuries he was remembered mainly as the masterly biographer of one of the great literary figures of 18th-century England, Doctor Samuel Johnson (1709-1784), though it was recognised in general terms that as well as having been an outstanding writer, Boswell had been a bit of an ass, and more than a bit of a rake. Then, in the 20th century, his manuscript autobiographical writings were rediscovered after a wonderful literary treasure hunt.[4] When these were published, in many volumes, they proved to be one of the most detailed and intimate autobiographical accounts of a life ever written, unique in the way they record events and examined conduct. They detail Boswell's excesses, and both his short-term delight in them and his repeated shame at his inability to control himself. One moment he is defying convention and proclaiming his freedom to act as he wishes, the next he is writhing in agonies of guilt and deep depression. In between, he traces a huge panorama of 18th-century life and people.

James Boswell (1740-1795) was the son of a Scottish judge and landowner of stern, Calvinistic outlook. His rampage through life has often been seen as a reaction against this disapproving father, but in many ways Boswell's attitude to himself was strongly influenced by the Calvinism he rejected. He constantly examined his conscience in an introspective, Protestant way, lamenting his sins, promising reform - and then returned to his former indulgences. He is an impossible man to sum up in a few words. He was indulgent and conscience-stricken. He was painfully aware of all his faults, and savaged himself for them, but he was also, when young at least, convinced of his own outstanding genius – but never found quite what the field was in which his genius lay. He became a lawyer to please his father, but hated its drudgery. He was obsessed with talking to great men, partly because he hoped for father-like advice from them, partly because he hoped that some of their greatness would rub off on him. He is a paradox.

Take the occasion on which he forced himself into the company of the great French philosopher, Jean Jacques Rousseau (1712-1778). Boswell worshipped Rousseau, regarding him as a great radical thinker and a champion of liberty. Yet, when he met Rousseau what he most wanted was to talk about his own attitude to sex and to seek Rousseau's approval for it. Boswell's naivety and self-centredness shine through. He has been privileged to meet a great philosopher – and all he can think of asking him about is his own sexual frustrations. Boswell put to Rousseau a fantasy of sexual behaviour. In spite of his frequent support for liberty and freedom, his male sexual vision of freedom is deeply feudal and authoritarian. He, Boswell, would succeed (soon, hopefully) to his father's large country estate. There, he could choose peasant girls - young, virgin and willing - from tenant families as mistresses. When they became pregnant or he tired of them, he would marry them off to tenant farmers, giving them substantial dowries. In Boswell's vision, there would be no losers. He would get all the girls he wanted. The girls would be flattered by his attentions, get a taste of the life and manners of the rich, and through the dowries they gained would get a better class of husband than they could otherwise have attained. The farmers who married Boswell's cast-offs would be delighted to have wives with unexpectedly large dowries – and, often, of proven fertility.

The vision is of course, typical of sexual fantasy, being utterly absurd and unreal, wildly naive. Escaping the constraints of reality is, after all, what fantasy is for. But it is characteristic of Boswell not just to have a fantasy of an endless supply of willing women, but to elaborate it to the point at which it came to seem a suitable matter for debate with a philosopher as a model for human sexual relationships. Rousseau, not surprisingly, dismissed the feudal fantasy, and lectured Boswell firmly. Boswell was impressed. He took Rousseau's words so deeply to heart that he swore to give up prostitutes. His resolution lasted nearly a month – which was pretty impressive for Boswell. Later, incidentally, he had an affair with Rousseau's long-term mistress.

Boswell can sound appalling – and he could be. But he was very good company, not only a good talker, but a patient and thoughtful listener. Sometimes his ideas were a bit wild, sometimes his behaviour was too, but he was someone most people in his society liked. He might be distinctly flamboyant, and some aspects of his life might be seen as reprehensible, but he was deemed great company, intelligent, witty, and lively. His company was sought and he became a known figure in both Edinburgh and London. So far as Boswell was concerned, however, Edinburgh was a backwater. It was in London that he wanted to shine. He was deeply ashamed of being a provincial Scot, and tried to anglicise himself, yet he intermixed this rejection of his background with a proud, defiant assertion of Scottish identity. And though he hoped to become very correctly English, he was often garrulous and informal in ways which made the English wince.

So far this picture of Boswell shows him as gregarious but light weight - engaging but outrageous. But there is also a far more substantial Boswell. Politically, he was for 'liberty.' He befriended the maverick radical John Wilkes (1729-1797), at times when keeping company with the outcast was likely to damage his reputation. His first substantial literary work was written in defence of liberty – and became a best seller. That it was written about Corsica may seem strange, but in the 1760s the island's government fascinated radicals, for it was the nearest thing to a democracy in Europe. A long war had largely driven out the Genoese, the country's former rulers, and the Corsicans had established a republican type of government under the inspiration of General Pascale Paoli (1725-1807). Paoli became a hero to European lovers of liberty, but there was frustration at lack of news about the situation on the island, which was regarded as difficult and dangerous to visit. Boswell may have talked to Rousseau about sex, but he also talked about liberty and Corsica. He decided to visit the island and interview Paoli. This was in 1765, and in 1768 Boswell published *An Account of Corsica, the Journal of a Tour of that Island, and the Memoirs of Pascal Paoli* (London, 1768). This was something of a literary coup, and 'Corsica' Boswell became famous.

In 1773 Boswell persuaded that great English literary figure Dr Samuel Johnson to come to Scotland, and accompanied him on the tour which led to the publication of Johnston's acclaimed *Journey to the Western Isles of Scotland* (1775). Boswell's own account of the tour appeared in 1785. In 1777 to 1783 Boswell contributed a regular column to the *London* Magazine under the name (very appropriately) of 'The Hypocondriack.' Finally, *The Life of Samuel Johnson* was published in 1791, and was soon hailed as a masterpiece which set new standards for biographers. When his autobiographical writings published over two centuries later are added to these works, Boswell emerges as a writer of major achievement, outstanding both as a biographer and an autobiographer. That he accomplished so much in a life in which he devoted so much time to drinking and whoring is remarkable.

How does Boswell's Freemasonry fit into his remarkably active life? His journals are an astonishingly rich source for cultural history. Among the aspects of his life that he records, he devotes some attention to his masonic activities. Most diaries and journals by freemasons say nothing of the Craft. What Boswell records is, it has to be said, in some respects disappointingly limited, but nonetheless, he says much more than anyone else.

Boswell was initiated in Lodge Canongate Kilwinning, Edinburgh, in 1759, at the age of eighteen. His uncle John Boswell was Depute Master of the Lodge at the time, and later Boswell's brother David was also initiated in the Lodge. Several relatives were members of other Edinburgh Lodges - though his father was not. Boswell served as Junior Warden of his Lodge in 1761, and as Depute Master in 1767-9,[5] after he returned from his Corsican ventures. Such promotions indicate that he was taking an interest in Freemasonry, but in his autobiographical writings he makes no mention of his connection with it until in 1772.[6] Freemasonry was not a side of his life, it seems, that inspired much thought and reflection – though as he spent much time in London and on a Grand Tour in Europe in the 1760s, his opportunities for attending his lodge were limited.

We do, however, have one reference to Boswell's masonic connections from early in his career, in a letter written to him in 1763 when he was visiting Holland. The writer was his uncle, John. The two men had recently met in London, and their friendship had become closer than in the past. Uncle John referred to this in masonic terms:

> I hope the friendship that is begun will increase and although never Mason could say more heartily than you and I "happy to meet, happy to part" yet above all happy in the thought to meet again.[7]

Note that John Boswell wrote 'happy to meet, *happy* to part,' whereas the modern version of the saying is 'happy to meet, *unhappy* to part.' I suggest that Boswell's version reflects the original form of the saying. Parting was natural, and partings were therefore to be happily accepted as an element of life, though in the confidence that people would meet again.

In the years 1772 to 1781 there are over fifty references to Freemasonry in Boswell's journals. Most simply note his attendance at his lodge, but some are more informative. An undated note gives us his wife's opinion of Freemasonry. She was a long-suffering woman, not only putting up with her husband's sexual exploits and his tendency to throw the furniture around when drunk, but with having to listen to his detailed confessions of his whoring, and being begged for her forgiveness. He thought he could claim virtue in boasting of his being a freemason. She was not impressed, saying that she 'had no high opinion of the Society of Free Masons, thinking us an indiscriminate, confused Rabble.' He responded indignantly, talking of the origins of the Craft at the building of Solomon's Temple. She hit back with the claim that the Tower of Babel was more likely to have inspired the Craft.[8] Boswell at least must take the credit for recording this exchange in which his wife silenced him. It may be worth lingering on the terms in which Mrs Boswell denounced Freemasonry – assuming she choose her words carefully. Freemasons were an 'indiscriminate, confused rabble.' Indiscriminate because in lodges men of differing social statuses met on equal terms. This was a common complaint against 18th century clubs in general. They mixed up people which the proper hierarchy of society kept at a distance. There was thus a lack of order in lodges – members met as a confused rabble and drank too much. There was a strong feeling that men meeting on their own, without women present, was a recipe for disaster. In lodges not only was the constraint of social hierarchy weakened, but the constraint of female presence on brutish male conduct was removed. A Scottish doctor of the day pronounced gloomily that the only reasons that men had for meeting socially in the absence of women was so that they could get drunk and talk obscenely, becoming slovenly and brutish because they had escaped women's civilising influence.[9]

The first dated mention of Freemasonry in Boswell's journals, in 1772, is brief. Having primed himself with two bumpers of brandy, he went to a lodge meeting and was 'solemn and well' – 'well' meaning that he was in good spirits.[10] In June 1774 he was elected to be the Master of his Lodge, which he just notes in passing.[11] He was more forthcoming when he was re-elected the following year.

> 'I was but moderately in Mason humour; though I have associated ideas of solemnity and spirit and foreign parts and my brother David with St John's Lodge, which makes it always pleasing to me. Such agreeable associations are formed, we know not how, as the foam of the horse was by the dashing down of the painter's brush on the canvas. I suppose the picture might be easily washed off. But it would be losing a satisfaction which perhaps we cannot equal by design.'[12]

Boswell is trying to express something of what Freemasonry meant to him, but what he wrote takes some interpretation. Attending the lodge has connotations of solemnity – through, presumably, masonic rituals and the ideals of the Craft. It makes him think not just of his Brethren who are present but of others far away, like his brother David, and it makes him think of foreign parts, through the consciousness that though he and a few friends are meeting in one small Lodge room, what they are doing makes them part of an international movement. Typically, Boswell tries to dig deeper. He was not quite clear in his own mind as to why the Lodge meeting brought him such agreeable feelings, but it did. He resorted to metaphor. It was like the painting of a racing horse. One flick of the painter's brush, and one gets the impression of the foam flying from its mouth as it gallops. Look at that brushstroke closely and it is not convincing – it is not foam. But stand back and take in the overall effect, and it is satisfactory. Boswell was admitting that he was unsure what it was about being at this lodge meeting that gave him satisfaction and contentment – but, overall, it did, and perhaps it is best not to risk undermining these sensations by examining them too closely.

Boswell also provided a second account of this June 1774 meeting when he was re-elected Master, for he also wrote the formal Minute of the meeting in the Lodge Minute Book:

> The Lodge having met, although there were very few brethren present, for which, those who were absent should be reprimanded, the evening was passed in social glee, every bother having sung, though not as a precedent.[13]

It has been noted that the Minute is defaced by a large splash of wine, the implication being that the 'social glee' had been a bit boisterous.[14] In fact the Minute was written more than two weeks after the event, so the accusation is unconvincing.

Boswell enjoyed another lodge meeting a month later, though the problem of low attendance continued: only six were present, 'But my spirits made a choice meeting'. As so often, Boswell believed he was the 'belle of the ball', and doubtless he talked, sang and drank to excess.[15]

The journals recall a number of visits to other Lodges. In December 1773 Boswell was 'assumed' as a member of Lodge Holyrood House.[16] In 1775 he and a coach load of his brethren went to the Lodge in Leith. 'My spirits were vigorous, and I sang my nonsensical song, "Twa Wheeles." '[17] Some months later he visited St Giles's Lodge. He had already dined and claret at dinner 'had enlivened me pretty well, and then' 'Some negus which I drank at the lodge put me in such a frame that I could not finish the evening but in merry company'. In other works, after the lodge meeting was over, he spent the rest of the night drinking and gambling.[18]

Boswell also took part in public masonic events. In 1774 he officiated, as Master of the Lodge Canongate Kilwinning, at a masonic procession and feast to mark St Andrew's Day.[19] On the same day the following year he walked with most of the members of Canongate Kilwinning in a procession from Parliament House to the Theatre Royal, with blazing torches. 'I was in perfect good spirits, and harangued and sung with ease and vigour'. The feast was held in the theatre as the usual meeting place, the Assembly Rooms, was being redecorated. From the stage Boswell made some joke about it being his first appearance on the stage, and was pleased at its reception. 'It had a cheerful influence like one of Burke's sallies.' Boswell thus happily compared himself to the noted orator, Edmund Burke.[20]

Another masonic activity bringing freemasons from a number of lodges together was attending performances of plays. Special performances of plays were commissioned, presumably by a number of the Edinburgh lodges joining together to make this possible. One night in 1775 the freemasons saw two comedies 'The Recruiting Officer' and 'Love Alamode'.[21] These were old pieces (first produced in 1706 and 1759 respectively) but clearly still in favour.

Lodge meetings could become fairly noisy and boisterous. Boswell records a quarrel occurring on one occasion. On visiting St Andrew's Lodge, the Junior Warden, an Irish student, was drunk and 'spoke a little impertinently.' Another visitor, Captain Hamilton of the 31st Regiment's military Lodge, took offence and wanted to fight him, and they had to be separated. Not very fraternal![22] However, Boswell was on good terms with Hamilton, for shortly afterwards he let the 31st Regiment's Lodge use the Canongate Kilwinning Lodge room.[23]

Boswell also considered, while he was Master, using the lodge room in pursuit of the most macabre of his many obsessions. He was fascinated by public executions. When in London he often struggled to get the best viewpoint to watch hangings, and he also sought to talk to condemned prisoners to find out how they viewed their coming fate. When his own clients were found guilty and faced death he harassed them with questions about how they would die. In 1774 he and others with similar morbid interests, were excited by theories that it might be possible to revive the corpse of a hanged man. They resolved to experiment with one John Reid – one of Boswell's own clients. But where to take his body after he was executed to attempt the resurrection presented difficulties. They thought of renting rooms near the place of execution, but, sensibly, realised that landlords might object to having corpses brought into on the premises. Boswell then had a bright idea. They could use Canongate Kilwinning Lodge room. 'I was master, and could excuse myself to the brethren.' The plan was abandoned, however, as the Lodge room was too far away. Smuggling a corpse through the streets would be difficult.[24] It seems remarkable that

Boswell evidently was unaware that his proposed raising of the dead on masonic premises might seem to be a mockery of aspects of masonic ritual.

In June 1776 Boswell had to resign as Master of Lodge Canongate Kilwinning, having served three years.[25] But promotion beckoned, for his notoriously dissipated lifestyle was not seen as a bar to progress in the masonic world. On 21 November Sir William Forbes of Pitsligo (1739-1806), a banker who was a close friend of Boswell, was about to be elected Grand Master Mason. He urged Boswell to become his Depute. Boswell was reluctant, but accepted when Forbes made it clear that he would take it as an obligation, putting him in Boswell's debt. That night he dined at Forbes's house with ten other freemasons 'to concert measures.' The occasion seemed, for once, to overawe Boswell, or at least to disconcert him. 'We talked with most serious importance, and I looked around the company and could not perceive the least ray of jocularity in any of their countenances.' A masonic meeting that did not give him a chance at least to laugh was, it seems, for Boswell almost a contradiction in terms. The solemnity inspired him to further thought. He 'wondered about how men could be so much in earnest about parade which is attended neither with gain nor with power.' The dinner party was discussing with deep earnestness details of processions and procedures and elections, and all to further an organisation that would bring them neither power nor money. Boswell loved being a freemason. It suited his immensely sociable nature, his love of good company, talk and song. Its rituals must have attracted him greatly, for, reacting against his Presbyterian background, he had an appetite for display and ritual and processions. Roman Catholic church services awed him deeply – and he flirted with joining that church several times. Yet perhaps he was awed by spectacle and performance rather superficially. It was the show that counted, rather than the meanings and beliefs that underlay the rituals. Now he was becoming Depute Grand Master Mason and found himself in this room of solemn men. No gaiety. It made him think about what Freemasonry was really about, what he was doing there. But, typically, he quickly rallied. 'I considered that it was really honourable to be highly distinguished in a society of very universal extent over the globe, and of which the principles are excellent.'[26]

This is the most revealing of Boswell's journal entries on Freemasonry, but it only makes the reader wish for more. If only he had recorded what he took the excellent principles of Freemasonry to be. Nonetheless, it serves again to demonstrate his occasional naivety. It is as though he had been much enjoying his Freemasonry, and has been Master of a Lodge, but needed to be reminded that it is supposed to be, at heart, something serious.

Shortly after Forbes and Boswell were installed in their new Grand Lodge roles in 1776, they and other freemasons went to the theatre and saw *Cymon*, a 'dramatic romance'. and *The Apprentice*, a farce (1767 and 1756 respectively). This was a splendid occasion, attended by no fewer than five Past Grand Master Masons, including the first ever, William St Clair of Roslin. 'I like to see respect paid to his worth'.[27] Though Boswell does not say so, the occasion seems to have been organised to celebrate the fortieth anniversary of the creation of the office of Grand Master Mason.

The following year, 1777 the freemasons' play was Goldsmith's 'She Stoops to Conquer' of 1773,[28] and in 1778 the theatrical masons of Edinburgh were right up to date, seeing Sheridan's 'The School for Scandal' in the year after its first production. In this case at least, the audience was not entirely masonic. Boswell sat with the Grand Master Mason, the Duke of Atholl, during the first act, and then moved to join his wife in a box.[29]

As Depute Grand Master Mason, Boswell took part in processions and visited Lodges, often with the Grand Master Mason. In 1781 two entries in his journal show his continuing connection with Freemasonry. He attended a meeting of his own Lodge when the Honourable George Cochrane was initiated. On St Andrew's Day (30 November) when Grand Lodge officer-bearers were elected he did not attend the meeting, but he had spent most of the day in the company of the Grand Master Mason (the Earl of Balcarres) who was about to be re-elected, which suggests he was actively involved in planning (not to say deciding in advance) the elections.[30] Boswell lived until 1795, but these are the last occasions on which he mentions Freemasonry.

One of the aspects of Freemasonry which attracted Boswell was, as we have seen, the idea of it as a universal institution, connecting men in various countries. But his many visits to London and his travels on the Continent did not inspire references to the Craft in his writings. A great many of the men he met were freemasons, including Voltaire and Rousseau, but Boswell never seems to have exploited this as a potential bond. His masonic interests seem to have been purely Scottish.

The one exception is so marginally masonic that it is hardly worth mentioning. It is a stray anecdote in Boswell's *Life of Johnson*. Boswell and Johnson attended the funeral of a freemason, which was accompanied by solemn music on horns. Johnson was notorious for complete indifference to - even antagonism to - music. It was just noise to him. But at the funeral he said in surprise 'This is the first time I have ever been affected by musical sounds.' And he went on to comment in his ponderous way, beloved by Boswell as a sign of genius but nowadays often derided as pomposity. The music, said Johnson, made him melancholy. If this was intended to put them in the right mood for having 'salutary feelings' about death, this might be good. But insomuch as it was melancholy *per se* – melancholy for its own sake - it was bad.[31]

Why was James Boswell a freemason? As we have seen, a number of the features of the Craft attracted him. But none were unique or distinctive, and this should not be expected. Becoming a freemason was not an exceptional act in his age and culture, but something extremely common for gentlemen. Like many others, Boswell was attracted by the sociability of the Craft, and the Lodge structure which it provided to support that sociability and the bonds it created. On the one hand you had your 'club' of yourself and your friends, with a good deal of autonomy, on the other you felt linked with a much wider, even universal, beneficent organisation. To Enlightenment thinkers, civic and sociable behaviour on the part of men was central to their being civilised. Being solitary was dangerous and anti-social. The age was rich in institutions catering for male sociability, and Freemasonry was the outstanding success story among them, in Britain and abroad. Masonic ritual and ceremony must have appealed to Boswell's taste for display in his reaction against the starkness of Presbyterianism. Perhaps the fact that his father was not a freemason made the Craft all the more attractive to him. How 'masonic' his rather intermittent passion for liberty was is unknown, but clearly the it linked up with the Craft's values.

Clarke and Jones, in their article on why Boswell was a freemason, eventually accepted that there were no motives distinct from those of many other freemasons. But they then produced a second question that it is tempting to see as having underlain the original one from the start. 'How could ... a man become a freemason at a time when his religious attachment was doubtful and his future uncertain?' This is really a very odd question. Certainty as to the futures has never been a qualification for entering the Craft. And though Boswell wavered between Protestantism and Catholicism, he never had any doubt as to there being a God, a supreme being as required by Freemasonry. And, of course, one of the central and liberating features of Freemasonry was that it did not enquire about sectarian religious affiliations.

Clarke and Jones struggled to define what they were really asking, which comes down to: 'How could such a man as Boswell have been *allowed* to become a freemason?' This they reach in a third question. How could the Craft have admitted Boswell 'in spite of the shortcomings in his private life' and 'the selfish traits of his character'?

They had an idealised idea of what freemasons should be like, and Boswell did not fit – and nor, they reluctantly accept, do many other 18th century freemasons. Freemasons should have exemplary private lives and not be selfish. Boswell was not the sort of Brother Clarke would have found it easy to welcome to his lodge.

From Boswell's own day, we have a thoughtful note on his character from the man who had persuaded him to become Depute Grand Master Mason – an act which in itself that indicates he had no qualms about Boswell's qualifications for or commitment to Freemasonry. Sir William Forbes wrote after Boswell's death:

> I have known few men who have possessed a stronger sense of piety or more fervent piety (tinctured, no doubt, with some little share of superstition, which had been probably in some degree fostered by his intimacy with Doctor Johnson), perhaps not always sufficient to regulate his imagination or direct his conduct, yet still genuine and founded both in his understanding and in his head.[32]

That Boswell was outstandingly pious is Forbes's basic message, and to the modern ear it seems an astounding judgement. But note that after claiming piety for Boswell, Forbes then qualifies that by admitting his old friend's piety was 'perhaps not always sufficient to regulate his imagination or direct his conduct'. Forbes is not using the word 'piety' to indicate a conventional outward religiousness, but rather inwardness. However shocking or silly or unpleasant some of Boswell's outward behaviour might be, he had impressed Forbes by how he was obsessed with trying to interpret himself, reaching inwards for an understanding of his conduct that he never achieved, struggling with religious feelings that were deep but troubled. Forbes admired this striving to comprehend, and was impressed with how genuine it was even if though it failed to influence Boswell's conduct. Boswell might sin, but he also repented. From a modern perspective, it might be felt that often what Forbes admired as Boswell's 'piety' were in fact symptoms of Boswell's manic-depression, an introspection and self-examination that was often destructive. In some brands of religious culture, an impression of sanctity can be achieved simply by being wretched and full of guilt.

In choosing Boswell to be his Depute, Forbes was choosing a friend whom he knew had problems, but whom he believed had an impressive seriousness underlying his frequent exterior flamboyance. And in having Boswell as his Depute Forbes doubtless welcomed the flamboyance as an asset – here was a man of wit and easy, confident manner to be at his side and put others at ease at official functions when the atmosphere seemed to be flagging. Boswell was very suitable in a number of other respects as a Depute Grand Master. He was a gentleman of an old landed family – such things were important – who had become a well known literary figure. Clarke and Jones seemed to think that Boswell's presence besmirched Freemasonry, and this is understandable, but is also possible to see him as someone whose reputation brought honour to the Craft and to the office of Depute Grand Master Mason. As so often with Boswell, the conclusion is a paradox.

***

NOTES

1 R. Clarke & G.P. Jones: *AQC*, vol. 79 (1966), pp. 90-92. This article drew much on A.F. Calvert: 'James Boswell as Freemason', in *The Freemason's Chronicle*' (21 January 1939), pp. 39-41 & 46. I acknowledge my debt to both articles, and thank the Library and Museum of Freemasonry at UGLE for supplying me with a photocopy of Calvert's work.

2 Clarke was a freemason but Jones was not, a point I owe to Prof. Andrew Prescott (Sheffield).

3 L. Stone: *The Family, Sex and Marriage in England, 1500-1713* (London, 1975), p. 575.

4 F.A. Pottle: *Pride and Negligence - The History of the Boswell Papers* (New York, 1982).

5 A. Mackenzie: *History of the Lodge of Canongate Kilwinning, No. 2, compiled from the records, 1677-1888* (Edinburgh, 1888), p. 85. At the time of his Initiation Boswell was eighteen, just a few weeks short of his nineteenth birthday.

6 *AQC*, vol. 79 (1966); *Private Papers*, vol. xvi, p. 105n.

7 *Boswell in Holland, 1763-5*, ed. by F.A. Pottle (London, 1952), p. 58, quoted in *AQC* vol. 91 from Calvert, 'James Boswell as Freemason'.

8 *The Private Papers of James Boswell, from Malahide Castle* (19 vols., London, 1928-37), vol. 13, p. 298.

9 W. Alexander: *The History of Women* (3rd edn., 2 vols., London, 1782: 1st edn., 1779), vol. 1, advertisement & pp. 475, 486 & 493-4.

10 *Private Papers*, vol. 9, p. 254.

11 *Boswell for the Defence, 1769-1774*, ed. by W. K. Wimsatt & F. A. Pottle (New Haven, Conn., 1960), p. 200

12 *Defence*, p. 225; *Private Papers*, vol. 9, pp. 126-7.

13 Mackenzie: *op. cit.*, p. 97.

14 F. Brady: *James Boswell - The Later Years, 1769-1795* (London, 1984), p. 87.

15 *Private Papers*, vol. 9, p. 134.

16 R.S. Lindsay: *A History of the Masonic Lodge of Holyroodhouse (St Luke's), No. 44. Holding of the Grand Lodge of Scotland with Roll of Members, 1734-1934* (2 vols., Edinburgh, 1935), vol. 1, p. 229.

17 *Private Papers*, vol. 10, p. 97.

18 *Op .cit.*, p. 252.

19 *Op. cit.*, p. 61.

20 *Private Papers*, vol. 11, p. 23.

21 *Op. cit.*, p. 32.

22 *Op. cit.*, pp. 28-9.

23 *Op. cit*, p. 43.

24 *Op. cit*, p. 231.

25 *Boswell in Extremes, 1776-8*, ed. by C. M. Weis & F. A. Pottle (London, 1971), p. 8. See also *Private Papers*, vol. 12, p. 12.

26 *Boswell in Extremes*, p. 58; *see also Private Papers*, vol. 12, pp. 85-6.

27 *Op cit.*, p. 64; *see also Private Papers*, vol. 12, p. 95.

28 *Op. cit.*, p. 199; *see also Private Papers*, vol.13, p. 80.

29 *Private Papers*, vol. 13, p. 188.

30 Boswell, *Laird of Auchinleck, 1778-1782*, ed. by J.W. Reid & F. A. Pottle (New York, 1977), 411; *Private Papers*, vol. 15, pp. 16 & 45.

31 *Boswell's Life of Johnson*, ed. by G.B. Hill & L.F. Powell (6 vols., Oxford, 1964), vol. 4, p. 22.

32 Calvert: 'James Boswell as Freemason', quoted in *AQC*, vol. 79 (1966), pp. 90-92.

*****

9

'You will prise our noble companionship':
masonic songbooks of the 18th century - an overlooked literary sub-genre

by

Andreas Önnerfors

Introduction

Wo man singt, da lass Dich ruhig nieder,
böse Menschen haben keine Lieder.

Johann Wolfgang von Goethe

'Where people sing, there one may sit down quiet, evil people do not own any songs' – this famous quotation from the German 18th-century poet Goethe explains one of the main reasons for why people gather in order to sing. It is a way to find a common tuning and create companionship 'among Persons that must have remained at a perpetual Distance', to paraphrase some words from Anderson's 1723 *Constitutions of the Free-Masons*. It is obvious that Freemasonry, as a form of human cultural activity, would also include music. But because it is acknowledged that the way Freemasonry stages its culture was - and is - rather different from mainstream culture, it is not surprising that - besides quite trivial uses of music - music and songs play an important role in the creation of the symbolic universe of Freemasonry generally. Precisely in the same way that the ritual texts define action within the lodge, songbooks and their texts can be interpreted as an affirmation of attitudes and values within Freemasonry. By combining text with music and repeatedly (we may even call it ritual) in singing, the text message was established as a powerful means of masonic education.

However, masonic songbooks belong to an overlooked literary sub-genre within Freemasonry. Masonic scholars have generally neglected song texts and text collections as sources for the study of masonic thought and history. Whereas much effort has been put in recovering ritual texts and in later years also into the study of drama and prose influenced by masonic motives, song texts, and speeches in lodges have rarely been treated. This may have been caused by an old-fashioned distinction between 'high brow' and 'low brow' literature. Scholars tend to pay more attention to the writings of established poets instead of analysing the functionality of literature in a larger context. Masonic speeches, commemoration literature and song texts played to a high extent a fixed functional role. They were mostly written for the use at special occasions and are thus referred to as 'casual poetry' or *Gelegenheitsdichtung*. Casual texts of the 18th century were composed of a language that to a large extent was determined by the heritage of antique mythology and antique rhetoric tradition. They were not intended to compete with the literary elegance and originality of a Lessing, Goethe or Mozart. Song texts, speeches and commemorative literature had a purpose beyond the purely literary ambitions of their time. It is, therefore, wrong to judge them from the viewpoint of established literary sciences. Moreover, it is not fruitful to apply the majority of literary theories upon this very functional genre of texts. There is still an important difference compared to articles in newspapers or educated journals (that we probably instantly would regard as merely functional). Song texts do not communicate information. They communicate rather fixed sets of motives, concepts and ideas. And it is due to the relatively poor developed poetics within them that we are able to extract these motives, concepts and ideas. Therefore, song texts can play a major role in order to enhance our understanding of concepts and ideas of the enlightened 18th century.

Different purposes of masonic songs

Masonic songbooks were and still are wide-spread in some Orders. A masonic system without songbooks is unlikely. But what did these songbooks look like in the first and constitutive century of Freemasonry? What areas of masonic activities and motives did they cover? And what is the relationship between texts, ideology and ritual? Sion Honea examined masonic songbooks of the 19th century[1] and made some crucial distinctions regarding their uses that may be applicable to the present study:

> On the face of the evidence itself, music was an important part of Masonic life at least as early as the mid-eighteenth century, by which time it had stimulated the production of songbooks directed exclusively to Masonic audiences. The music itself can be divided into three broad, overlapping categories: functional music for lodge rituals, music of edifying nature explicitly or implicitly Masonic in sentiment, and non-Masonic music of a social or entertaining nature.

Honea later explained these three different levels more closely:

> Functional music was intended to accompany or illustrate the variety of ritualistic or formal activities of the lodge. Somewhat different is the large amount of music of a serious and edifying nature that was not intended to accompany the rituals, but tended to extol Masonic ideals and virtues. The innumerable parties, banquets, festivals, and drinking bouts of the fraternity called for accompaniment by another type of convivial music, sometimes reflecting its specifically Masonic context. The latter two categories of non-ritualistic music seem designed for the broader purpose of providing entertainment or filling the needs of the lodge singing club.

These three levels - *functional, edifying* and *convivial* - are a point of departure for the analysis of 18th-century songbooks upon which I shall elaborate later. As Honea stresses, these levels may also well overlap. The entertaining song may also have an edifying impetus and the functional song may also have been sung in an 'entertaining' context. However, at least another level may be added to the list. When going through the song texts of the 18th century, a considerable motive is made out of what - in modern studies on identity formation - is called 'othering'. Many texts deal with the surrounding world that does not understand and wants to harm Freemasonry and that it is a goal for freemasons to prove the excellence of the Brotherhood. Although we as well may call such an intention 'edifying', the purpose of such songs is clearly directed outwards, whereas songs which deal with fraternal love and refer to virtues that are a constitutive part of the ritual plot - e.g., beauty, strength and wisdom - primarily have an internally affirmative function. As a strange sub-motive of 'othering', at least in Swedish songbooks of the period, we can extract 'absence of the opposite gender'. The repeated occurrence of songs that treat the fact that no women are allowed among the fraternity and the fact that they are absent makes it necessary to find a reasonable explanation. If masonic lodges and Orders in the 18th century would have belonged to a clearly gendered zone (one that was open to men only) these songs would not have played a significant role at all. Why sing something about the absent gender if there anyhow never would have been a possibility to gather? It seems more likely that the songs were affirmative for the male gendering of Freemasonry as such. To explicitly regret the absence of women is to hail the presence of men. There must be very important reasons to gather only among men, so important that even women not are allowed. If we contextualise Freemasonry as a phenomenon within the age of the Enlightenment, this sub-motive of 'othering' – to project a quality upon A in order to elaborate the quality of B – becomes perfectly clear. What for the conservative and deliberately gendered 19th century was a matter of course (the exclusion of women from public space) was still a motive for the 18th century, where women and men gathered in different kinds of societies and associations. The absence of women was such an apparent trait of Freemasonry that it had to be explained.

Taken together, masonic songs from the 18th century may be characterised as programmatic. They contained a well-defined message within a solid frame of motives and they served a predictable set of purposes. The meta-frame was made out of enlightened philosophy and a strong belief in the ennoblement of mankind.

Different levels and purposes of masonic songs

Level	Purpose	
(1) functional ('liturgical')	to accompany lodge rituals	
(2) convivial	to provide with entertainment	
(3) internally edifying	to praise masonic virtues and values	may overlap
(4) externally demarcating	to establish counter -propaganda; 'othering', projection	

In his *Heredom* article, Honea gives different explanations for the roots of masonic song-tradition:

> The repertoire itself is drawn from an extremely wide range of sources: classical art, music, traditional tunes, hymns, drinking songs, popular songs of the day, light choral music, and instrumental works. It consists mainly of part songs, typically for three voices of the glee type, but also includes a wide variety of solo songs, duets, rounds, catches, and instrumental pieces.

Focussing on the song tradition in the USA, Honea argued further that this repertoire provides an index to the actual musical life of middle-class America in the nineteenth century. As such it offers the researcher a large number of intriguing questions.

The extensive catalogue of 'intriguing questions' Honea raised in the subsequent part of the paper is, of course, useful in the study of 18th-century songbooks as well:

What are the exact components of the repertoire? What do they say about society at the time? Who were the composers that reached into this substratum of middle-class life? What was the repertoire of traditional tunes utilized? What were the hymn tunes? What was the relative influence of secular versus sacred sources? How did the repertoire change over time and how did it remain the same? Are there indications of social change in the changes detectable in the collections and their contents? What conclusions can be drawn concerning the penetration of classical music into the popular realm? What types of ensembles were typical? What were the musical resources commonly available? What do the printing and publishing practices indicate about the dissemination of the music in relation to the larger music market of the time? The list might well continue almost indefinitely.

Having in mind that the last sentence opens up for a research project that would reach far beyond the scope of this paper, which is limited to a consideration of masonic songbooks that were known and disseminated in Sweden throughout the 18th century.

The songs of *L' Ordre des Franc-Maçons trahi* (1745)

In 1745 the famous exposure of Freemasonry *L'Ordre des Franc-Maçons trahi et l'Ordre des Mopses revelée* was published in Amsterdam. Besides a thorough description of Freemasonry and the Order of Mopses, there is an interesting 'Appendix' that contains masonic poetry and song-texts as well as some engraved plates of tunes – a quite expensive technique then. Five songs were included in the Appendix: one for each of the first three degrees, one for the Wardens and one sung in the general assembly of masons.

The song for the first, or Apprentice degree apparently was intended to be sung at the table:

Freres et Compagnons De la Maçonnerie,
Sans chagrin jouisson Des plaisirs de la Vie.
Munis d'un rouge bord,
Que par trois fois un signal des nos verres,
Soit une preuve que d'accord
Nous buvons à nos Freres.

The song of the second, or Fellow Craft degree, is – compared with that of the first degree – far more dedicated to the values of Freemasonry as such:

Art divin, l'Etre suprême
Daigna te donner lui même
Pour nous servir de Remparts:
Que dans notre illustre Loge Soit celebré ton èloge,
Qu'il vole de toutes parts.

The song for the third, or Master's degree (fig. 13) goes in the same elaborated direction. The most symbolic song is that of the Wardens. It contains references to the mythological history of the Order:

> *Adam à sa posterité*
> *Transmit de l' Art connoissance;*
> *Et Caïn par l'experience*
> *En demontra l' utilité.*
> *C'est lui qui bâtit une Ville*
> *Dans un paijs de l'Orient,*
> *Où l'Architecture Civile*
> *Prit d'abord son commencement.*

The publication of *L'Ordre des Franc-Maçons trahi* throughout Europe with its engraved tunes surely gave the impression that songs and texts like these were normal ingredients of masonic culture.

Odi profanum vulgus – the first Masonic songbook in Sweden

The first masonic songbook edited in Sweden was published in 1759 in Stockholm by Johan Israel Torpadius (b. 1722).[2] He became First Master of the St. John's Lodge *Sankt Erik* in Stockholm, founded in 1756. Torpadius was initiated into the Lodge *St. Jean Auxiliaire* in 1752 and was given the Scottish degrees in a St Andrew's Lodge, *L' Innocente*, which was also founded in 1756 and with which his friend, Carl Friedrich Eckleff, was associated. Torpadius was a founding member of the first Swedish Chapterial Lodge with the same name, *L' Innocente* (founded in 1759). With Eckleff, Torpadius was also a member of a literary society, the *Tankebyggarorden* ('The Order of Thought-builders') through which several of his literary works were printed. In his non-masonic life, Torpadius carried a number of high-ranking political and juridical positions. He died in 1760 but his songbook, *Frimurarewisor* and *Frimuraresånger* ('Songs for Freemasons'), was edited no fewer than twelve times between 1759-1824 without any substantial changes in the texts. The first edition – for some reason – was printed in Copenhagen and several later local reprints, in Stockholm, Karlskrona and Gothenburg, also appeared. In some editions the thrilling subtitle, *Sjungas efter sina särskilta behageliga Melodier* ('to be sung according to their special convenient melodies'), was added. This, of course, raises the question how these 'convenient melodies' were spread throughout the Swedish lodges.

The first edition colophon carries the rather elitist phrase from Horace *Odi profanum vulgus et arceo*, which we can interpret as an affirmative slogan of 'othering'. Freemasonry is not at all profane and it takes place within definite demarcation from the profane world. Torpadius songbook contains about twenty songs, sometimes with some local amendments, like in the edition from Gothenburg, which closed the singing with an elegy on the 'pearl, the beauty city of the Western coast of Sweden that brings prosperity through trade and commerce'.

It is unclear why the publication of editions of Torpadius' 'Songbook' ceased in 1824. Either it was replaced by a more updated and even more local version that was kept within the lodges or it was simply no longer popular. His texts are rather naïve and adapted to the rhetorical tradition and language of Enlightenment. The keywords may not have appealed any longer to users of the songbook. The convenient melodies – sung for more than six decades within Swedish Freemasonry – may also simply have been forgotten. The singing tradition – unless it was a distinctive part of the ritual – is unfortunately not easily traceable within the source material of Freemasonry.

However, a masonic scholar in 1956 stated that the solemn hymn of the Swedish Order that still was in use at that time, was translated and spread by Torpadius, which means that it basically was sung for two hundred years within Swedish Freemasonry.[3] According to the preserved manuscript, the song in question was a translation from a French original written by a 'brother Lança' and later on included in a printed edition of masonic songs *La Lire maçonne* from 1766. It is said that even Lança himself not was the composer of the song, but that he translated it from an English original. If this is true, it appears that masonic songs and the way they were communicated throughout Europe would be an interesting topic for further research on trans-cultural communication. It is also remarkable that the text of Torpadius' songbook basically remained unchanged during six rather dynamic decades, when new rituals and a new organisation were worked out and implemented.

The first song praises masonic virtues and their respect for the order of the state, which the first verse perfectly proves:

> *Frukta Gud och Kungen ära*
> *Nästan som sig sjelf ha kär*
> *Okränkt lyda Lagens lära*
> *Undfly alt hvad lastbart är*
> *Billigt tala, tänka, göra*
> *Höra, pröfva, döma rätt*
> *Aldrig svek på Tungan föra*
> *Det är Brödrens lefnads-sätt*

[Translation:
Fear God and honour the King/Love them nearly as much as you love yourself/Without harm obey to the teachings of the Law/Escape from all that may be vicious/Speak, think and act righteous/Listen, proof and judge in a right manner/Do not ever carry betrayal on your tongue/That is the way of life of brethren.]

The first lines paraphrase some of the main rules of Swedish Freemasonry as they are formulated in the General Rules of the Order (*Ordens allmänna Lagar*) and are also in line with one of the laws that make out a cornerstone of the Swedish constitution: The Bill of Press-freedom of 1766. From this year on it was allowed in the Swedish realm to print everything that not was directed against religion, law and good manners. The 'escape from virtues' is a motive that occurs in several parts of the ritual text and thus can be interpreted as an allusion. The same applies to the motive 'betrayal'. To think, speak, listen and judge righteous – a cornerstone of Enlightenment ideology – is the exact opposite of arbitrariness and prejudices.

The 1799 edition of Torpadius' songbook shows on its title page an angel-like figure with a burning torch. Song No. VI is dedicated to the new brother:

Välkommen du, som har idag
Vårt värda sälskap velat öka
Du prisa skal vårt sälla lag
Då du vår lefnad får försöka
Om blott af förvett du gjort rön
Så skal förundran bli din lön

[Translation
Welcome You, who today/ wanted to enrich our chosen society/You will prise our
noble companionship/When You try to our way of life/If you on beforehand only have
gained knowledge by speculation/astonishment will be your salary.]

The first verse presents some key motives: Freemasonry is a way of life and the
brother who not has spoiled his curiosity will be rewarded. Especially the second
motive is quiet interesting from a phenomenological point of view. It states clearly
that knowledge within Freemasonry is created through experience. It is not wrong to
have an idea about Freemasonry, but there is a limit where the process of knowledge
is spoiled by too much *Vorverständnis* ('pre-conception' in Habermas' sense).

The second verse elaborates clearly upon the virtues of Freemasonry and is a
good example of an edifying ambition:

Här ser du dygd från skrymtan ren
Hur den med egna färgor prålar
Här finns inga villo-sken
Och intet gift i gyldne skålar
Här ser du konst förutan gräl
Och frihet, dygdens egen träl.

[Translation:
Here You see virtue, pure from exaggeration/how it glooms by own colours/here will
not be any wrong lights/and no poison in golden cups/Here You see art without
quarrel/And freedom, the slave of virtue.]

The subsequent verses of the song go in the same direction: they hail the qualities of
the brotherhood and communicate to the new brother among them the moral benefits
of his membership.

A German masonic songbook in Sweden

A rather peculiar songbook was published in Stockholm in 1787, the songbook
of the German-speaking Lodge *Carl*, entitled *Freymaurer Lieder der Teutschen
Nationalloge in Stockholm* (see fig. 14).

Since mediaeval times German immigration to the Swedish realm was
substantial. It grew considerably after the Thirty Years' War when the Swedish
monarchy was compensated for its warfare with dominions in the Holy Roman
Empire. The most intense cultural encounter between Sweden and one of the German
possessions developed in Swedish-Pomerania. A whole district in the capital
Stockholm was inhabited by Germans who were naturalised Swedish subjects. There
existed a German church, parish and school. It was a natural step that the German-
speaking Lodge *Carl* (or simply 'The German Lodge') was founded in 1761. One

year before it seems to have ceased its activity officially, the songbook was published. It did not simply contain of a translation of Torpadius, but of eleven rather well composed texts that mirror different aspects of Freemasonry. One can probably claim that the German songbook already was influenced by the *Sturm-und-Drang* literary movement.

The first song text starts of with a philosophical reflection:

> *Richter freygeschaffner Geister*
> *Grosser Welten grosser Meister*
> *Blick auf unsre Maurerey*
> *Uns befällt ein heilig Grauen*
> *Was wir hier im Dunkeln bauen*
> *Bleibet nicht von Fehlern frey.*

[Translation:
You judge of free-created minds/Grand Master of grand worlds/watch our Masonry from above/We are struck by a holy fear/What we build here in the dark/remains not free from defect.]

Also the subsequent verses are dominated by a solemn intonation. The majesty of the mighty Master is praised and shines in so many worlds, but even in locked rooms, without rays, only with a tiny gloom his glory is enhanced. He is asked to make the whole world notice the edifice of the brethren 'that now hardly and only is perceived by random'.

The second song is dedicated to the new member of the lodge:

> *Wackre Brüder stimmet an*
> *Auf, begrüsst den braven Mann*
> *Der in unsern freyen Orden*
> *Eben aufgenommen worden*
> *der nicht weiss, wie ihm geschah*
> *Ob der Wunder die er sah.*

[Translation
Dear brethren, sing the tune/Alas, let us welcome the honourable man/Who was received into our free Order/Who does not know what was done to him/Concerning the wonders that he saw.]

The first verse stipulates in similarity with the Swedish text that the newly received member has no clear knowledge about his own Initiation. When the Torpadius songbook points out that experience can be spoiled by too much of knowledge in advance, the German text clearly states that it is impossible for the candidate to know how the 'wonders' that he perceived during the Lodge of Initiation were performed.

The following verses are directed towards the newly received Brother.

> *Lieber Bruder, freue dich*
> *Wir auch freun uns inniglich*
> *So du als Maurer handelst*
> *Und der Weisheit Pfade wandelst*
> *Hüllest mit der Zeiten Lauf*
> *Neue Wahrheit dir sich auf.*

[Translation
Dear Brother, be content/we as well are deeply filled with joy/As You will act as a Mason/and walk the path of wisdom/with the proceeding time/a new Truth will be revealed for you.]

The third verse contains the popular motive of the relationship between darkness and light.

Senke, Bruder, nicht den Blick
In die Finsternis zurück
Forsche tiefer in die Wahrheit
Von der Dämmerung geh zur Klarheit
Wandle sicher! Strauchle nicht!
Bis Du fleugst von Licht zu Licht.

[Translation:
Do not lower your eyes, brother/back to darkness/Investigate deeper into truth/Walk from twilight to purity/Wander secure! Do not stumble!/Until you fly from light to light.]

The song also depicted a common motive that was used in all kinds of masonic texts: the motive of the non-understanding world outside the Order (i.e., 'othering').

Sey getrost, und achte nicht
Was der Thor und Heuchler spricht
Sie, die uns im Finstern richten
Lügen an die Wahrheit dichten
Was gehn einen braven Mann
Alle Splitterrichter an?

[Translation:
Be sure and don't listen to/ what the fool and hypocrite are saying/They who doom us in the dark/and attach lies to the truth/What does a honourable man care about/all judges that only create disharmony?]

It is not known to what extent the songs included in the German songbook were imported from the Holy Roman Empire or whether they were composed in Sweden. Furthermore we do not know whether it was planned as a supplement to Torpadius or if it was intended to replace it, at least within the German Lodge. It is, however, somewhat strange that a lodge with a printed songbook ceased with its activity within a year of the publication. During 1788, Sweden entered the war against Russia. Due to the growing opposition against King Gustav III that ended with his assassination in 1792, it seems likely that several lodges were closed in order to gain control over potential meeting places for the opponents of the monarchy. Even the extremely successful military lodge had to cease with its activity during the Swedish-Russian War, probably because several serving and high-ranking officers had announced their negative attitude concerning the politics of King Gustav III.

Songs in the *Acts of Eckleff* (1765)

With the songbook of the German Lodge in mind, it is interesting to notice, that masonic songs were spread from Sweden to the German masonic culture. When the Swedish Rite, in the version of the so-called *Acts of Eckleff*, was exported to Prussia in 1765, Swedish songs apparently were regarded a part of the ritual. The German translation contains several Swedish songs (one that can be found in the songbooks of Torpadius) and also a song in French for the Scottish Fellowcraft degree (which was apparently sung in its original language in Sweden as well). It is remarkable that there was effort put in the translation of song texts, which may proof their value as a constitutive ingredient of the masonic play.

The first song included in the *Acts of Eckleff* that were handed over to Zinnendorff in Berlin is a song written by Eckleff himself: '*Freimaurer Lied, zusammengesetzt von Hochw. Großmeister für die siebente Loge in Stockholm, Br. Carl Friedrich von Eklöf [sic]*' ('Freemason's song, composed by the Honourable Grand Master of the Seventh Lodge in Stockholm ...').[4]

Swedish original	German translation
Hwem Frimurar lott har vunnit	*Wer Freimaurer Loos gewonnen*
Lärlings och Gesällers tropp!	*Lehrling oder Geselle!*
I som hvad I sökt ha funnit	*Wer darin gefunden, was er suchte*
Och som bygger Logen opp	*Wer an der Loge baut*
I utvalde ämnes vänner	*Auserwählte Mitbrüder*
Hvem som hvandt vårt hopp och mål	*Wer unsre Hoffnung und unser Ziel*
Hvem som Frimurarlösen känner!	*erfüllet*
Dricke våre Bröders skål.	*Wer Freimaurer Loosung kennt*
	der trinkt auf unser Brüder Wohl.

Without knowing Swedish it is easy to notice that the German translation did not at all reflect the ABAB-rhyme of the original text. This is, of course, quite puzzling. Probably the German translation was not intended to be used for singing purposes but just to provide an explanation of the Swedish text. If that is the case, the idea of including the song in the *Acts of Eckleff* might have been to let the German brethren sing a Swedish song. Where the first verse is rather simple and ends with a toast to the fraternity, the second verse is directed against curiosity, envy, blindness and philosophical speculation. Curiosity may guess what the delighted society deals with, envy 'thunders', blindness does not move the Order and the Philosopher seeks an answer upon what the highest Good may be. And the answer is: 'to be a worthy mason-brother is the highest of my hopes'. The third verse is even more edifying as it elaborates upon the motive of equality among brethren: neither royal nor imperial dress are greater than a mason's apron. Distinct masonic motives continue in the subsequent verses. Freemasons can be proud that there are brethren in all countries scattered around the surface of the whole world, 'because the guests of the ruined temple/are to be found in another district' (*Ty förstörda Templets gäster/Råkas sån i annan trakt*). It is interesting that a song devoted to the Entered Apprentice and Fellow Craft degrees contains an allusion to the destroyed Temple. No further explanation is given, but the last verse opens up some further thought-provoking ideas as well. Among an illustrious Brotherhood the art of architecture is well known that corresponds to that transferred from the Orient (the Swedish original has: 'showed from', the German translation has: 'received from the Orient'). This knowledge among the intimate brethren is the basis of all construction. It gives lustre and reason to the lodge where the last light will be spread.

Eckleff's text starts off as a harmless convivial drinking song among Brethren and develops via an edifying elaboration upon virtues of Freemasonry and bad qualities outside the lodge to an ideological crescendo, hailing some of the key elements of esoteric Freemasonry so typical for the Swedish rite such as the destroyed Temple, the transfer of knowledge from the Orient and allusions to light symbolism.

The origin of the 'Scottish Fellow Song' that was included in the *Acts of Eckleff* among the rituals of the Fourth and Fifth degrees is unknown. It may have reached Sweden in its French original, as Eckleff himself is supposed to have received his acts from a Chapter in Geneva.

The first verse does not explicitly refer to Scottish degrees. It stresses innocence, religion, justice and goodness, fidelity and friendship as basic secrets for *tout Maçon parfait*. The second verse however turns into a decent comment upon the ritual play:

> *Dans une route obscure*
> *Et par milles detours*
> *J' errais a l'aventure*
> *Sans guide et sans secours*
> *Dans le temple a peine suis-je èntre*
> *Qu'un globe de lumiere ...*

This is the exact opposite of the song in Eckleff, a song devoted to the Scottish Fellowcraft degree, which ends with a verse that mainly stresses the convivial features of Freemasonry.

Conclusion

Masonic songbooks and songs served different and sometimes multiple purposes. One the one hand, they played a rather trivial role by providing entertaining songs at banquets and meals among the brethren. On the other hand, songs that stress virtues and values of Freemasonry may well have been an active part of the ritual play itself. They accompanied rituals and must therefore be dealt with as we deal with ritual texts. As in the case regarding the songs included in the *Acts of Eckleff*, we can see a mixture of purposes ranging from drinking toasts to esoteric ideology. Unfortunately, however, in most cases, we do not yet know under what conditions these songs were used. It is, therefore, especially challenging to put more effort in a thorough study of Lodge Minute Books or other kinds of supplementary description that provide us with additional information on what occasions songs were a part of the ceremony or were even a constituent part of the ritual play. As has been pointed out already, the edifying level of masonic song texts carried an important affirmative function. These songs rephrase the complex ideology and ideas of Freemasonry in a condensed way, adapted to the overarching philosophy of Enlightenment. Special attention should be paid to texts that are a clear statement against the ignorant surrounding world or to texts that express motives like the absence of the opposite gender. They formulate a world-view based upon demarcation against something that is conceived as foreign to Freemasonry and thus express its values indirectly. We should not be trapped by the wrong conception that song texts are too trivial to deal with. Rather the opposite is the case: the fairly simple coding of the moral message makes them a perfect tool in order to reveal masonic motives of the time. Songs can be interpreted as a commentary upon the cultural phenomenon of Freemasonry, a kind of meta-text that we need to decode further. Singing and songs within the lodges of the 18th century can be regarded as a rather harmless activity, but on the other hand they represent a gateway into the philosophy of Freemasonry and the spirit of the time.

***

Fig. 13 'Song for the Master's Degree',
in engraved tunes from *L' Ordre des Franc-Maçons trahi* (1745)

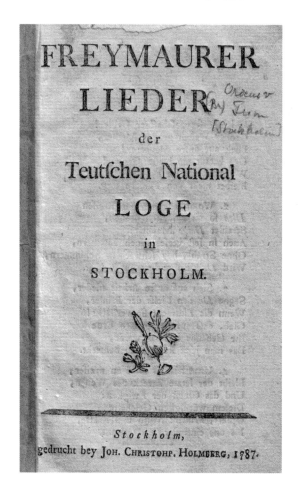

Fig. 14 Title page of a Swedish masonic songbook in German translation (1787).

NOTES

1 S.M. Honea: 'Nineteenth-Century American Masonic Songbooks', in *Heredom* vol. 6 (1997), pp. 285–304.

2 Notes on Torpadius' biography were made in *S:t Johannes logen S:t Erik 1756-1956*, Stockholm (1956), pp. 39-40.

3 P. Lindfors: '*Musiklivet under 200 år i S:t Johannes logen S:t Erik*', in *S:t Johannes logen S:t Erik 1756-1956.* Stockholm (1956), pp. 182-184.

4 According to a copy of the MS of the *Acts of Eckleff* owned by the author of this article.

*****

10

Wolfgang Amadeus Mozart and his contribution to the Craft

by

John Wade

[*Editor's Note: this is a revised version of John Wade's illustrated talk which he gave to the conference. The nine musical illustrations were provided by soloists, the Sheffield and District Masonic Choir and instrumentalists of his acquaintance. The points at which these extracts of Mozart's delightful music were provided are indicated by the notes shown below in square parentheses.*]

his paper has no pretensions to scholarship with regard to either Mozart or the Craft, but is intended to provide the contextual framework for delegates to this conference to hear something of the story of this most remarkable man, Bro Wolfgang Amadeus Mozart, and to share in a performance of some extracts from his masonic music. My text is heavily indebted to a paper by Bro Frederick Smyth,[1] a Past Master of *Quatuor Coronati* Lodge, and to two books by Bro Professor H.C. Robbins Landon[2], but I have also drawn on a range of other sources.

Mozart was born in Salzburg, Austria, on 27 January 1756. He was baptised Johann Chrysostom Wolfgang Theophilus Mozart, but in later life he preferred Amadeus, the Latin version of his fourth Christian name, Theophilus, both of which mean 'Dear to God'.[3] His father, Leopold, was a very good singer, competent violinist, organist and later deputy *kappelmeister* at the court of the Prince-Archbishop of Salzburg.[4] Leopold was also a prolific composer who was well respected by his contemporaries. In Sacheverel Sitwell's words 'he was dutiful, conscientious, respectable and dull',[5] but he did publish a treatise on the violin in the year of Wolfgang's birth which became the standard manual for violin playing in Germany during the later 18th century.[6] His mother was Anna Maria Pertl, daughter of the secretary to the Salzburg Exchequer, and she would seem to have passed on to Wolfgang his *joie de vivre*. Despite having six siblings, the only other survivor was Mozart's elder sister, Maria Anna (Nannerl), who was also very musically gifted.[7]

By the age of four Mozart was playing simple pieces on the clavier, having watched his sister studying the piano. Within a year he was also playing the violin and composing short pieces at the keyboard which were written down by his father. At the age of five and a half years in 1761 he was performing pieces such as K.1, composed by Wolfgang but taken down in Nannerl's music notebook in their father's handwriting.[8]

[Musical Illustration 1: Mozart K. 1, played on the piano by Bro David Rogers]

Leopold now decided to take both his children on an extended concert tour across Europe, displaying their talents to the most influential people of the day at the courts of Vienna, Munich, Frankfurt, Brussels, Paris and London. Wolfgang's sight-reading of very difficult scores and the outstanding maturity of his compositions astonished all who heard him: this included some of the leading figures in European music circles. His first published works appeared in Paris in 1764 when he was 8 years old, being two sonatas for violin and piano.[9] From Paris the family travelled to London in April, where they stayed for over a year, appearing before King George III and Queen Charlotte on two occasions, the first of which was within two weeks of their arrival, and receiving a fee of 24 guineas for each appearance. There were many public concerts in London and other cities, such as Canterbury, as well as parties in private houses. While Mozart was playing at one of these, an incident occurred which was described by an amateur musician, the Hon Daines Barrington, as follows:

> 'Whilst playing to me, a favourite cat came in, on which he left his harpsichord, nor could we bring him back for a considerable time. He would also run about the room with a stick between his legs by way of horse.'[10]

The Mozarts left England at the beginning of August and although there were plans for a return visit in later years, this did not take place. During a visit to Italy in 1769 Mozart went to Rome, where he copied down from memory Gregorio Allegri's *Miserere*, which was an extremely complicated piece performed only by the Papal Choir and only during Holy Week, the secrecy of which had been hitherto preserved by the threat of excommunication.[11] Of course we now listen to this piece almost daily on the radio! In Italy Mozart received many honours, including being made a member of the Philharmonic Academy of Verona and being knighted by Pope Clement XIV with the with the Knight's Cross of the Order of the Golden Spur.[12]

Before his fourteenth birthday he had composed his first opera, *Mitridate, re di Ponto*, which was commissioned for the 1771 Milan season after the young man had impressed the Italians with several sample arias on a visit to that city in 1770.[13] It is interesting that within another two years he had composed a short song for tenor soloist and organ, entitled *O heiliges Band* K. 148, the words of which were written by Ludwig Friedrich Lenz (1717-1780) and have the following meaning:

> O holy bond of friendship's loyal brothers,
> Like the highest happiness and Eden's bliss,
> Friendly to religion, but never set against
> The world, well known and yet full of mystery.[14]

There is an obvious connection of thought between these words and Freemasonry, but this work pre-dates his initiation into the craft by some twelve years. Although this apparent masonic influence has led some writers to argue that its position in the Köchel catalogue is incorrect and should be moved to a composition date of 1784/5, and thus to a time after his Initiation,[15] it could well be the case that Mozart was encouraged to set these words by one or other of several masonic friends he had made prior to his joining the Craft.

[Musical Illustration 2: Mozart K. 148 *O Heiliges Band*, sung by Bro Mike Teanby]

Up to 1772 the Mozarts' travels had been possible because of the generous leaves of absence granted by Archbishop Sigismund Schrattenbach of Salzburg. Unfortunately, his successor, Hieronymous von Colloredo, did not possess the same musical appreciation. This led to greater difficulties in gaining permission for further travels. When Leopold's application for another extended tour was refused in March 1777, father and son were so exasperated that they wrote rather hastily and in strong words to the Archbishop, leading to their services being summarily dispensed with.[16]

Wolfgang, who was determined to make the tour, resigned from the Archbishop's household and, accompanied by his mother, set off from Salzburg for Germany and thence to Paris without Leopold. This was not what Leopold had wanted – it was to lead to a period of strained relations with Wolfgang, especially after Anna Maria, who did not have a strong constitution, died in Paris in 1778.[17]

Mozart returned to Salzburg and reluctantly re-entered the Archbishop's service, becoming court organist in 1779. However, within two years a bitter quarrel with the Archbishop Colloredo, whom Mozart regarded as 'an unworthy ruler, benighted, parsimonious and unjust',[18] led to his decision to move to Vienna and establish himself as there as a composer and teacher. Leopold did his best to intercede and calm matters down but Wolfgang was adamant about leaving Salzburg and arrived in Vienna on 16 March 1781. By July of the following year Mozart had composed his first German opera, *Die Entführung aus dem Serail* ('The Abduction from the Seraglio'), which was a great success, the librettist being Johann Gottlieb Stephanie (1741-1800), an actor and stage manager, who was a member of a group of freemasons which included Dr. Franz Anton Mesmer (1734-1815), the famous hypnotist. Mesmer had first met the Mozarts on a visit to Vienna in 1773.[19] So, as early as 1782 Mozart was regularly in the company of freemasons and within two years he was to become one himself.

In August 1782, despite Leopold's bitter objections,[20] Mozart married Konstanze Weber, who, according to Smyth,

> was not, unfortunately, an ideal wife for him, being a bad housekeeper and failing to provide the domestic comfort so badly needed by her overworked and often over-worried husband.[21]

Bro Robbins Landon has more recently tried to show that the assessment of Konstanze by German musicologists over the years has presented an unfair picture of her character. He cites, amongst other evidence, the description of her by Bro Franz Niemetschek (1766-1849) in 1798:

> 'Mozart was happy in his marriage to Konstanze Weber. He found in her a good and loving wife, who was able to fall in with his every mood, and thereby win his complete confidence and exercise great influence over him. This, however, she used only in preventing him from making hasty decisions. He loved her dearly, confided everything in her, even in his   petty sins - and she forgave him with loving kindness and tenderness. Vienna was witness to this and his widow still thinks nostalgically of the days of her marriage.'[22]

The young couple's first child was born on 17 June 1783 and was christened Raimund Leopold, but during a visit to Salzburg in an attempt at a reconciliation with Leopold, the Mozarts learned of the death of this baby who had been left in the care of a nursemaid in Vienna.[23] The *Mass in C Minor*, K.427 which was another attempt at a family reconciliation, received its first performance in October 1783, although, like the later *Requiem Mass*, it remained incomplete.

During this period Mozart had many friends among those who were promoting German art and culture at the highest levels of Viennese society. A significant number of these were freemasons, so it is quite unsurprising that on 5 December 1784 the Viennese Lodge *Zur Wohlthätigkeit* ('Charity') sent the following Summons to its sister Lodges:

Proposed Kapellmeister Mozart - Our former Sec'y Bro Hoffman forgot to register this proposed member at the most honourable sister Lodges. He was already proposed four weeks ago at the honourable district Lodge and we should like therefore in the coming week to take steps for his admission if the most honourable sister lodges have no objections to him.

In the Orient of Vienna
5 Dec. 1784   Schwanckardt: Secr.[24]

Mozart was initiated on 14 December 1784 into this Lodge, which had only been founded in the previous year. Indeed there was a close link between the sister Lodges in Vienna and 'Charity' Lodge frequently worked with *zur wahren Eintracht* ('True Concord') Lodge. The latter had been founded in 1781 and had quickly reached a membership of some two hundred members. The Master who initiated Mozart was the author and dramatist, Baron Otto Heinrich von Gemmingen-Hornberg (1755-1836), Palatine Chamberlain and Privy Councillor.[25]   He is frequently mentioned in the Mozart family correspondence as a good friend and it would seem highly likely that it was largely through his influence that Mozart joined the Craft.

Now that we have Mozart in the Craft we shall hear our first definite masonic musical illustration – the *Opening Ode* K.483 which was actually composed just over a year later for the inaugural meeting of a new Lodge called *zur neugekrönten Hoffnung* ('Newly Crowned Hope'), which was an amalgamation of three lodges, *zur wahren Eintracht* ('True Concord'), *zu den drei Adlern* ('Three Eagles') and *zum Palmbaum* ('Palm Tree'), following an imperial decree that there should be no more than three lodges in each of the principal cities in Austria.[26] The piece is set for tenor soloist, chorus and organ.

[Musical Illustration 2: Mozart K. 483, 'For the Opening of the Lodge' sung by the Choir with Bro Mike Teanby, tenor soloist]

There were in 1785 eight lodges in Vienna. Among the smaller ones were the 'Three Eagles' and 'Steadfastness'. The latter included among its members Karl Ludwig Fischer (1745-1825), the first Osmin in *Il Seraglio*; the composer's brother-in-law, Joseph Lange (1751-1831), who was responsible for the famous, though unfinished, portrait of Mozart painted in 1789-90[27]; and Christoph Torricella, who published works by Haydn and Mozart. The other smaller Viennese lodges were 'Three Fires', founded in 1783 and 'St. Joseph', of which Lorenz Leopold Haschka (1749-1827) was a member. The latter was the author of the 'Emperor's Hymn' which was set to music by Joseph Haydn (1733-1809) in 1797. The other Lodge was 'Palm Tree'.[28]

On Christmas Eve 1784, just over a week after his Initiation, Mozart visited 'True Concord' Lodge and then on 7 January 1785 at the same Lodge he was passed to the Fellow Craft degree by the Master, Ignaz von Born (1742-1791), a leading scientist and one of the most prominent freemasons in Vienna. The Mozart family had been on familiar terms with Von Born from at least 1777[29] and there can be no doubt that he had played a leading part in Wolfgang's admission to the Craft. Mozart attended the next few meetings of 'True Concord' and certainly hoped to be present for the Initiation of his friend Josef Haydn on 28 January, but Haydn was unable to attend, possibly because of the short notice about attending the meeting.[30] When finally Haydn was initiated on 11 February, Mozart was unable to be present, since his father had arrived that day from Salzburg and Wolfgang was to give the first of six subscription concerts, playing the solo part in the first performance of his Piano Concerto in D minor, K.466, although a reference in *Grove's Music Dictionary* suggests that it is likely that Haydn's interest had received greater encouragement from his circle of colleagues in his post as *kapellmeister* to the Esterházy court.[31]

On 6 April 1785, Leopold Mozart was initiated into 'Charity' Lodge - the same Lodge as his son had joined some four months earlier. The relationship between father and son had suffered greatly since the death of Anna Maria in Paris in 1778. Their separation through Mozart's decision to move to Vienna and his subsequent marriage did not help matters. It may be that Mozart involved Haydn in persuading Leopold to join the Craft, 'hoping that the Masonic tie might improve the atmosphere between father and son'[32] but Nettl points out that even if this were the case it was not very successful in that Leopold continued to be unforgiving with regard to the marriage to Konstanze. On 16 April at a meeting of 'True Concord' Leopold was passed to the Fellowcraft degree, and it is believed that Wolfgang had set *Gesellenreise* ('Fellowcraft's Journey') to music with this in mind, although it was actually composed on 26 March, some days before Leopold's Initiation. The words of *Gesellenreise* have the following meaning:

> You who approach a new degree of understanding,
> go steadfastly on your road, knowing that it is the
> path of wisdom. Only he who perseveres may draw
> near to the source of light.[33]

[Musical Illustration 4: Mozart K. 468, sung by Bro Roger Hart, tenor]

Either on or by 22 April Leopold was raised to the Master Masons degree - the lodge Minutes are not very clear about the actual date of his raising.[34] We do not know when Wolfgang was raised, but it would seem from his many subsequent attendances and from some of his letters that he and his father had both been through the third degree ceremony.[35]

While contemporary English lodges consider that not having a ceremony and having to have a 'talk' or some sort of demonstration indicates a 'problem' in their programme of meetings – and these are often poorly attended – it was quite usual in both England and in Vienna during this period to have a meeting with the express intention of hearing a performance of music or a learned discourse from a leading scholar.[36] It was in this context that a benefit concert was given in aid of two clarinet and basset horn players from Prague on 24 April 1785 in 'Newly Crowned Hope' and a lengthy programme of symphonies, cantatas and concertos etc. in another concert at the same Lodge on 15 December 1785.

On 24 April 1785 there was a special meeting of 'Newly Crowned Hope' to honour von Born, who had very recently been raised to the nobility by the Emperor Joseph II for his scientific discoveries.[37] Among the music, which played an important part in the proceedings was Mozart's cantata *Die Maurerfreude* ('The Masons' Joy'). This work is for solo tenor a three-part male chorus and small orchestra. The words, which were in praise of both the honoured Brother, von Born, and the Emperor who had honoured him, were written by Franz Petran, a priest from

Bohemia, who had recently joined 'Newly Crowned Hope'. The opening words are as follows:

> See how, to the keen eye of scholars,
> Nature by degrees reveals herself;
> how she fills the mind with wisdom
> and the heart with virtue. That is
> pleasant for the Mason to see and
> gives him great happiness.[38]

[Musical Illustration 5: Mozart K. 471, part of which was sung by Bro Roger Hart, tenor soloist, with the Choir]

The deaths within twenty-four hours of each other on 6 and 7 November 1785 of Count Franz Esterházy von Galantha, the court Chancellor of Hungary, and H.R.H. Georg August Duke of Mecklenburg-Strelitz, the youngest brother of Queen Charlotte of England, both of whom were members of 'Newly Crowned Hope' occasioned a Lodge of Sorrow on 17 November.[39] Bro Frederick Smyth is, in fact, mistaken when he comments on the short notice and pressure put on Mozart for the composition of music for the remembrance of these two distinguished brethren, as the piece was actually composed for a third degree on 12 August, as Philippe Autexier has correctly noted.[40] Regarded as one of Mozart's finest compositions, in Smyth's words

> The real importance of this work is that it perhaps expresses something of Mozart's personal attitude to death, an attitude which had been coloured by his Masonic experience in the letter to his father.[41]

Bro Professor John Morehen has drawn attention to the scoring of the piece for two oboes, clarinet, basset horn, double bassoon, two horns and strings, and that a further two basset horns were added later.[42] Elsewhere he notes that

> the plaintive timbre of the basset horn, an obsolete member of the clarinet family of alto pitch, is prominent in all Mozart's five identifiable pieces of Masonic instrumental music.[43]

As it was composed originally for the third degree ceremony just mentioned, Mozart entitled the piece 'Master Music' and it was scored for men's chorus and orchestra. It would appear that he was not completely satisfied with the reduced version produced for the Lodge of Sorrows which did not contain the vocal parts. Hence, for a third performance on 9 December 1785, he added the new low wind parts which emphasise the gloomy mood of the work, and this is the version which has come down to us today as the 'Masonic Funeral Music'.

[Musical Illustration 6: Mozart K. 477, *Die Maurerische Trauermusik*, played by Bro David Rogers on the piano, with the Choir adding the original vocal parts]

The absence from Köchel's catalogue of any masonic composition written between early 1786 and the latter half of 1791 led Bro Smyth to assume that quite a number of pieces written for the lodges may have become lost when they finally closed down.

At about the beginning of May 1791 Mozart was concentrating all his efforts into writing the music for *Die Zauberflöte* ('The Magic Flute'), K.620,[44] his last opera, which received its first performance on 30 September 1791. *Die Zauberflöte* is, of course, well known to the popular world as being of especial masonic significance, although this traditional assumption has been challenged recently by Bro Jans Morgens Reimer,[45] who concludes that

> *The Magic Flute* might have been meant to be a joke, a satire, or a way of exposing the stultification of the ignorant bourgeois. It might have been meant to be a populist form of entertainment, as well as a way to expose the superstitious side of the epoch of New Romanticism, and last but not least, a very effective way for a peripheral theatre to sell tickets and earn good money, all the while the play continued to run.

The words were by Emanuel Schikaneder (1751-1812), a member of the *Karl zu den drei Schlüsseln* ('Charles to the Three Keys') Lodge in Regensburg.[46] One could spend a whole talk on this work alone but now we perform only one item from it, the chorus 'To Isis and Osiris', which is a thanksgiving to the gods. Darkness is in retreat before the brightness of the sun. Tamino, the young hero, is coming into possession of a new life; soon (the word is sung in solemn three-fold repetition) he will be an initiate.

[Musical Illustration 7:   Mozart K. 620, *The Magic Flute*, Chorus: 'To Isis and Osiris' sung by the Choir]

Research by Bro Robbins Landon and, more recently, by Solomon has shown that Mozart's financial problems, which had been a constant worry, 'had already begun to ease considerably, although they were far from over' and that there were prospects of a considerable increase in his income from various sources. [47] Following the success of *Die Zauberflöte*, Mozart worked on his *Clarinet Concerto in A major* K.622. The work was composed originally for an instrument something akin to a basset-horn[48]. He had completed it for a first performance on 16 October and then turned his attention to a Requiem Mass which had been commissioned by an unknown nobleman under rather secretive circumstances back in July,[49] but had been delayed by the completion of other works including *Die Zauberflöte*. A further delay had occurred with a trip to Prague for the coronation as King of Bohemia of the new Emperor, Leopold II, and a number of performances, including the premiere of the opera *La Clemenza di Tito* in late August. Here Mozart had become ill, but had managed to finish off the last few sections of *Die Zauberflöte* by 28 September, in time for its premiere on 30 September.

It would seem that the *Requiem Mass* was actually composed between 8 October and 20 November, when Mozart became too weak to leave his bed.[50] Konstanze had persuaded him to lay it aside and to work on a masonic cantata, *Eine kleine Freimaurer-Kantate* ('A Little Masonic Cantata'), K.623, the last work which Mozart himself completed.   It was at one time thought that the text was by Schikaneder, the librettist of *Die Zauberflöte*, but it seems likely that it was written by Karl Ludwig Gieseke (1761-1833), a member of 'Newly Crowned Hope', for the consecration of their new Temple on 17 November.

This final masonic work, scored for three soloists, chorus and orchestra, was completed by 15 November in a very short space of time (within about two weeks) and the MS reveals very little in the way of correction in a single draft. It was then performed as arranged two days later on 17 November. Mozart returned from the Lodge very satisfied with his efforts.[51]

[Musical Illustration 8: Mozart K. 623, *Eine kleine Freimaurer-Kantate*, Chorus: '*Laut verkünde unsere Freude*' sung by the Choir, accompanied by Bro David Rogers.]

Mozart turned once more to the Requiem Mass, but his last illness from 20 November prevented him from completing the score, although he was working on this until the final hours of his life. He was confined to bed in great pain and died of acute rheumatic fever on 5 December 1791.[52]

The title of this paper referred to Mozart's contribution to the Craft. I can only quote from the oration delivered by Karl Friedrich Hensler (1759-1825) at the Lodge of Sorrow held at the next meeting of 'Newly Crowned Hope' following a third degree ceremony:

'It has pleased the Eternal Architect of the Universe to tear from our chain of Brotherhood one of its most deserving and beloved links. Who did not know him? Who did not esteem him? Who did not love him, our worthy Brother Mozart.

Only a few weeks ago he stood in our midst, glorifying with his magical music the dedication of our Temple. Who among us would have thought then how soon he was to be taken from us?

Mozart's death is an irreplaceable loss to art. His talent, which already showed itself when he was a boy, made him one of the wonders of our time. Half of Europe esteemed him, the great called him their darling, and we called him *Brother*!

He was husband and father, a friend to his friends and a brother to his brothers. He only lacked riches to make hundreds of people as happy as he would have wished them to be.'[53]

Well, in Bro Smyth's words, 'we are left in no doubt whatever that Mozart had left his mark as a Mason.'[54]

[Musical Illustration 9: Mozart K. 484, 'For the Closing of the Lodge' sung by the Choir with Bro Steve Palfreyman, tenor soloist]

***

NOTES

[1] F. Smyth: 'Bro Mozart of Vienna', in *AQC* vol. 87 (1974), pp. 37 – 73.

[2] H.C. Robbins Landon: *Mozart and the Masons - New Light on the Lodge 'Crowned Hope'* (London & NY: Thames & Hudson, 1982; 2nd edn., 1991); and his *1791- Mozart's Last Year* London: Flamingo, 1989).

[3] O.E. Deutsch: *Mozart - A Documentary Biography* (London: Simon & Shuster, 1965), p. 9.

[4] M. Solomon: *Mozart - A Life* (London: Hutchinson, 1995), pp. 21–33.

[5] S. Sitwell: *Mozart* (London: Nelson, 1932), p. 9.

[6] Solomon: *op. cit.*, p. 32.

[7] K. Thomson: *The Masonic Thread in Mozart* (London: Lawrence & Wishart, 1977), p. 20.

[8] Smyth: *op. cit.*, p. 39; Solomon: *op. cit.*, p. 38.

[9] Deutsch: *op. cit.*, p. 29.

[10] Sitwell: *op. cit.*, p. 14.

[11] Sitwell: *op. cit.*, p. 17; G. Rech: *The Salzburg Mozart Book* [trans. G. Schamberger] (Salzberg: Residenz Verlag, 1991).

[12] Solomon: *op. cit.*, p. 78.

[13] Deutsch: *op. cit.*, pp. 128 – 9; Solomon: *op. cit.*, p. 84.

[14] Translation from *Songs for Solo Voice and Piano, Wolfgang Amadeus Mozart* (NY: Dover Publications, 1993), p. 93; cf. Smyth: *op. cit.*, p. 61, where alternative composition dates are discussed.

[15] e.g., H.C. Robbins Landon (ed.) *The Mozart Compendium* (London: Thames & Hudson, 1990), p. 332.

[16] Solomon: *op. cit.*, pp. 112ff.

[17] Rech: *op. cit.*, p. 44.

[18] Solomon: *op. cit.*, p. 241.

[19] Thomson: *op. cit.*, pp. 20, 52.

[20] P. Nettl: *Mozart and Masonry* (NY: Dorset Press, 1957), p. 53.

[21] Smyth: *op. cit.*, p. 41.

[22] H.C. Robbins Landon: *1791 - Mozart's Last Year* (1988; 2nd edn, 1989), p. 189; F.X. Niemetschek, *Leben des k. k. Kapellmeisters Wolfgang Gotlieb Mozart nach Originalquellen beschrieben* (Prague, 1798; Eng. trans.,1956) p. 72.

[23] Solomon: *op. cit.*, p. 268.

[24] Smyth: *op. cit.*, p. 44; *also* Robbins Landon, H.C.: *Mozart and the Masons* (London: Thames & Hudson, 2nd edn., 1991), p. 7.

[25] Nettl: *op. cit.*, pp. 14 – 15; Robbins Landon : *op. cit.*, p. 8.

[26] Smyth: *op. cit.*, p. 43.

[27] Robbins Landon: *op. cit.*, p. 55.

[28] *Op. cit.*, pp. 9 – 10.

[29] Thomson: *op. cit.*, p. 62.

[30] Robbins Landon: *op. cit.*, p. 10.

[31] J. Webster: 'Haydn, (Franz) Joseph', in *New Grove Music Online* ed. by L. Macy. (Accessed 22 May 2005), http://www.grovemusic.com

[32] Smyth: *op. cit.*, p. 45.

[33] *Op. cit.*, p. 56.

[34] So Smyth: *op. cit.*, p. 45. However, Robbins Landon: *op. cit.*, p. 18 is quite sure that it was 22 April.

[35] Smyth: *op. cit.*, p. 45.

[36] *See*, e.g., the discussion in Stewart, T.: *English Speculative Freemasonry - Some possible Origins, Themes and Developments* [Prestonian Lecture for 2004], *passim* but especially p. 51ff.

[37] Smyth: *op. cit.*, p. 48.

[38] *Op. cit.*, p. 56.

[39] *Op. cit.*, p. 49.

[40] P.A. Autexier: 'Preface' to *Meistermusik fur Mannerchor und Orchester, c-moll, Wolfgang Amadeus Mozart, Rekonstruktionsversuch und Klavierauszug* (Poitiers, May 1985). N.B. Katharine Thomson had already noted, in *The Masonic Thread in Mozart* (1977), that the original composition dated to July 1785 from the entry by Mozart in his own catalogue, but this was ignored until Autexier's research was published in 1984–5.

[41] Smyth: *op cit.*, p. 49. For the letter to his father: *see op. cit.*, p. 44.

[42] 'Masonic Funeral Music', transcribed for organ and ed. by J. Morehen: *Oxford Organ Music* (O.U.P., 1975), Preface.

[43] J. Morehen: 'Masonic Instrumental Music of the 18th Century - A Survey', in *AQC*, vol. 89 (1976), p. 178.

[44] Solomon: *op. cit.* p. 475.

[45] J.M. Reimer: 'Mozart, *The Magic Flute*, Freemasonry and Rosicrucians - An Antithesis', in *AQC* 116 (2004), pp. 268-72.

[46] For discussion on Shikaneder's masonic career, see Nettl: *op, cit.*, p. 61ff.

[47] Robbins Landon: *1791 – Mozart's Last Year*, pp. 44–47; Solomon: *op. cit.*, pp. 476f.

[40] Robbins Landon: *op. cit.*, p. 146.

[49] The secretive circumstances have been exaggerated over the years by suggestions of an allegorical summons to the Underworld and various conspiracy theories, but it seems that, according to Solomon (*op. cit.*, p. 483), Count Walsegg had intended to use Mozart as a 'ghost writer' for the commission, and to pass the work off as his own composition.

[50] Robbins Landon: *op. cit.*, p. 149–152.

[51] Solomon: *op. cit.*, p. 490.

[52] Robbins Landon: *Mozart and the Masons*, p. 60; also Solomon: *op. cit.*, p. 491.

[53] Nettl: *op. cit.*, p. 22; *also* Smyth: *op. cit.*, pp. 55f.

[54] Smyth: *op. cit.*, p. 56.

*****

INDEX